4CLOVER SERIES BOOK TWO

Shauna
X

SHAUNA McDONNELL

Contents

Dedications

For those we love, those who lost us amongst their struggle, those who lost the fight — may you rest peacefully, and those who are still battling with alcohol addiction.
This one is for you.

To Elle Maxwell, you claimed Cillian as your book boyfriend from the very first page, this is me gifting him to you.

Author's Note

This book is written in British English, spellings may differ from American English. A lot of my characters have Irish names. So, I've made a pronunciation chart.

Cian (Ke-ane)
Cillian (Kil-e-an)
Ciaran (Kier-on)
Conor (Conn-or)
Croí (K-ree)
Sean (Sh-aun)
Bronagh (Bro-NA)
Roisin (Row-sheen)

My goal was to make this book as interactive as possible; each chapter has a song for a sub-title. If there is anything, I love more than reading, it's music.

The playlist is available on Spotify: Love, Boys of 4Clover. Happy listening.

Shauna's Guide to Irish Slang

Gobshite/eejit - Idiot
Bellend - Dickhead
Pissed - Drunk or Angry (depends on the setting, LOL)
Garda - One policeman
Gardai - two or more policemen
Lilt - Twang or Sound
Plaster - Band aid
Playschool - Preschool
Debs - Prom
Secondary School - High school
Nineteen-o-splash - A long, long time ago
Solicitor – Lawyer

About the Author

Shauna lives in the small townland of Oldtown, North County Dublin with her Fiancé. She is a boy-mom of two tiny hellions, also known as her children. When she isn't busy trying to keep her children alive, she loves to lose herself in a good romance novel. Her other hobbies include singing, art, all things spiritual, song writing and binge-watching Netflix series. She believes we all have a little light inside us, but it's up to us to let it shine. Love is her second novel; it is book two of the deliciously sinful Boys of 4Clover Series.

"What if the love you deserve is love you never find? I've learnt in love and death we don't decide. If only you could see yourself in my eyes, you'd see you shine. You shine."

Lost, Dermot Kennedy.

Prologue

Mr. Almost by Meghan Trainor

<u>Starz Unveiled</u>

Sean and Rosie are getting hitched!
Well, ladies and gentlemen, today is the day.
The biggest wedding of the year is finally here.
The only daughter of Michael Mulligan, (4Clovers
manager and part owner of Sham Rock Records) and the
son of Patrick Morgan, (founder of Ireland's largest
entertainment law firm, Morgan & Son) tie the knot.
The extravagant ceremony is set to take place in the
spectacular gardens of the Powerscourt Hotel Resort Spa,
at two p.m.
The guest list for this special day is jam-packed with
A-listers, including Ireland's hottest indie rock band,
4Clover. The band's lead singer, Cian Mulligan (the
bride-to-be's brother) will be amongst many of the famous
faces in attendance today. A source close to the band has
said although lead guitarist, and close childhood friend of
the family, Cillian O'Shea, has flown back to Dublin for
the big day, he will not be attending the wedding
ceremony. We at Starz Unveiled are wondering why that
is?
We have been led to believe, that Mr. O'Shea and Mr.
Morgan do not see eye to eye. We can't help but wonder
if the history between the raven-haired beauty and the
broody musician is the cause?

What do you think, readers?

Rosie

Well, today is the day.

The day most little girls dream of.

The dream dress, the dream venue, and most importantly, the dream man.

You guessed it; it is my wedding day. But, contrary to what my younger, more naive, ten-year-old self thought — this is not the dream day I once envisioned it to be.

I am not radiating happiness, and that I'm so in love glow everyone blabs on about, is virtually non-existent.

There are no nervous jitters, no sweaty palms, no butterflies of anticipation fluttering around my stomach.

Just complete emptiness.

Let's just say, my feet are so far beyond cold, I can no longer feel them.

I'm so numb, I can't even appreciate the fine details, the intricate design, the beautiful decor. I'm an interior designer for Christ's sake, detail is my Nutella. I live for that shit. But, no... this nightmare wedding has sucked the joy right out of my happiness, making what was meant to be the happiest day of this girl's life, possibly the worst.

I should be impatiently waiting to walk down the aisle into the arms of my happily ever after. Instead, I am camped out, sulking in an outrageously large marble bathtub, in an overpriced, vintage lace, Vera Wang gown. Hiding from the reality of what in the actual fuck did I sign myself up for.

Today, I should marry the man of my dreams, my best friend, the person I want to build the rest of my life with, not the man of my father's dreams.

Alas, here we are, mere hours away from my inevitable nuptials and I'm spiralling. When exactly my love life turned into a business transaction, I'm not quite sure.

All I know is, it's unavoidable. A necessary evil to help protect someone I once — and if I'm being completely honest — still love. When I envisioned this day throughout my teenage years — we all do, don't deny it — was it my soon-to-be husband's face I saw waiting for me at the altar? No, it was not.

Who did I see?

The man of my actual dreams, the same man who haunts my subconscious whether I want him to, or not.

Cillian O'Shea, 4Clovers lead guitarist, my best friend's older brother; and my brother Cian's best friend. Cillian was my first kiss, my first love, my first heartbreak. He was my first everything. I know what you're all thinking. It's a little too late for me to be questioning my life choices, and you're right. But, let's get one thing straight… this was not my choice.

I was given an ultimatum; one I could not refuse. Also, I know most arranged marriages went out of fashion in the eighteen-hundreds or whatever, but when Michael Mulligan wants something, he stops at nothing to get it. Even if that means his daughter will be miserable for the rest of her life.

Here's the thing about Sean, he is boring. Personally, I've had more exciting conversations with myself. The only thing he really has going for him, is his looks.

Without sounding extremely vain right now, the man is a solid eight. But, is he marriage material?

Most definitely not.

So, my guess is, you're all wondering how I ended up with the knight dressed in shiny aluminium foil, instead of my one and only true Prince Charming?

Well, let's take it back to the beginning and find out.

Chapter One

Dirty Little Secret by The All-American Rejects

Rosie

October 2013

"The black one."

That's Lily for you, allergic to every colour that isn't black, and on occasion, yellow. Tightening the lid of the matte black nail polish she's applied to her long coffin-shaped nails, she spins around on the desk chair to face me. The plastic wheels glide along the laminate floor, echoing a sound resembling nails scraping along a chalkboard.

I examine the two t-shirts closely. "Are you sure?"

They're almost identical, well, except for the colour. The one in my left-hand harbours a shade of obnoxious hot pink, and the one in my right, inky black mirroring my hair.

Lily stands, snatching the top from my hold. "Definitely the black one." She scrunches the pink tank into a ball, then throws it across the bedroom with a grunt. "Sorry, not sorry, my eyeballs are genuinely in pain here. Whoever invented that shade of pink should be executed. It's horrific. I should unfriend you for even considering wearing that monstrosity."

Classic Lily, always so dramatic.

Lily plonks herself on the edge of my double bed, her reflection visible in the floor-length mirror I'm facing. "So, Ro…" Her eyebrows wiggle suggestively. "What's the game plan tonight?"

Pulling the black lace tank top over my head, I smooth it over my slender frame with the palms of my hands. "I've told you already, there is no game plan. I'm not trying to impress your brother."

Lily is forever hoping I'll marry her brother and have pretty blue-eyed babies. *Her words, not mine. Although I have thought about it, I will not admit that to anyone.*

Her mouth forms the perfect O as her eyes widen with an all-knowing look. "Ohhh-kay, and I'm entering the Rose of Tralee contest." One thing you need to know about my fiery red-headed best-friend is sarcasm is her first language.

"I'm nineteen, Lil. I've never had a boyfriend because I compare everyone to Cillian. I've decided that it will stop tonight. I can't do it anymore. I'm done waiting for him to make up his mind." I pull on my favourite black leather Freddy jeans and examine myself once more. *Cute.* "Tonight, is about finding a nice lad, one who will hopefully like me as much as I like him." *I don't know who I'm trying to convince more; me, or her.*

"Whatever Ro! You can keep telling yourself there's nothing between you and my brother, but we all know different. I see the way he looks at you when he thinks nobody is looking." Her eyes find mine through the reflective glass. "He has a pet name for you for Christ's sake. One of these days, my brother will realise, he is in fact, head over heels about his little Snow White, and it won't matter in the slightest what The Big Bad Wolf, Cian, has to say about it."

I love Lily to pieces, but she needs to come to terms with the fact Cillian and I are not some real-life fairy tale.

Am I in love with Cillian O'Shea? Yes. I've loved him for almost half my life; ever since he kissed me in a game of kiss chase when I was ten years old. He is a tortured boy with a guitar, calling out to be rescued from his demons, yet, he never allows anyone close enough to save him. Not even me, and trust me... I've tried.

After painting my lips with my signature cherry-red lipstick, I turn to face Lily. "You do realise The Big Bad Wolf is Little Red Riding Hood, not Snow White? Besides, he has been calling me Snow since we were kids. Ever since we forced him to watch it on repeat for months on end. It's just a silly nickname, it means nothing. Cian has one for you too. Does that mean he is madly in love with you?"

"Okay, that's actually laughable. Your brother calls me Snot Face. It's hardly a compliment. Besides, Cian is a gobshite. My brother, on the other hand, compares you to a princess, one of these days he'll realise he is your prince."

There is no talking to Lily when she gets on one of her "you two belong together" speeches, so I continue getting ready in silence and let her believe that she is right. Lily loves when she is right.

* * *

We get to Lily's house just after ten, the place is already jammed. Mama O'Shea would be pissed if she found out about this. We push our way through the crowd, making our way through the kitchen.

"Who the hell are all these people?" Lily scans her living room with wide eyes. "I doubt this is what Ma meant when she said he could have a few friends over."

Eventually, we make it through the horde of people and my heart stops beating in my chest. Standing directly in front of me, in all his six-foot-two glory is none other than, Cillian O'Shea. He is leaning back against the countertop. His chestnut hair is tossed in a messy, just-fucked look. The overhead light catches his eyes, reflecting against the melting earthy hazel colour I love so much. A black Thin Lizzy t-shirt is painted across his lean toned chest. Black, ripped jeans paired with his favourite black Converse, finish off his tall, dark, and broody image.

I swallow down the marble sized lump in my throat. Not tonight. I will not let him affect me anymore. Just then, those earthy coloured, hazel eyes lock on mine. Do you know the butterflies everyone talks about? Yeah, well, I don't get those. What I get are elephants, a whole herd of elephants, stampeding around my stomach. Even at twenty-one, Cillian O'Shea is all man, wide shoulders, lean toned waist, sexy arm porn forearms, and God must be trying to kill me dimples. He flashes his signature, sexy smug smile at me and I have this sudden urge to fling myself at him. I don't do that though.

Why? You ask.

Because that is a God-awful idea.

Cillian has gone through more girls than I have tampons, and frankly, I don't want to end up just another name on his, "been there, banged that" list.

Cillian pushes himself off the counter and the rest of the room suddenly fades away. He stalks towards me, making me feel like one of those poor helpless animals on one of those Discovery Channel shows. The ones who are trying to mind their own business when suddenly, a big scary alpha lion comes out of nowhere; and they realise they're fucked.

Yep, that's me right now, completely and utterly fucked.

"Snow… you came." He wraps me up in his arms, pulling me in against his hard chest and leans forward so his mouth hovers over my ear. His breath tickles my neck, sending the best kind of shivers throughout my body.

The scent of his aftershave fills my nose. It's uniquely him. Like freshly cut grass on a crisp Spring day, mixed with the malty smell of whiskey. "Are you trying to kill me, Snow?" His hands grip my hips. "How am I supposed to keep my hands to myself when you're walking around looking like that?"

I shift, trying to pull myself free from his hold; but it's no use. He tugs me closer, leaving me flush with his very hard man bits. *Sweet. Baby. Jaysus!*

"Every time I see you… I lose my mind. It's getting harder to stay away from you. Pun intended."

Well shit! That was the last thing I expected to leave his mouth. Normally, I would laugh at cheesy lines like that, but the rough tone of his voice makes me swallow my tongue. Cillian is never this forward, at least not with me anyway. *He must be hammered.*

Feeling bold, and hopeful he'll forget all about this tomorrow, I push myself up onto my tippy toes. Our lips are almost touching, but not quite. "Well, then don't. The only thing standing in your way is yourself."

Cillian's body tenses when the words I've spoken register. *If I could high five my lady balls right now, I totally would.*

"Fuck, Snow. Don't say shit like that, you know we can't. Cian would kick my ass for touching his baby sister." His toned, tanned arms tighten. A complete contrast to what his words are saying.

I want to yell, fuck Cian. Who gives a shit what he thinks? But I already know the answer to that... Cillian. Cian has been his best friend for most of his life, and apparently, rule number one of the bro-code states... thou shalt NEVER touch a fellow bro's sister. Do you know what I want to do with that bro-code? Shove it so far up my overprotective big brother's ass, it would tickle his tonsils.

I try my best to hide the disappointment showing on my face. "Whatever, Cillian. I need a drink."

I pry myself from his hold and turn to walk away, keeping some of my ego intact. I'm done with this, the constant back and forth. Cillian's hand captures my elbow, halting me mid-turn.

"Snow, wait."

Peering back over my shoulder, my eyes lock on his. There is a sadness in his gorgeous muddy green eyes that wasn't there before. "Dance with me, please. Just for a moment, let's pretend we're the only ones here that exist."

His pleading stare burns through my skin; making promises we both know he won't keep. I release a defeated sigh.

"Okay, Cillian. One dance. Just one."

Chapter Two

Iris by The Goo Goo Dolls

Cillian

Rosie Mulligan, my Snow White.

She's my forbidden fruit of Eden.

The one girl in this shitty little town I can't ever have.

Unfortunately for me, I've loved her almost my entire life.

Rosie is the girl people write songs about. Onyx black hair that falls to the centre of her back. Crystal clear, ocean blue eyes that light up every room she walks into. Her porcelain white skin turns a pretty shade of pink when she blushes, making her my perfect Snow White. A shy but sultry smile frames her pouty, natural red lips to perfection, making me want to wrap her five-foot-two frame in my arms and hold her forever, but I can't.

Rosie is selfless, she finds the good in everything. She's the only girl I've ever met, who looks through my darkness and loves me even more for it. She deserves the world, not some broke musician with a guitar, and a shitload of family issues. Maybe in a few years, after she's finished with college, and the band hits the big time, I can give her everything she deserves. But, until then, I need to keep her at arm's length.

I can't let her get too close. I need to make something of myself first. If I let her in now, I know, I'd give it all up for her. I can't do that; music is all I have in the world. I need it to breathe; it is the medicine for my mind. The only thing that drags me away from the demons that haunt me.

Then there's Cian, her overprotective big brother and my best friend since playschool. Cian has been warning me off his little sister since I first kissed her, back when I was just twelve years old. He beat the shit out of me, threatening if I ever so much as looked at his sister again, he'd rip my balls off.

If I didn't love Cian like a brother, I wouldn't care what he thinks, but I owe that shithead more than I could ever repay him. So, if I've to stay away from Rosie until I can prove to Cian, I deserve her. That's what I'll do.

Rosie is the glowing light at the end of my pitch-black tunnel. If I start something with her before I figure shit out, I will suck the light right out of those pretty, ocean blue eyes.

Having her here in my arms is not helping the situation. I'm desperately trying to fight a war between my head and heart.

Rosie sways her curvy hips to the music, rubbing up against my body. Every argument my brain has on why I should walk away, vanishes.

Whose bright idea was it to ask her to dance, anyway?

Oh yeah, that honour would have to go to the third opponent in this raging battle. My dick.

Instantly, the recognizable guitar strum of Iris by The Goo Goo Dolls, blasts through the speakers, drowning out the noise of the surrounding crowd. I tighten my arms around Rosie's waist, pulling her a little closer.

She rests her head against my chest, tucking herself under my chin. Together, we sway to the steady beat as I sing the words softly to her. I breathe her in, committing every second this moment has to offer into my brain.

Rosie shifts in my arms, resting her back up against my chest, she links her fingers through mine and rests them on her hips as she sways back and forwards to the heavier guitar solo. I lean down and place a small kiss on her right shoulder.

I softly whisper in her ear, "Someday, Snow. Someday, I will give you forever, I promise." I don't miss the shiver that runs over her skin as she melts back into my chest. I know that if this moment could last forever, I'd never want to be anywhere else.

I'm so lost in her; I don't even realize Cian is barrelling across the sitting room like a bat straight out of the gates of hell. *Shit!*

I pull Rosie behind me, blocking her from Cian's line of sight. This has nothing to do with her.

I come nose to nose with her brother, ready to take whatever shit he wants to spew at me.

"Cillian. You better take your hands off my sister before I remove them from your fucking body." His eyes are burning with molten rage. If looks could kill, I would be six feet under right now.

Suddenly, the fiery little redhead I call my sister puts herself in between me and my best friend. Lily may be tiny, but her attitude is far from it. "Cian, will you calm your nuts for just one second? They're just dancing, you'd swear from the way you're reacting he had his thrill drill housed in her toolbox."

Jesus Christ! Where the hell does she come up with this shit? I got to give it to her; the girl has a way with words.

"Stay out of this, Lily! This has nothing to do with you. Your brother's 'thrill drill', as you so elegantly put it, has been inside more than half the girls at this party, at some stage or another. I'm just making sure he knows to keep it the hell away from my baby sister. She deserves better, and he knows it."

Fuck, he's pissed.

I know Cian detests the idea of me and Rosie together; he has been warning me off her for years. Cian knows all my secrets, the nightmares that keep me awake at night. He knows the struggles I face and the vices I use to numb the pain. I don't blame him for wanting more for Rosie. I want more for her, too. I want to be more.

Yes, I've had my fair share of girls over the years, but they were all the 'love 'em and leave 'em' kind. Girls like Rosie, you don't find very often, and once you do, they're the 'forever and always' kind. Well, at least for me anyway.

How do I make her brother see that? I know she's my forever girl, even if she is not mine right now. I'm just biding my time until I can make her mine, because as much as I hate to admit it, Cian is right. I don't deserve her, not yet; but I will. Someday.

Until then, I'll bite my tongue and walk away, leaving my heart in the hands of the blue-eyed beauty. I pray to God she doesn't shatter it before I get my shit together.

I look Cian straight in the eye and tell him exactly what he wants to hear. "It was just a dance, chill the fuck out! It means nothing, right Snow?"

The hurt that crosses her face, shatters me and I want to kick my own ass for it. I despise the next words that come out of her mouth; they hit me right where it hurts, but honestly, I deserve it.

"Yep! Just two friend's dancing. No need to worry Cian. All Cillian and I will ever be, are friends."

Rosie turns on her heels and walks away, making me feel like the biggest dickhead ever. I've hurt her feelings and believe it or not, that's the last thing I wanted to do.

Cian pats me on the shoulder in good faith. "Okay, man, I believe you. Just keep your dick away from my sister, and we won't have a problem. There's plenty of other girls here. Find one who isn't related to me."

I hear the warning loud and clear. He walks around me, tapping me on the shoulder with his tattooed hand. "Understood?"

I grit my teeth together, forcing the next words out. "Yeah, understood," I hate lying to my best friend, but right now, it's necessary. The only girl I'm going to find is Snow. I need to apologize and explain why the hell I said what I said.

Rosie

I pace back and forth in Lily's bedroom. I am so frustrated right now.

Can you fucking believe that asshole? Really, what an idiot! Friends! Argh, he drives me insane sometimes. I swear he has some sort of split personality disorder.

One minute he is all touchy feely and full of promises about someday, then the next: Oh, it means nothing Cian; we are just friends.

The nerve of him.

I have never, and I mean never, wanted to punch someone in the balls as much as I do right now. He either wants me or he doesn't. Whichever he decides, it better be fucking quick, because my patience level is running dangerously thin. I am getting sick and tired of waiting.

"Rosie! Are you up here?" Cillian's raspy voice calls me from the top of the stairs.

The rubber soles of his converse squeak against the hardwood floorboards. He makes his way across the landing before his footsteps silence, right outside the bedroom door.

Knock knock.

"Snow, open up. I know you're in there."

I'm not answering him. Nope, I'm not doing it. He can kiss my ass.

"Please, open the door." A deep sigh leaves him. "I just want to talk to you."

Well, too bad, because I have zero interest in speaking to you. Cillian O'Shea meet my good friend, the silent treatment.

"Please Snow."

Even though I can't see him, he seems defeated. "Just five minutes, please."

Do you know what he can do with those five minutes? He can take them and shove them right up where the sun doesn't shine.

I am not giving in this time. I always give in. I'm sick of it, of all the games, this cat-and-mouse thing we have going on is getting old. I'm over it! Cillian O'Shea needs to learn that I am not a toy he can play with. I am a person. I have real feelings and he hurt them.

I am determined to stand my ground. I'm taking my power back. *I am a strong independent woman. I don't need a man!*

A few minutes pass by, and I'm still pacing back and forth. Surprisingly, I have stayed silent, not given in to Cillian's requests. Finally, he gives up. *Thank Christ for that, because my resolve's wearing thin.*

Next thing, I hear some sort of commotion coming from the hallway. I press my ear against the wooden door, straining to hear what is going on.

Lily's tough as nails voice echoes through the closed door. "When the hell are you going to man up, Cillian? Anybody with two eyes can see you're crazy about that girl. Why don't you just tell Cian to back off and mind his own business?"

"It's not that simple, Lil, and you know it. What can I give her? Nothing. I've just finished school, and I'm not doing the whole college thing. The band is only taking off. Rosie deserves better and I can't give her that, at least not right now." Cillian's voice trembles with emotion. *Good, he deserves it!*

"You're so full of shit. The band is doing great with all the gigs, and Michael said he is so close to getting you guys your big break. You're so talented Cillian. Nobody writes or plays the way you do. If Jimi Hendrix and Bob Dylan had a love child, you'd be it. Stop selling yourself short; we both know you're making excuses because you're scared. One of these days, that girl in there will find someone who isn't afraid to fight for her. And you and I both know… it will break your heart to see her with someone else. Do you really want to spend your life wishing you claimed what could have been yours all along? Don't wait until it's too late. She idolizes you. She always has. If you won't do whatever it takes to make her yours, maybe Cian is right. You don't deserve her."

"Fuck you, Lil."

"Truth hurts big brother."

That right there is why Lily O'Shea is my best friend. Everyone she loves, she loves fiercely. She is honest, opinionated and loyal to a fault. It's what I love most about her.

A little tap comes from the door.

"Open up Rosie, it's Lily."

I slowly turn the handle, pulling the door ajar, just enough to make sure her brother's gone. When I see it's just her, I open it fully so she can make her way inside. I wrap my arms around her and pull her into a big hug. "Thanks for sticking up for me."

"No problem, Ro. It's not like it was something he didn't need to hear. I love my brother. I really do, but sometimes his head is so far up his own ass, he needs his little sister to pull it out for him."

Lily steps out of my grip; she rests her arms on my shoulders, checking my face for any sign of tears. "So…" Her eyes roam over my face with pity. "I take it you heard all that then."

She knows full well how I feel towards her brother, and I hate the way she gets caught in the middle of us from time to time.

"Yep," I reply, putting an extra pop on the p.

"And..." She places her hand on her hip, arching her pencilled eyebrows and pursing her dark stained lips, perfecting a stare that forces me to elaborate.

"And what, okay so he cares, just not enough." I shrug like it doesn't bother me, but we both know differently.

A defeated sigh falls from Lily's lips. "Fair point. Look, let's get back to the party and try to forget about my brother. Ciaran and Conor just arrived, and Ciaran is overdue for his daily dose of reality."

"Lead the way."

I follow Lily back downstairs. It's time to follow through with my original plan. Find a nice boy, no more pining. Times up, Cillian. I'm not waiting for you anymore.

Chapter Three

In the Blood by John Mayer

Cillian

Goddammit!

I'm such an idiot.

Why can't I let myself have her?

Why can't I admit what everyone already knows?

Why not tell Cian that I'm madly in love with his sister?

So many questions that I have no answer for. I slump back into the only free armchair left in my overcrowded living room. My idle fingers pick at the old brown leather, peeling off the worn arm. Ma really needs to toss this hunk of shite.

I fucking hate this chair. He used to always sit here, right beside the fireplace, blocking any heat from escaping into the rest of the room. Every night, he would come home from the pub after working on whatever the hell job he had that day and plonk himself into this chair. He'd kick his tattered boots off and order my mother to go grab him a can of stout from the fridge. *Woman get me a Guinness.*

Just thinking about him makes my fucking skin crawl.

For years, he has been a vice around my neck, his toxicity poisoning my every thought. He's like an unbearable itch I can never relieve myself of, no matter how hard I try.

I reach for the full bottle of Jameson sitting on the rickety oak coffee table in front of me. I need it, especially if I have to endure this sham of a party. I lift the green glass bottle to my lips, swigging back the amber liquid like a can of soda. The golden liqueur burns its way down my oesophagus, taking away all the bad memories I don't want to face.

Alcohol does a great job of drowning out my emotions, it's the only thing I can count on to take away the ache in my chest.

I scan the room, trying to make out all the blurred faces. Clearly, I've had a little more to drink than I originally thought. Sitting back, I close my eyes and allow my mind to drift away from the noise, back to a time where I believed a man like me could have his happy ever after.

"Mammy, are princesses real?"

"Yes baby, of course they are, and one day, when you're older you'll find your very own princess. You'll fall in love and live happily ever after."

Her hazel eyes — that are the mirror of my own — sparkle like diamonds against her stress-filled face.

"But Mammy, I think I already found her... she's in the garden."

She lets out one of her big, hearty, belly laughs. Her hands ruffle my hair and the smile on her face spreads further. "That's great, baby, what's her name?"

She takes my hands in hers, listening intently to every word I have to say.

"I don't know, but she's out in the garden. She's playing with Lily." I pull her towards the window above the kitchen sink; and point towards the little girl with the black hair my sister is playing with. I don't know her name, not yet! "Can you see her, Mammy? Isn't she pretty? She is gonna be my princess. She looks just like Snow White."

"Yes sweetie, I see her. She is very beautiful, just like a real princess."

With my voice full of hope, I ask, "Do you know her name, mammy?"

"Rosie." She squeezes my tiny hand with hers. "Her name is Rosie."

I grip the bottle a little tighter, forcing myself to push the memory back. I must have been about five or six the day I decided Rosie was the one for me. I didn't understand what love meant back then, but looking back on it now, I realise I've loved Rosie Mulligan from the very first moment I saw her.

I lift the bottle to my mouth again, draining the rest of the amber liquid in two mouthfuls; hopefully, it will make me forget, even just for a little.

Once the bottle is empty, I fire it across the sitting room; getting great satisfaction when it crashes against the wall and explodes into a million tiny pieces.

"Jesus Christ Cillian! Who the hell pissed in your breakfast cereal this morning?" Ciaran pipes up from his spot on the couch.

He may be one of my best friends, but I am not in the mood for his shit this evening.

Ignoring him, I take my favourite guitar out from behind the chair and run my fingers across the strings — my body instantly relaxes. Nothing could ever compare to the calmness my guitar gives me. Tucking the body of it under my left arm, I strum a few chords.

With each stroke, I allow the melody to flow through my body, filling my veins with peace only music can provide. I search my mind for a song, one that portrays my present mood. When I come up empty, my fingers start to play a new tune, blending a string of chords together to form the perfect melody.

I feel someone's gaze on me as the song takes me under. I don't need to look up, I know exactly who it is… Rosie. I can feel her eyes roaming over my face, as she listens intently to every chord I strum. I take that moment to lock my eyes on her baby blue ones; and suddenly, the rest of the room fades.

It's just me, her, and the tortured tune. I continue to play, to her, for her.

My singing voice is raspy from all the years of smoking cigarettes, but if anything, it has added more of a unique tone, one I have come to love. I feel each of the lyrics as they leave my tongue, each word chosen by me to fit the situation perfectly.

"How does it feel to watch her and love her from afar? If only he could tell her, she's his northern star. How does it feel to want her, when she's so far out of reach? If only he could be the man, the man he knows she needs.

How does it feel to break a heart, when it is your own? If only he could turn back time and make her finally see. That everything he does for her, is so he can be the man she needs.

I know that it's not easy to love someone who's broke. Just give him time to heal his mind of all he's ever known. He promises you, baby, that there will come a time, in this war he's waging, when your two hearts will entwine.

So please don't be mad love, he just wants you to know You're holding his forever, so please don't let it go.

Oh, please don't let it go."

My eyes search her face, hoping she hears the meaning behind each word I sing. I am expressing myself the only way I know how, through music.

Her eyes close as if she's forcing her tears not to fall, then she does the last thing I was expecting, she turns and walks away; taking what's left of my heart with her.

✻ ✻ ✻

My knuckles turn white as I clench the neck of my whiskey bottle. Gritting my teeth together, I force the jealous rage to stay buried beneath my not so calm surface.

My eyes narrow in on the guy across the room, the same guy who has his arms wrapped around Rosie's waist.

Tall, blonde and full of shit.

Anyone who's had the displeasure of meeting Sean Morgan knows he's a pretentious asshole. He walks around as if he owns the place, using his daddy's money to get whatever he wants. Tonight, he's set his sights on Rosie. My Rosie.

Two hours I've been sitting here contemplating my next move. It's taken every bit of willpower I have not to lay him out, but I've decided that killing Sean Morgan is not an option. But so, help me God, if he doesn't stop his roaming paws soon, I might change my mind.

Watching them interact together, smiling, laughing, and dancing is torturous. Now and then Rosie looks my way, I can still see the hurt behind her fake smile. This is my fault; I did this, I pushed her away.

I'm halfway through my second shoulder of whiskey when my little red-haired sister takes it upon herself to remove it from my hands.

"What the hell are you doing? You're pissed, Cillian!"

Pulling the bottle back from her grasp, I lift it against my lips and swallow a generous gulp. "Mind your own business, Squeak."

Lily stabs my chest with a pointed finger as her nostrils flare with annoyance.

"Listen here, Asshole, if you want to drink yourself to death, be my fucking guest; but don't do it in front of me. I love you way too much to let you become him, and from where I am standing, looking at your pathetic drunk ass, you're halfway there."

Angry tears roll down her cheeks, staining her face with the black eyeliner that surrounds her eyes.

Rising from the chair I step into her space. I'm more than a foot taller than her but she doesn't cower away. "I'm nothing like him! How dare you compare me to that fucking prick!"

Lily pushes herself up onto her tippy toes, her next words filled with hurt, venom and anger.

"Really, Lurch? Maybe you need to take a very long, hard look in the mirror because seeing the state you're in now, I understand why they say the apple doesn't fall far from the tree. You're a disgrace.

On the verge of becoming an alcoholic at the ripe old age of twenty-one. You're just like our worthless father. Get a grip on your life, or you will end up just like him; rotting in a prison cell with no one to blame but yourself. Wake the fuck up before you lose it all. The band. Rosie. And me."

I hand her the bottle defeated by the truth behind her words. I won't become him. I will not become my father.

Chapter Four

Oceans by Seafret

Rosie

I'm trying to ignore the heated conversation Cillian and Lily are engaged in on the opposite side of the room, but it's proving rather difficult.

Every hurtful word they spit at each other pierces my heart a little more. Everyone—except Cillian—knows his drinking has been getting progressively worse in recent weeks. Honestly, I don't think I've seen him sober in months.

The hand resting on my waist tightens, dragging my gaze away from my best friend and the beautifully broken man.

Sean Morgan and his aquamarine eyes scan my body from head to toe, making me feel wanted, and desired. His handsome, yet boyish face looks at me as if he's waiting on the answer to his question.

"I'm sorry," I apologize for my ignorance. "What did you say?"

His soft chuckle makes his shoulders shake. "It's okay. I was just saying, it seems O'Shea is still a drunken asshole."

With a raised brow, I step out of his reach. "Excuse me?"

Sean takes hold of my hand; he notices the look of horror on my face because he's sure quick to apologize. "Shit! I'm sorry. I shouldn't have said that. I know you two are close. It's just... I've watched you follow him around for years, and he's too stupid to realise you're standing right in front of him."

He reaches up, pushing a stray hair from my face. "You deserve better than that. Any man lucky enough to have your attention should kiss the ground you walk on."

I wanted this, a man who sees me. I drink in his features. He looks nothing like Cillian. His ashy blonde hair, cut tight to his scalp; his aquamarine eyes — so light, they're almost transparent — rest under his naturally furrowed brow and a sharp jawline that could carve glass frames his face; technically, he's gorgeous, but I don't feel... it.

The heart stopping, earth quaking, soul claiming, rush I have when I'm around Cillian.

But, isn't that what tonight is all about? Letting all those daydreams I've spent years living in, go; to move on from the boy whose heart is undeniably unobtainable.

Glancing over at Cillian once more, I wonder if letting him go is an option. That's when I see it. My heart, breaking right before my eyes. He's leaning back in the old leather armchair with his eyes closed. But that's not what's caused my stomach to drop ten thousand feet. No, it's the girl straddling his lap and the way his arms are clutching her waist as her lips travel over the protruding vein that creeps out of the neckline of his t-shirt. The blatant disregard for my feelings, and the deafening sound of every promise of someday, crashing with a heavy ear-piercing silence against the floor.

I watch the way his hand teases the hem of her crop top, and suddenly, all the air in the room dissipates. I need to get out of here; away from him and the feelings that are threatening to pull me under.

"I'm going to head home."

Sean's eyes crinkle with disappointment at my announcement, but I can't stay here a second longer. I'm well aware, whatever it is between Cillian and I, it does not resemble a relationship; and that I'm all sorts of crazy for getting jealous over someone I haven't kissed since I was ten years old.

But I can't help it; I'm not like Lily. I can't acknowledge my feelings and then tell them to fuck off.

They're very present and staying here will only aggravate them more.

After walking over to the coat rack, I pull on my leather jacket and head for the door; but right before I turn the handle, Sean gently grips my elbow. "Rosie, wait up."

Spinning in place, I face him.

"It's dark, let me walk you home?"

"Thanks, but I'm only one field over. It won't take me long," I reassure him.

"Please, I'd feel like a complete dick if I let you walk home at night on your own."

Holding his hands up, in an 'I mean no harm' gesture, he adds, "I'll even promise to keep these to myself." His smouldering smirk makes me blush.

"Fine, but if I even see so much as a fingernail emerging in my direction, I won't be responsible for your death. Deal?"

He shoves his hands deep into the pockets of his washed-out denim jeans, laughing off my teasing. "Deal."

✻ ✻ ✻

Together, using our phones as torches, we trail through the grass field between the O'Shea house and mine. Glancing down at Sean's no-longer-pristine white Nike's, I cringe internally at the sticky, wet, muddy grass stuck to the soles. I nervously look around at everything but his face. The quiet night air does nothing to fill the silence.

"I'm sorry about your shoes."

"Eh, it's alright. They're old anyway."

I don't miss the twitch above his brow as he responds to my apology or the way his face scrunches after he steps into the puddle beneath his feet. "Shit!"

Coming to an abrupt halt, I stop him in his tracks. "Look, I really appreciate you wanting to walk me home, but it's just through that gap beside the oak tree." I point in that general direction, using my flashlight app to light the way. It's about one-hundred meters from where we are standing.

Sean looks between me and his Nike's. "Are you sure? I… I can walk you the whole way."

"I'm sure. It's not that far. I've been walking these fields since I was six years old. I'll be fine. Promise."

"Okay, if you're sure. But, before you go…umm, I was sort of hoping you would have dinner with me sometime? I know you have a thing for Cillian, and I'm probably an idiot for even asking, but I like you, Rosie. I think you're smart, pretty, and we would have a lot of fun together. Who knows, maybe it's me you're supposed to be with, and not that clueless drunk. I'm sorry — no, you know what, I'm not. That's what he is, a clueless drunk idiot to not recognize what an amazing girl he has right in front of him."

Taking my hand gently he looks deep into my eyes. "But I do Rosie. I recognize how amazing you are, and I would love to take you out. What do you say?"

I should be mad at him for speaking about Cillian that way. I should tell him to take a hike… but then I remember that girl all over Cillian, and all the hurt it caused me. Pulling a deep breath in through my nose, I blow it out and give in to his request. "How does next Saturday sound?"

"Really?" I smile at his reaction.

"Yes, really. Why not?"

"Oh, okay. Great. I'll pick you up at seven. Night Rosie."

He gives me one more shy smile before he turns and walks away.

"Night, Sean."

I head towards the tree lining both properties, but instead of walking past it, I head up the handmade wooden ladder and into the tree house. I need to process all the events of this evening and this place is exactly where to do it.

Once I climb inside, I pull out my old purple throw, a few pillows, my sketch pad and pencils. I spend the next hour bleeding my thoughts onto paper. The pencil rushes across the page, line after line until finally, I look down at the drawing.

Cillian, always Cillian.

Cillian

The red glow coming from the small digital clock resting on my bedside locker illuminates my otherwise dark bedroom. It's nine forty-five and I've barely slept a wink.

Rolling over onto my back, I release a frustrated groan. Between the alcohol and everything else that went down last night, my mind wouldn't shut off. I know I need to fix this, and not just with Rosie, but Lily too. She shouldn't have to see me like that. Especially after everything that went down with Da over the years.

I was so far out of line I couldn't even see the damn thing.

I behaved like a total wanker, one that deserved every word she spat at me. I know my drinking habits bother her, and usually, I'm more conscious not to overdo it around her. Today's agenda: apologies for acting like a dickhead.

Gently, I lift my weighted head up from the pillow. Jesus Christ, how much did I drink last night? The groggy heaviness from all the alcohol I consumed forces me to slump back down. The potent smell of liquor fills the surrounding air, its stale scent burning my nostrils with every breath I inhale.

Fuck me, I need a shower.

After dragging my lifeless body from my bed, I make my way to the small connecting bathroom between Lily's room and mine and try my best not to wake her, not yet, I still can't face her after being such an asswipe last night. I twist the temperature dial on the shower up to the hottest setting; hoping to sweat the rest of last night out through my pores.

Once I'm finished, I pull on my clothes and head back to my room. Grabbing my notepad and pen from my desk, I sling my guitar case over my shoulder and head for my thinking spot. I need somewhere I can breathe.

Oldtown is a twenty-minute drive from Dublin City Centre, but to the city slickers, it's the sticks. There's not much to look at around this part of the country; unless you like green fields and back roads; but I love it here. It's peaceful.

The next house is about one kilometre down the road, and it belongs to Cian and Rosie's parents. The place is about three times bigger than ours; and they own all the land surrounding it. Their fields stretch right to the boundary of ours, divided by a thorn hedgerow and a large oak tree. I make my way over to the old tree that separates the two properties. When we were kids, our Ma's let us build a treehouse in it. I still come here every now and again, it's where I go when I need space to write, or just think.

Climbing my way up the old rickety ladder, I take extra care on the rotten step.

It's hard to believe this place is still standing; we must have been only twelve when we built it with Ma and Maggie. When I reach the top, I spot the old treasure trunk in the corner. Lily and Rosie thought it would be a great idea to store blankets and cushions in it, for the cold Irish summer evenings. I lift the lid, and sure enough, there they are.

Rosie's lavender and apple scent immediately floods my senses. She must have been here recently. She always loved coming out here to draw; and judging by the new art pinned on the wooden walls — that's exactly what she was doing.

My eyes scan each piece, everything from roses and thorns to birds and trees, then finally, a broken man and his guitar. His head's bent, and his eyes are closed as if he is letting the music take control. She must have been here this morning because every detail of this drawing is identical to how I looked last night.

I can never understand how she does it, capturing a moment so perfectly with just a pencil and paper.

Gently, I take the picture from the wall, folding it carefully and sticking it into the pocket at the front of my guitar case. Placing the purple rug and a few pillows from the box onto the floor for comfort, I take a seat and grab my guitar.

The morning sun rises over the horizon, glowing through the cut-out Perspex windows. The birds sing in the trees. Chirping with the promise of a new day. I pull out my worn leather-bound notebook and pen.

Dear Snow, for every picture you draw me, I'll write you a song.
Love, Charming.

My fingers move across the strings as a new melody forms in my mind. This is what I do, I write music.

I let each note take away the worries of yesterday. I lose myself in every chord. Lyrics push to the forefront of my mind and I scribble them down as they come.

"I pray to God above that he will save me. Cause the devil's sent a fallen one to claim me. The lust I feel inside, this greed to make her mine. Her beauty has got me falling on my knees.

She's the girl all the others envy. Skin as fair as the winter's snow. I'm a glutton for her eyes, the colour of the bluest sky. Anywhere she goes, I will follow.

This war going on between us, is one they never meant for me to win. My heart belongs to a fallen angel. Who's wrapped up in seven deadly sins!

Lips redder than the apple of Eden. Hair black like an onyx stone. Oh, it is not a lie. She will be my demise. Straight to the gates of hell is where I'll go.

I pray to God above that he will free me, the devil took my soul for her to keep. I try to fight against the wrath inside me. But her heart is the only one I seek.

This war going on between us, is one they never meant for me to win. My heart belongs to a fallen angel. Who's wrapped up in seven deadly sins!

Oh, my heart belongs to a fallen angel. Who's wrapped up in seven deadly sins.

Rosie, always, Rosie.

Chapter Five

All or Nothing by Wild Youth

Rosie

So, this date is going down as the worst date in the history of all dates. Who knew Sean could be so... bland?

"So, Rosalie, where do you see yourself in five years?" Sean questions while chewing a mouthful of his overpriced steak.

Reaching for my glass of sparkling water, I lift it to my lips washing away the disdain I feel towards his blatant lack of table etiquette. "I'm studying design at the National College of Art and Design. I'm not sure which path I'll take yet, but I'm leaning towards interior."

I get that he is just making conversation, but seriously! I'm nineteen; my life goals consist of what I'm doing next Saturday. I feel like I'm at a job interview, not a first date. I scan the expensive restaurant, it's full of businessmen in stuffy suits. Was this supposed to impress me? If so, it's an epic fail. What twenty-year-old brings their date here? I couldn't even read the goddamn menu — it's in French.

Honestly, I would have preferred a cheeseburger. Fancy is not my style; I feel out of place and extremely uncomfortable. Also, let me just add; I hate when people call me Rosalie. I'm Rosie.

Sure, Rosalie is my birth name, but nobody calls me that — bar my Grandmothers and occasionally, my Da. I prefer Rosie. It's more, I don't know.... me.

"Interesting choice. But isn't designing more of a hobby than a career path?"

Lord, grant me patience because I'm seconds away from throwing my main course over his egotistical head.

"Wouldn't you rather do something more," he pauses, searching for the right word I presume, but we all know no matter what leaves his mouth next will be the wrong choice, "challenging."

Okay, I've had enough of him and his backward, downright insulting opinions. I need out, and I need it now. *W.W.L.D? What would Lily do?*

Lily's sharp sarcastic wit fills my thoughts. "Bitch, if it were me, I'd have climbed out the bathroom window by now, that boy would put an insomniac asleep."

I look up at Sean, who has his face planted into his phone. Fuck this, I'm out of here, time to call the rescue squad.

Rosie: SOS! I need you. Please, SAVE ME!

Lily: LOL! Wait for it… I told you so. (God, that felt good.) Sean's about as entertaining as watching paint dry. Give me thirty. Lily "the boss bitch" O'Shea, to the rescue.

Rosie: THIRTY MINUTES? I could be dead by then.

Lily: Eh, dramatic much? Hakuna your tatas! Help is on the way. Don't kill me... oh, and if you do, bury me in my Doc Martens. They're the only love of my life.

Rosie: Lily! What did you do?

Rosie: What help?

Rosie: LILY!!!!!!!!

"So, Rosalie."

I'm not a violent person, but I swear if he calls me Rosalie one more time, I'll stab him with one of the four forks sitting on the table. Who the hell needs four forks?

"Rosie." My name comes from somewhere behind me. A deep velvet voice that could drop the knickers off a nun. One I would know anywhere.

Cillian. What is he doing here?

I spin around in my chair and sure enough, Cillian O'Shea is barrelling straight for me, with a look in his hazel eyes that would send a bold child scurrying.

Lily! I'm going to kill her!

Cillian strides towards us at a thunderous pace; when he reaches the table, he slams his two hands flat on the surface, rattling the half-full glass of wine in front of Sean.

His murderous eyes lock on Sean, but his direct commanding words are all for me. "Get your coat, Snow. We're leaving."

Who died and made him Hitler?

"Morgan, did I or did I not explain to you on more than one occasion, that Rosie is off-limits? Did I not make myself crystal-fucking-clear that Rosie is unavailable?"

Sorry, what the fuck? Off-limits? Unavailable? Has he lost his mind?

Sean swallows his tongue with an audible gulp, he's completely frozen in his seat, and if I wasn't so aggravated at Cillian's little show of possession, I'd probably find Sean's reaction hilarious. The other patrons stare as Sean sits there with his mouth agape.

Cillian faces me and his hardened expression softens. "Come on, Snow. I'll take you home."

I go willingly, even though his whole, Me Tarzan, you Jane act is not acceptable. Better the devil you know, than the devil who thinks he's God!

The whole way to the car, Cillian guides me with his hand gently resting on my back. We reach his cherry red golf and he holds the door open for me to get in.

I take my seat, then turn to scold him. "What the fuck was that? Would you like me to lie down so you can piss all over me some more?"

"Don't, okay. I'm not in the mood for your sass tonight. Sean Morgan is a dickhead. He's been that way since we were kids and you know it. Lily called me and said you needed rescuing, so here I am. So, save your ear bashing for someone else. Also, you're welcome."

Twisting the key in the ignition, the old car rumbles to life.

"I'm welcome? Do you think it's okay for you to storm into a five-star restaurant and go full caveman? Who do you think you are, demanding me to leave? You're not my dad."

He tries to speak, but I cut him off by continuing with my rant. "Oh, and don't get me started on the whole, Rosie is off-limits. Rosie is unavailable," I taunt, mocking his earlier tone.

Cillian mumbles something under his breath, but I don't quite catch what it was. "Excuse me? What did you just say?"

His calloused hands grip the wheel, his knuckles turning white from the pressure he is putting into his grasp. He looks at me, eyes burning with... with, I don't know what, to be honest.

Grinding his teeth together, his head whips around so fast, I almost get whiplash. "I said, you are unavailable. You will never be available, Rosie. You. Are. Mine!"

Oh, hell no! Mine? Mine? What am I, a fucking teddy bear? I belong to nobody.

Pulling the door handle, I pop it open before he drives off. I need to leave this car right now. I've had enough assholeness tonight to last me a lifetime.

Twisting in the seat, I flick my feet out onto the tarmac, but Cillian's hand comes down on my shoulder, holding the rest of me inside the car.

"Where are you going?"

"Listen, Cillian, I don't have the time — or the crayons — to explain this to you. So, when you figure out what's wrong with this whole 'prince on his white horse, coming to save the day' act, you have going on, come find me. Until then, this princess will rescue her-fucking-self."

With that, I leap from the car and storm across the car park. Take that, Disney. This princess doesn't need a man. I make it about eight meters before the heavens open and God rains all over my parade. Literally! Fuck you rain. Fuck you very, very much.

Before I can process how I'm going to get home in the lashings of rain, two strong arms wrap around me from behind. The all too familiar earthy scent gives away his identity.

"Rosie. Get in the car, now. It's lashing."

When I refuse to move, Cillian lifts me, throwing me over his shoulders like a bag of coal.

"Put me down," I scream, punching his back with my fists. I mustn't be that strong because his shoulders shake with laughter as he stalks back to the parked car.

He gently places me in the passenger seat and kneels in the doorway so he's at my eye level. He places a soft, gentle kiss on my forehead.

"You might not be mine, Rosie. But, I'm definitely yours."

With that he closes the door, leaving me with my mouth agape as he rounds the front of the car to the driver's seat.

Cillian

The ten-minute car ride back to my house is filled with awkward silence. I'm still processing the fact, Rosie was on a date, and with Sean, the king of all dickheads. In all the years I've known Sean, we've never got along.

The fact he's been googly eyed over Rosie since we've been kids might have something to do with that. I'd like to think it's because he's a wanker in general—he doesn't deserve someone as pure as Rosie—but that would be a lie.

The second Rosie sent Lily that first SOS message, my keys were in my hand and I was out the door quicker than Lily could respond. Which is most likely the reason my conniving, little brat of a sister read Rosie's text aloud; she knew I would go running, and I proved her right.

There wasn't a chance in hell I was standing idly by while Sean Morgan tried to stick his dick in my girl. Okay, so she's not mine, not yet… but after tonight I'm hoping to change that.

It's been a few days since the party, and I've done nothing but think of ways to tell Rosie how I feel. I've spent years going between avoiding her and trying to be her friend. I've spent countless nights trying to fuck her out of my system with any girl who was willingly throwing themselves at me.

Nothing ever worked; she was always there reminding me; she is what I need.

The only other solution is to give us a shot. Try being together, boyfriend and girlfriend. Although, I still have reservations about that. There are a lot of risks, Rosie's friendship with Lily could suffer, not to mention the band, and God only knows how Cian will react to it all—but, I want to try; I don't think I'd be able to live with the regret otherwise. I'm finally ready to face the wrath of her brother. I can't fight my feelings any longer. Cian knows deep down I would never intentionally hurt his sister; she means far too much to me.

Taking my eyes off the road for a split second, I steal a glance at the raven-haired beauty beside me.

Her head rests against the glass as she watches the world fly by with wide blue eyes. I need to talk to her. I just haven't figured out how yet. Focusing back on the narrow country road that leads to my house, I reach across the centre console and take her hand in mine.

"I'm sorry, Ro."

Those three words linger in the air around us, and although I'm not looking at her, I can feel her eyes on me.

Seconds pass before finally — she squeezes my hand a little tighter. I intertwine my fingers with hers, hoping to assure her I'm ready. I want this, and I want it with her.

Nearing our houses, I ask, "Do you have to head straight home, or can you hang out with me for a while?"

She's hesitant for a moment as she contemplates what my suggestion means. Eventually, after what feels like forever, she breaks the silence with four simple words that fill my chest with hope. "I could hang out."

Sneaking another peek at her, I spy the small smile that forms on her plump red lips. She drags her bottom lip between her teeth and nibbles a little. *My Jesus, she will kill me, yet.*

Pulling into my driveway, I put the car in park. "How does the rooftop sound?"

Rosie raises her eyebrow while huffing out a sweet laugh. "Eh, wet?"

The rain pounding against the hood of my car supports her theory. "Okay, fair point. How about a movie?" Why am I so nervous? "I'm sure we still have Snow White on VCR."

The smile on her gorgeous face makes my chest tighten. "Aren't we a little old for fairy tales?"

I push back a stray hair that's kissing her rosy cheek. "We're never too old for a happy ever after, Snow."

With every ounce, of willpower I possess, I pull back and suppress the urge I've to kiss her. "Let's go, princess. Disney waits for no man."

I hop out of the car and rush around to open her door. Taking her hand in mine, we walk up the gravel drive and into my house.

* * *

I pick up yesterday's dirty laundry up off my bedroom floor, throwing it in the wash basket. "Sorry about the mess."

My room is not the tidiest. There are clothes thrown across the chair that sits in the corner, and the bed is unmade, but other than that, it's reasonably clean. Well, for me.

"It's fine, Cillian. Stop fussing."

I watch as Rosie makes her way over to the accented wall. It's completely covered with all the old records I collected over the years, giving it a wallpaper effect. Lily showed me the cool idea off some app on her phone; Pin-it or something like that.

Sitting proudly in the centre of the records is a large framed painting of Jimi Hendrix shredding his guitar. The background behind him is tea-stained sheet music for 'Little Wing'. The man was a musical genius, the greatest instrumentalist in the history of rock.

I adore this painting. Rosie painted it for me for my twenty-first birthday. She is an amazing artist; she doesn't give herself enough credit for how talented she is. Rosie runs her fingers over the glass protecting the artwork.

"You... you had it framed."

Stepping in behind her, I wrap my arms around her waist. Her back is flush against my chest and I rest my head on top of hers, tucking her in under my chin. "Yeah, of course, I did. I love it, it's probably the best gift I've ever gotten. It means a lot to me, especially because of who painted it." I kiss the top of her head and breathe in her cherry apple scent.

Turning in my arms so we're face to face, she looks up at me with eyes full of questions. "What are we doing here, Cillian? I can't handle all this back and forth. The all-or-nothing facade is wearing thin. I can't keep putting my heart on the line for you. Not when every time I do, you stomp all over it."

Taking her face between my palms, I search for assurance in her clear blue eyes. "This is me Rosie, all of me. If you want me, I'm all yours. I promised you someday, and today is that day." I kiss her forehead as she wraps her arms tighter around my waist. "We both know, whatever it is between us, it's always been more than friends. There's something magical about us, and I'm done fighting it. You make all my darkness brighter. I want us to try, Ro."

A small tear escapes her eye. I gently brush it away with my thumb. Resting my forehead against hers, our noses touch, and our lips are a breath apart. "I tried so hard not to fall for you, Snow. But I've realised lately, I'm already free falling without a parachute."

Rosie lifts her hands, covering my chest. I'm sure she can feel how fast my heart is beating. I just laid it all out, hoping she feels the same.

"I fell a long time ago, I'm just waiting on you to catch up," she whispers against my lips.

I close what's left of the little space between us, the need I have to kiss her taking over. When our lips finally touch, it feels like I'm drowning; and Rosie is the air I need to breathe. It's all-consuming, the softness of her mouth pressed against mine, the sweet moan that leaves her lips. The way her delicate fingers tease my hair. I sweep my tongue over her bottom lip, begging for entry and she immediately responds. I brush the tip of my tongue against hers, and I swear my soul screams at me. Hello forever!

I kiss her... I kiss her the way an addict would kiss a cigarette. Pulling her close against my lips, I cup my hands around her body, setting her on fire. I breathe her in, letting her fill my lungs and squeeze my heart. I breathe her out, knowing well, she's become my new addiction.

Finally, after what seems like hours, we break apart, both of us gasping for air. We're consumed by the need for each other.

The smile on Rosie's face is infectious. "I thought you promised me some happy ever afters," she teases with a cheeky smile.

"Lead the way, Princess. Lead the way."

Chapter Six

Rosie by The Kooks

Rosie

*T*wo weeks.

That's how long Cillian and I have been sneaking around.

Sharing stolen kisses and mid-night cuddles while the rest of the world is fast asleep. After that night in Cillian's room, we kept our newfound relationship status a secret. Giving us time to enjoy being a couple, without having to deal with the inevitable backlash, bound to come from Cian when he finds out his best friend is dating his sister.

Lily is the only other person privy to the new development between Cillian and me. Being the best friend, she is, she's been covering for us when I say I'm spending the night at her place, when in fact I've been curled up next to her brother.

I can still hear her say, "What are friends for? Just no loud sex noises, please. I draw the line at hearing my big brother banging my friend into next week."

But, like all secrets, it's becoming increasingly harder to keep. Not being able to kiss, touch or even look at Cillian for too long in public, is almost unbearable. Not to mention, how hard it was to sit idly by at the last two local 4Clover shows, while every girl, mother and granny fawned over Cillian as if he was a pot of gold at the end of a rainbow.

That leads me to the last and final problem I have with our little secret relationship, my Da and his unwanted matchmaking.

Somehow, he found out about my recent kind-of-date with Sean Morgan. To say he is ecstatic by that news would be the understatement of the century. My Da has been friends with Sean's father, Patrick, for years; ever since they attended Trinity College back in nineteen-o-splash. And contrary to the truth, he believes Sean and I would make a perfect pair. *Please hold while I find a puke bucket.*

"Rosalie, darling, I don't understand your hesitation. Sean Morgan is a lovely young man and a joining between you two would do wonders for our business."

To say I don't agree with my father's statement, would be a gross understatement. I've been trying to avoid Sean like the plague since our epic dinner fail went down in flames. Now, to make matters worse, my Da is insisting I attend this business meeting tonight, per Sean's request.

"Da, I don't want to go. I've already made plans." *With Cillian, but he doesn't need to know that piece of information.*

"Rosalie. Don't be so childish. You will attend this dinner and you will behave; with the good manners we raised you with. Sean Morgan is the kind of gentleman you should spend your time with. He's well-bred, with a good education. A romantic union between the two of you would benefit our record label, hugely."

Has he lost his mind? A romantic-fucking-union? Is he for real?

"Da, there will be no," using air quotes I accentuate my next word, "union of any kind. He is, how do I say this nicely... more boring than the colour beige."

"Listen here, young lady. You're going to this dinner despite your childish feelings. You will dress up and play nice with Sean and his family. This business deal is crucial to the success of 4Clover. Without Patrick Morgan's contacts, your brother and his friends will end up wasting their talent in shitty dive bars. You and I both know those boys are star quality."

Taking two steps forward, he closes the space between us. "So, you will do what you're told, do you understand me? I will not have this little crush you've been harbouring for a certain guitarist, fuck this up. The future of 4Clover depends on this deal. If that means you have to schmooze Sean — that's exactly what you will do."

Lowering my head in defeat, I release a heavy sigh. "Yes, Daddy."

He played his hand nicely. He knows full well, I would do anything to help 4Clover succeed. They deserve their big break. Let's just hope Cillian will understand that too.

* * *

Standing in front of the floor-length mirror in my bedroom, I examine my reflection with zero enthusiasm. My black hair is curled and flowing freely down my back.

Except for my favourite bold red lipstick—Ruby Woo by MAC, I kept my make-up simple; with just a light dusting of sun-shimmer.

I run my hand over the satin wrap dress, it's beautiful—long sleeves that cuff around my wrist, a deep plunging V-neckline that accentuates my collarbone and elongates my neck. The figure-hugging material stops mid-calf, giving off a classy, elegant look with just the right amount of sex appeal.

Normally, I would give my left tit to wear something like this, but tonight, it feels wrong.

I still haven't told Cillian about tonight; he's been at rehearsals all-day. I sent him a brief text asking him to call me, but I got no reply.

Taking one last look at myself, my stomach fills with dread. The last thing I need is for Sean to think I dressed up for him, when in reality, I'm doing this for Cillian, Cian, Ciaran and Conor. Their music career depends on this meeting going well and I'm willing to sit through a meal with Sean if it ensures 4Clover's success.

To finish my look, I slip into my favourite pair of silver holographic stilettos and slide the silver Tree of Life, Ani and Alex bracelet onto my wrist.

A gentle tap on my door grabs my attention.

"Who is it?"

"It's me." Cillian's unmistakable raspy lilt echoes. "Can I come in?"

Shit! What's he doing here?

Pushing the panic bubbling up my throat, back down, I force myself to open the door, even though I'm certain I'm not ready for what's bound to transpire when Cillian finds out where I'm going tonight.

Cillian's heated stare travels over every inch of me, causing shockwaves of desire to erupt along my skin. His hazel eyes darken with something that can only be described as unerasable hunger. "Jesus, Snow. You look beautiful."

Stepping forward, he claims the room with his presence. Without taking his lustful eyes off me, he closes the door and strides towards me like a man with a purpose. "Wouldn't want anyone to witness me kissing the ever-loving shit out of those blood-red lips."

No matter how hard I try, I can't seem to get words to leave my mouth. I just stand there as Cillian wraps his arms around my waist, engulfing me entirely.

"Fuck, I missed you today." He places a loving kiss on the tip of my nose. "Where are you off to, looking like every man's wet dream? Hot date?"

His tone is light and teasing; it breaks my heart that he thinks I'm dressed up for him — well, I suppose in a fucked-up way I am, but I can guarantee he won't see it like that. Swallowing the bowling ball sized lump in my throat, I search my mind for the words I need to say. *Yes, I have a date, a dinner date. And no, it's not with you.*

"Erm, actually… I… umm."
Jesus, why is this so hard?

He steps back, the hunger in his eyes disappearing, replaced by something much darker. "Spit it out, Rosie."

The sharp edge in his voice makes me flinch. Curling into myself, I look up at him through my lashes. "I have to accompany my Da to a business dinner." *Omitting isn't lying.*

"Oh! Right, okay. How come? Isn't that Lily's domain?"

He's right, Lily is normally the only one to attend this kind of thing. She's been interning at Da's new record label ShamRock Recordz since we left school last year. Schmoozing clients is one of her greatest attributes. Her small doll-like frame makes people underestimate her; then she unleashes her fiery, take no shit attitude and gets shit done. Her ability to bring men twice her size to their knees is frankly terrifying, and that's what makes her a shark in the music business.

"It's-at-Sean's." The words come out so fast, they're blended.

"Sorry, what did you just say?"

Pulling up my big girl knickers, I inhale. "The business dinner. It's with Sean's father. Da didn't ask Lily because my presence, was the one they requested."

"Please, tell me you're joking."

Cillian's normally cocky demeanour vanishes. He's hurt. I can see it in his eyes. "You're not going, Ro. No-fucking-way."

"I've no option. I have to go, Da insisted. It will help him secure the contacts to further the band's career. There's a lot resting on this. It's just dinner. It means nothing."

For a split second, I get a glimpse of the little boy I once knew. The boy he was before he had to grow up too fast. Then suddenly, as if he never showed his vulnerability, the wall he hides behind, slams up, his fists clench, and his anger takes over.

This is the Cillian I don't like—arrogant, aggressive and almost emotionless.

"Do you know what, Snow? You're right. Go enjoy your dinner with Mr-fucking-fancy-pants because just like that stupid kiss ass meal, this," he motions between us, "means nothing to you."

Before I have a moment to catch my breath, let alone reply, he's out the door, slamming it shut behind him. I want to chase him, to explain why this stupid dinner is so important; but knowing Cillian the way I do—he needs time to sift through his emotions.

* * *

"Rosalie, Darling. You look delightful."

The insincerity is clear in Alice Morgan's voice as she greets me and my father in the foyer of her extravagant home. No joke, this place is bigger than most hotels.

Also, I am well aware I look like shit lady, no need to lie. Who are you trying to fool here? That smile is as fake as your tits.

"Rosalie, you made it." Sean enters the bigger-than-my-house hallway.

His sandy blonde hair is slicked back and his aqua-blue eyes glisten with delight. But they can't hold a candle to the muddy hazel ones I love so much. The ones that belong to the boy who just stomped all over my heart.

Sean's long confident stride places him beside me within seconds. I take in what he is wearing and nearly choke myself trying not to laugh. A navy sweater vest with beige chinos and matching navy loafers. *Golf much?*

Quickly wrapping his arm around my shoulders, he pulls my body closer to his. *Ever heard of personal space buddy? Back the hell off!*

His face holds a look of triumph, with a slight hint of smugness. *Entitled asswipe.*

I don't know why Cillian and Sean hate each other so much, but whatever the reason, it feels like me being here, is a win for #TeamSean.

Sean is aware this is the last place I want to be. Even though I haven't verbally said it, I'm sure it's written all over my less-than-impressed face. The weight of his arm resting on my shoulders is making my skin crawl; I don't want him touching me.

Peeling his arm from my body, I level him with a glare; a silent warning to keep his hands to himself. *I don't bite, but I'm betting if I asked her; Lily would.*

My eyes scan the large entryway of the Morgan house. It is evident Sean's family comes from old money; it's practically dripping off the walls in solid gold blocks.

I need to get out of here as quickly as possible and find Cillian. I didn't like the look that washed over his face earlier. It scared me. I don't want him to do something he might regret—like go on a week-long bender and start a row with his own shadow.

Cillian's temper is explosive, all it takes is one flick of a switch and he automatically self-destructs.

Sean's hand settles on the curve of my back, forcing me to follow the rest of the group to the dining room. Slowly, I place one foot in front of the other. *Just one dinner. Just one dinner.* I repeat those three words over and over as if they're my own personal mantra. Hopefully, it will be over quickly.

Entering the dining area, I take in the over-the-top decor. An ostentatious chandelier hangs from the centre of the high ceiling, making the long dining table the centre focus in the room. Walking towards the only two free chairs available, I spot a small place card with my name resting on an empty plate. Right between Sean and my Da. *The universe must really fucking hate me.*

About an hour later, I feel something vibrate against my ankle; It takes a second to register it's my phone. Trying my best to ignore it, I sit up straighter, but the constant buzzing noise against the white parquet flooring is getting on my last nerve.

Not to mention the side glares I'm receiving from daddy dearest at each buzz.

I place, what I presume to be, my real silver cutlery gently on the table. "Sorry, please excuse me, I need to use the little girl's room."

"My dear Rosalie, by all means, don't let us keep you." Everything about this woman is so plastic. So much so, even China would deny making her. "It's just down the hall, the sixth door on your right."

Just down the hall my ass.

Hurriedly, I make my way through this maze of a house, finally finding the bathroom. Which, may I add, looks like something from MTV Cribs.

Clipping my small holographic clutch bag open, I pull out my phone and unlock it, only to find a ton of new messages. Not good!

All of which are from Cillian. Definitely not good!

Cillian: You broke my heart.
Cillian: I felt the pain.
Cillian: With every shot.
Cillian: I'll wash away.
Cillian: The taste of you.
Cillian: From off my tongue.
Cillian: Just one more drink.
Cillian: And I'll be numb.
Cillian: Oh, fuck you, Rosie. Rosie, fuck you.
Cillian: As you can see, my whiskey and I are doing fucking dandy without you. Hope you're having fun with Mr. Moneybags. At least, I can say I tried. Bye, Snow. Xx.

I read over every line, again and again, tears falling from my eyes. I don't know how to fix this. I don't even know if he wants me too. My heart tightens in my chest, struggling to beat in time. Every word he typed cuts deeper than a thousand knives. I need to get out of here; I need to find him and make things right.

I should have never come here in the first place. Fuck my Da. Cillian is all that matters, and I won't sit back and watch as he drinks himself into an early grave.

He has been on a slippery slope with his drinking for a while now, every time life gets too much for him, he drowns himself in alcohol. He is searching for something at the bottom of every bottle, but the only thing he finds is more pain.

He needs help; he needs support, and I intend to give him both.

Rushing from the bathroom, I make my way to the front door. I sneak past the dining room—like a goddamn ninja turtle—so nobody sees me leaving. Hopefully, by the time they notice I'm gone, I'll be far enough away that they won't bother coming to find me.

Chapter Seven

I'll Follow You by Shinedown

Cillian

Okay, I probably shouldn't have sent Rosie those messages, but you know what—hindsight is a real bitch.

I'm just so fucking pissed at her. I really thought we would make this work. I was ready to face the wrath of everyone so I could be with her. I almost told Cian today at practice—thank fuck I didn't.

When she dropped that Sean bomb, everything came crumbling down. At that moment, I realized I'll never live up to the person she's destined to be with. I don't come from money; my Da is a rotten apple who's in prison for the next three to five years; all I have is my old guitar and a few songs. How can I measure up to Sean when we aren't even on the same goddamn level?

I've been sitting in this pub since I left Rosie's house earlier, knocking the whiskeys back, one after the other, feeling the familiar burn with every sip. I hate this gnawing feeling, the one that reminds me just how fucked up I am. I'll never be worthy of a girl like Rosie Mulligan, not while I still fall victim to my childhood and the never-ending thoughts that I'm never good enough.

"Shut up, you fucking bitch. I told you to have my dinner ready. Do you call this fucking dinner? I wouldn't even feed that to a dog."

Fear covers her face. She can do nothing right, not for him. None of us can.

"I'm sor..." The force of his hand hitting her face, silences her words. The distinct sound of skin slapping skin ricochets around the kitchen.

I'm scared. Lily's scared. I squeeze her little hand a bit tighter — under the table away from his view. Silently, I tell her I'll keep her safe. That's my job. I'm her big brother. It doesn't matter how scared I am. I need to keep her safe.

"I told you to shut up. You better start doing what you're told, Mary. Do you hear me?" Another slap, this one leaving a small cut on her lower lip. Droplets of blood land on her white blouse. A potent smell of Guinness wafts from his skin and his clothes. Every word he speaks slightly slurred. "Bitch, I said... Do you hear me?"

He grabs a fist full of her auburn hair and drags her towards the old cooker to make him something new.

"Stop, stop hitting my mammy!" I think I'm bigger than I am, I'm only eight. What can I do? I can't stop him.

"Quiet boy, or you'll be next."

I immediately silence. I can't get hurt. Who will protect Lily if I get hurt? I swear once I'm big and strong, I'll kill him.

Shaking that memory away, I down another shot. Not tonight asshole, not to-fucking-night.

Waving my now empty glass at Bronagh — the barmaid and Conor's long-time girlfriend — I signal for another drink.

Clearly, I haven't had enough if the memories are still creeping in. Manoeuvring her way around the rest of the bar staff at The Golden Barrel, she finally reaches me.

"I think you've had enough already, Cillian."

I have a good mind to call Conor and tell him to get his woman under control. Can't a man get a fucking drink around here? And they call this place a pub.

"No... I'm pretty sure I haven't." Wiggling the empty glass in her face, I request another. "Double Jameson."

"This is the last one Cillian, I mean it. I've already texted Conor. He's on his way to take your drunk ass home."

"Whatever you say, Darling. I'm not leaving. Man Buns will have to carry me out."

She places the glass in front of me, muttering something, I don't quite catch under her breath.

Fucking Rosie, always messing with my head. When I saw her standing there looking like my wettest dreams coming true, I thought it was for me.

I was wrong. Jesus, I have a good mind to drive to Sean's house and beat the shit out of him. Fucking gobshite! If I could stand up straight, that's exactly what I would do.

* * *

A hand landing on my shoulder wakes me from my slumber. *Fuck, my neck is killing me. Where in God's name am I?*

"Fucking hell Cillian, how much did you drink?" Conor, the hand belongs to Conor.

Then I remember, I'm at the bar. *Shit! I must have dozed off.* Rubbing the back of my neck, I desperately try to release the crick. I need to get out of here, and now.

Slowly, I lift myself from the barstool, but my legs won't hold me. Conor grabs me before I land flat on my face. Wrapping my arm around his neck, he takes most of my all-but-dead-weight. He waves goodbye to his girlfriend, then leads me towards the door.

"Care to tell me why you're drinking yourself to death?" *Fuck you Conor. Why the hell do you even give a shit? I'm an adult. I'll drink if I want to drink. Jesus, I think I'm going to be sick.*

"I need Rosie. Where's Rosie?" *Oh, guess that cat is out of the bag.*

"Calm down! She's in the car waiting. I found her walking along the back roads on my way here."

The fuck! It's easily an hour walk from Sean's to her house. Has she lost her mind?

"Is she okay? I'll fucking end him if he hurt her."

"She is fine, man. Just worried about you and your drunk ass. If you would keep walking instead of swaying side to side, we'll get to her quicker. How does that sound?"

Like heaven.

"Lead the way, Man Bun. Lead the way."

My shaking legs can barely hold my weight. Each step I take is slow and sluggish from the fog of the whiskey. If it wasn't for Conor's tight hold, I would more than likely be face-first against the tarmac. Drinking always seems like a fan-fucking-tastic idea, until you've to do something as basic as, I don't know... walking.

Eventually, we make our way to where Ciaran and Rosie wait in the car. Conor opens the back-passenger door for me, and there she is. The light that illuminates my darkness. Rosie. My Snow.

Climbing — or rather falling — into the back seat, I lean my head back against the headrest for support. My head falls to the right, giving me the perfect view of the sombre girl beside me. She stares back at me, the weight of her silence removing all the air from the car.

She hates it when I drink like this, but she doesn't understand. She doesn't live in my head and with my guilt. I need to drink; the numbness helps me turn it all off. The memories and the pain that comes with them.

I hate the look she is giving me right now.

Sadness lines her beautiful face, the hurt I caused, dimming her bright blue irises which portray anger and... disappointment?

Reaching over, I claim her hand with mine. My fingertips trace little hearts on the underside of her palm. "I'm sorry."

Keeping my voice low, I try to keep this conversation between just Rosie and me. But Ciaran's eyes find mine in the rear-view mirror. He sends me a sympathetic look. He is the only one I spoke to about what was going on with Rosie. He also knows all about my past, he witnessed me at my lowest and he knows just how vicious my demons are.

Rosie's grip tightens in mine, causing my eyes to flicker to her face; but she is not looking at me, her gaze is on the window. Watching the little droplets of rain race down the glass. The rain always fascinated her. When we were kids, when it would rain, she'd run outside, open her arms out wide, lift her head up to the sky and just bask in it. If I remember correctly, she called it rain-gazing.

I once asked her why she loved the rain so much, her answer was so completely Rosie. "What's not to love, I love the smell of the wet roads, I love the sound of the raindrops ricocheting off the glass as I curl up inside with a good book. I love the moisture in the air, the greyness of the sky, watching the scurry of people trying to stay dry and the reflection of the world that mirrors in the large puddles. The list is endless."

Rosie always saw the best in everything. It's probably the thing I love most about her. She views the world for its potential, not its flaws. She sees the silver lining in every grey cloud. She sees the boy behind the suffering. She sees me.

✻ ✻ ✻

The stairs leading to my room are like Mount Everest. Each step makes me sway with defeat. I grab hold of the handrail, trying to steady myself.

"Let me help." Rosie's soft voice echoes from behind me. I tried making her go up first, but she insisted on being behind in case I fell backwards — not that it would help. I probably weigh double what she does; if I fall, she's going down with me.

Finally, we reach the top. Rosie leads me down the hallway to my room as my stomach rolls with every movement. I need to lie down. My head spins, a sure sign I'm going to be sick.

I take slow, steady breaths trying to contain everything I drank from erupting all over the floor. Thankfully, my bed comes into view, and I rush towards it.

Climbing up onto it on all fours, I roll over and lie flat on my back. The spinning gets worse, like I'm stuck on a carousel, starting slowly, but rapidly gaining speed. I close my eyes, trying to hold back the urge to vomit.

Rosie must notice my internal struggle because she pulls me into a sitting position, plants my feet on the floor and forces my head between my legs. She reaches over to the small waste bin beside my bed, quickly grabbing it and shoving it under my nose, just in time for me to empty the contents of my liver. *Attractive.*

Her small delicate hand rubs up and down my back in a soothing motion. Once I'm finished dry heaving, she carries the bin into the bathroom before returning with a washcloth.

"Will you stay?" The words come out just above a murmur.

She kisses me gently on the tip of my nose. "Of course."

Positioning herself behind me, she rests my sluggish head in her lap. The room spins once more, that combined with the feel of Rosie's fingers running through my hair makes my eyes drift closed.

"Sweet dreams, Snow."

"Sweet dreams, Charming."

Chapter Eight

Another One Bites the Dust by Queen

Cillian

Feeling like a dead man walking, I trudge over the cobble-stone pathway in Ciaran and Conor's back yard. Their Da is a local builder; and when we were all about ten or twelve, he decided that he had had enough of Ciaran constantly banging the whole house down with the racket of his drum kit. So, he built the two boys a safe place where they could both play till their heart's content—The Shed.

The soundproof structure has become the rehearsal slash hangout space for all the 4Clover boys. We have a show at The Golden Barrel on Friday night, so today we're nailing down the final set-list. But that's not what has me wound so-fucking-tight.

Today, I'm telling my best friend—of fifteen years—I'm in love with his sister. It's safe to say I'm sweating buckets, but I promised Rosie I would talk to Cian today and it's a promise I intend to keep.

I'm hoping the intense fucker is in a good mood. Maybe then, I'll have some sort of fighting chance of getting out of there in something less than a body-bag.

I've spent the better half of today torturing myself, mulling over how to broach the subject. Running through a few more scenarios, I figure out fairly quickly—I am in fact, fucked.

Cian, I love your sister, deal with it. No! Too forward.

Cian, just so you know, Rosie is my girlfriend. Yeah, that will go down like a lead balloon.

So, Cian, I'm planning to bang your sister for the rest of my life, and I thought you should find out from me. That one will definitely get me killed.

I think it's safe to say none of these are viable options—especially that last one.

Pushing open the heavy metal door, I find Conor and Ciaran flicking through my songbook—thankfully, Cian is nowhere in sight.

"Well, if it isn't the walking AA advertisement," Ciaran greets me from behind his drum kit. "Glad to see that you're alive and kicking today. You were in a way last night, my friend."

Genuinely confused, I ask, "Did I see you last night?"

Last night is still rather hazy, I remember Rosie putting me to bed, but how she got there remains a mystery.

Conor throws me a bottle of water from the mini fridge beside him. "Seriously O'Shea. Do you not remember how the hell you got home?" *That would be a definite no!*

They both erupt with laughter at the blank expression on my none-the-wiser face. Slumping back into the old leather couch, I swallow the entire bottle in two gulps.

"Is anyone going to enlighten me… what the fuck is so funny?"

"Okay… so, last night, Bronagh called me from the bar, told me you were absolutely shit-faced and maybe I should come get you. Amongst our travels, we find sweet little Rosie wandering the back roads in her bare feet, so she joined our rescue mission. When we arrived, I went inside to find you passed out, face first on the bar."

"Shit!"

"Oh, that's not all. I practically dragged your drunk-as-fuck ass out of there and back to the car. Finally, we got you settled in the back seat, where you then confessed your undying love for a certain someone's little sister — who may I add, is off-limits." Conor looks to Ciaran. "That's about it, right Ciaran?"

He nods his head in agreement. "Yep, sounds about right. So, how is Rosie? Did you work things out?"

Rubbing the back of my neck, I search for the right words to say. "Yeah, we did. I'll tell Cian about us as soon as we finish up here."

"Tell me what?" *Oh, shit!*

Three sets of eyes hone in on me, each pair portraying an entirely different emotion. Ciaran's are lit with amusement. Conor's are more apprehensive. Then there is Cian—always so intense, but slightly curious.

Time to man up Cillian, just tell him. "I'm-in-love-with-Rosie."

The words fly out of my mouth so fast, they're almost inaudible. The tick of the clock is the only sound as Cian stands there with wide-as-fuck eyes. I swallow. He blinks. And the twins watch in anticipation.

Finally, Cian's agape mouth forms words. "I'm sorry. Could you repeat that? Because I swear you just said you're in love with my sister. My baby-fucking-sister."

His steel-grey eyes darken with a murderous glare, directed straight at me. He steps towards me; his fists clenched tightly by his side. Standing from the couch, I drop the water bottle onto the side table and square my shoulders. I've wasted so many years hiding my true feelings towards Rosie. Now that I have her, there's no way I'm letting her go.

He's right in my face now, nose to nose. Pressuring me to back down, but guess what? That's not going to fucking happen. I meant every word I said to Rosie this morning. I am ready; if he wants a fight, then he'll get one.

Swallowing back the marble-sized lump forming in my throat, I say what I need to say.

"Because I did, I'm telling you out of respect for our friendship. I'd like you to be okay with this; because we are together, and regardless of what you think, it's happening. I love her, and she loves me. I won't hurt her."

Cian grips my shirt and forces my back against the wall. "If I ever so much as see you lay one fucking finger on my sister, I swear I will chop your dick off and feed it to my dog."

I push against his chest, forcing him to stumble backwards. "Fuck you, Cian. Rosie is my girlfriend, so you better get used to seeing us together. She's it for me."

Tweddle-D and Tweddle-Dumb think this is the perfect time to break into fucking song. Conor plays the opening bass line while Ciaran joins in with the heavy drumbeat. Is that Another One Bites the Dust? I try. I really do. And even though this is a serious conversation, I can't... my laughter erupts like a volcano.

Trust the twins to try to lighten the mood. But it doesn't last long, because next thing I know, the force of Cian's legendary right hook, connects with the side of my face. *Lights fucking out!*

* * *

Voices echo in my ringing ears, becoming louder as I reclaim my consciousness.

"Jesus Christ, Cian. How hard did you hit him? He's out fucking cold." Lily. When did she get here? "I'll go get him some ice."

"Do that, cause when his ass wakes up, I'm gonna knock him out again."

I'm vaguely aware of Cian's foot shaking my rib cage, forcing my limp body to wake.

"You're such a dick, Cian. Would you stop that?"

"No! He's fucking my sister. He's lucky he's still breathing."

"Cian!" The sweet sound of Rosie's voice warns him. "Stop. Now."

Blinking a few times, I rid myself of the black dots floating behind my eyes. Jesus that motherfucker can throw a punch.

A dainty hand gently caresses my face. "Welcome back, handsome." Rosie's beautiful blue eyes and bring-any-man-to-his-knees smile greets me. Cian can knock me on my ass any day if this is the angel I get to wake back up to.

"What the hell did I just tell you, Rosie? I always want ten feet between you and dickface. Move it. Now!"

"Cian, sit the hell down before I put you on your tattooed ass." Lily's sharp tone prevents him from coming near me. Laughable really, the girl is barely five-foot. She just about reaches his nipples for fuck's sake.

Rosie pulls my attention back to her. "How are you feeling? Does it hurt?"

Pushing myself up into a sitting position, I wrap my arms around my girl. I don't give a flying fuck what Cian thinks anymore; he took his free shot. Next time he won't get to. I've taken way too many hits over the years. If anyone can handle Cian Mulligan and his temper, it's me.

"If I say yes, will you kiss it better?" Rosie leans in, placing a little peck against—what I would say is—my very swollen cheek.

"ROSIE!" Cian barks. "Did you not listen to a word I said? Ten-fucking-feet, NOW!"

Squeezing her in closer, I allow her scent to fill my nose—fresh flowers with a hint of cherry red apples. She has always smelt like this, for as long as I can remember.

Rosie helps me to my feet, and I rub my dusty hands off my black jeans before tucking her under my arm. Kissing her gently on the forehead, I whisper so no one else can hear. "Can I take you on our first official date, now?"

A smile works its way across my face when she nods her head yes.

"Just give me a minute or two. I need to talk to your brother, then we can go."

Stepping from my hold, Rosie heads for the couch as I turn to face Cian—where he's still being held captive by my little hell-in-heels sister.

"Can I talk to you for a second?"

The glare I send Lily lets her know I mean alone. She quickly heads to the other side of the room; to where the others are all watching the exchange.

Taking a seat beside my best friend, I fidget with the sleeves of my hoodie. I don't want to fight with him over this. We've been friends since we were kids, but I won't give Rosie up. That's non-negotiable. I've tried to hide my feelings for her over the years. I tried everything to flush her out of my system, and nothing ever worked. Looking him straight in the eye, I try to explain to him how I feel.

"Look, man, I know you don't like the idea of Rosie and me together. I haven't exactly got the best track record with girls; but I love her, Cian. Looking back, I think I always have. Whatever you say, it doesn't matter, because we are giving this thing between us a shot — with or without your blessing. Although, I hope with. I would like it if my best friend could be happy for us. It's been years since I felt like I deserved to be happy, and with Rosie, I just can't help it."

I allow my eyes to wander across the room, Rosie's eyes lock on mine, giving me the courage, I need. "She brings light back into my life, Cian. She makes me want to be better, do better. Trust me when I say, I know she's too good for me; but I will do everything I can to be the person she deserves. I promised her this morning, there would be no more drinking, no more partying, I'm done. I'll give it all up for her." Releasing a heavy sigh, I take in the torn face of my best friend. "Please, don't make me have to choose between you and her, because even though you're my boy and always will be, I will choose her. Every-fucking-time."

I don't know what I said, but whatever it was, it worked. Cian's hardened demeanour softens. He looks over at Rosie, who's watching us from the couch, and a weighted breath escapes him. He looks torn. "Okay, I'll back off, but I swear Cillian, if one tear leaves her blue eyes because of you, I will put you in the ground. I mean that. And for the love of fuck, please don't be touching her in front of me. She is still my sister and this," Cian motions between Rosie and me, "will take me awhile to get used to. Now get the hell out of my face before I change my mind."

"I promise you, Cian. I'll never hurt her. In doing so, it would tear me apart, too." He nods his head, letting me know he understands. He slaps me on the back in a friendly man-to-man way. "I'm going for a smoke," he mumbles before heading for the door.

Well, that went better than expected.

Chapter Nine

Kiss Me by Sixpence None the Richer

Rosie

*T*he drive back towards my house doesn't take long, and before I know it, we are pulling into the barely-there gateway that divides our property lines. Cillian parks the car safely off the road and looks to me for a reaction.

"The treehouse?" I smile at the thought he put into tonight.

"Is that okay?" I can hear the nervousness and uncertainty in his voice. "I know it's not some fancy restaurant or anything, but I promise you one day, when I can afford it, I'll bring you wherever you want to go. But for now, this is all I can give you."

Leaning over the centre console, my hands grip his face. Our noses rest against each other, and our eyes lock. "I don't need or want fancy restaurants. This is perfect, Cillian. Absolute perfection."

Together, hand in hand, we travel along the small dirt track that formed over the years by our consistent footsteps. The normally dark, narrow trail is now lit up with hundreds of lit tea lights — each one enclosed into a masonry jar, keeping them sheltered from the night breeze. The soft romantic glow of each one lights up the now dusky evening. *How did he do this? When did he do this?*

Although Cillian was hesitant about bringing me here, I love it. It's thoughtful, personal to who we are. The treehouse has always held a special place in my heart. Right underneath this large oak tree is where Cillian and I shared our first kiss — almost nine years ago.

"Run, Rosie," Lily squeals. "Run faster... they're going to catch us."

Her laughter fills the summer air as she runs by me at lightning speed.

"I'm running as fast as I can, Lily," I lie. "I can't go any faster." I can run faster. I'm the fastest girl in my class, but if I run any faster, he won't catch me. I want him to catch me.

"Rosie, don't be such a girl. You're the fastest person I know. Run before he catches yooou." Sean grabs her around her waist, planting a big wet kiss, right on her mouth.

"Ewwww, get off me." She pushes Sean away and wipes her lips with the back of her hand. Sean is my daddy's friend's son. We don't like him that much. He smells like old cheese or smelly football socks. But my mammy said it's nice to be nice and to never leave anyone out. So, while his daddy and mine talk business, he's playing with us.

"I had to kiss you, Lilyanna. It's called kiss chasing. I caught you, so I kissed you... that's the rules." Sean stomps his little feet while shouting like a banshee at Lily.

I stop running to watch the commotion between them. Glancing towards Lily, I see she's super mad. She's standing in front of Sean with her hands on her hips, looking like she's about to pull his lips off; or worse... cry.

"I don't like this game! It's stupid and I'm not playing anymore!" she stomps off towards her house.

Just as I am about to go after her, two hands grab me by the waist and spin me around. "Caught you." A wide grin lights up his boyish face, his brown hair falling forward, shading his eyes from the summer sun. "Now, I can finally kiss you."

His hands run through his longish hair, sweeping it back off his face. Are boys meant to be pretty? Because that's the only way I can think to describe him. My eyes latch onto his, green with little flecks of golden browns.

Looking at him makes my chest feel funny and my breathing gets a little quicker. I'm not meant to like him, he's my friend's big brother. You should never kiss your friend's brother.

Oh, sparkle-nuggets, I am about to get my first kiss. Cillian O'Shea is about to kiss me. Before I can even process what to do next, it happens. His lips press to mine and O.M.G!

I try my best to kiss him back, but, I don't really know how. I have never kissed anyone before. He will think I'm a silly little girl. His hand loops around my waist, pulling me closer and sprinkles erupt through me. Fuzzy, I feel fuzzy.

I'm having my first kiss ever, and it's with Cillian O'Shea.

The large oak tree comes into view, forcing me to leave that memory behind. My eyes dance across the branches, my mind desperate to capture every detail of the tree now surrounded by fairy lights and lanterns. The sparkle of each light illuminates the darkness, giving the illusion of a thousand fireflies flashing. It's beautiful, magical, romantic.

"After you." Cillian gestures to the old wooden ladder that leads to our childhood tree house.

Carefully, I climb each step until finally, I reach the top, where my breath lodges in my throat. I was only here a few weeks ago, but he has totally transformed it.

More fairy lights are hanging from the rafters, the old, worn trunk I usually use to store blankets sits in the centre of the floor and is now acting as a small dining table. In the centre, sits a chipped glass vase, filled with some daffodils—probably from his Ma's garden. Two paper plates sit on the table across from each other.

My eyes wander around the rest of the space, in the far corner is a large fort made from large throw blankets and pillows. Cillian's guitar, and a laptop placed in the middle. I'm utterly speechless.

The place looks amazing. I can't believe he arranged all this. It's beautiful.

"Wow."

Cillian's arms wrap around me from behind. His head rests where my shoulder meets my neck. "Do you like it?"

Spinning in his arms to face him, I wrap mine around his shoulders. "I love it. This is amazing, Cillian. How did you do all this?"

He kisses the tip of my nose, then my forehead. "I may have had a little help from a certain sister/best friend." *Lily, of course.*

"Are you hungry? I had Lily pick up some pizza, she texted me and said it's in the insulated bag in the trunk." He releases me from his hold and kneels to retrieve the bag. "It might not be piping hot, but it should still be warm."

His hand rubs the back of his neck. *Is he nervous?* I take a seat on the pillow covered floor and give him a reassuring smile.

"Pizza sounds amazing."

After our pizza, Cillian and I curl up together in the little fort, completely oblivious to the outside world. It's just him and I, together, underneath the twinkling lights. Each bulb glistens above us, lighting up the wooden space and mirroring our own personal night sky. Everything about tonight has been amazing. I couldn't have asked for a better first date. Cillian's been so attentive, every detail perfectly planned, making tonight even more memorable.

Being here, now with him, I know I've never felt more loved and I want to show him just how much he means to me. I want him to have all of me.

I know he is more experienced than I am, but I want to share myself with him completely. I know I sound like a naive little girl, but I never imagined giving my first to anyone else but him. No one will ever make me feel the way he does.

Cillian is not one in a million, he's once in a lifetime.

I know he's said he'd be patient with me. That he's willing to wait until I'm ready—but I'm ready now. I don't want to give this moment to anyone else. It belongs to him. I've always wanted my first time to be his, mine, ours.

Us together wrapped up in the most intimate way possible.

Cillian already holds many of my firsts. My first kiss, my first love, my first official boyfriend. I want to share this part of me with him, too. I want him to be my first everything.

Forcing down my nerves, I turn and face him. "Cillian?" His name falls from my mouth like a question.

"Yes, Snow."

"I'm…" I search my mind for the right words. "I'm ready."

His hands still from where they were playing with the loose strands of my hair. He sits up, pulling me up with him. The words I spoke dangle in the surrounding air. Cillian's eyes search my face for any sign of hesitation. "Rosie, I... I didn't do all this for that reason," he assures me. "I'm more than happy to wait until you're ready. I don't want you to rush into this. This is important, you only get to lose your virginity once and trust me, I want you to wait until you're one-hundred-per cent sure. Don't get me wrong, I want nothing more than to share it with you, but I'm happy to wait until you're ready."

He's adorable right now. His eyes are so loving yet full of concern. If I could, I would snap a picture to keep forever.

Crawling up onto his lap, I straddle his waist and wrap my legs around his torso. Taking his face between my palms, I catch his eyes with mine. They're burning with a fire I can't quite describe. The smile on his gorgeous face takes my breath away.

"I'm ready, Cillian." I kiss his lips softly before pulling back a little. "I promise you; I've never been more ready. I want this, I want this with you. I love you, Cillian O'Shea. You and only you. So, please... make love to me."

Wrapping his arms around my centre, he pulls me closer. A smile that could light up the world painted across his face. Our breaths mingle in the small space between us. "I love you, too." His lips peck my nose. "You're sure?" He asks softly, his hand travelling slowly underneath the thin material of my white t-shirt.

"I'm positive." Two words. That's all it takes.

He slowly lifts the hem of my t-shirt up and over my head. His calloused fingertips — from years of playing the guitar — electrify my skin along the way. Once he lifts it completely off, he cups my ass in his palms, taking my weight off his legs. Laying me back gently on the array of blankets, he dots angel kisses along my exposed, porcelain skin.

Starting at the waistband of my black leggings, he travels upward. Each brush of his lips, lights me up inside. Goosebumps erupt along my arms as the cold breeze escapes through the small cracks between the wooden planks, but I'm burning up on the inside, overcome with desire and need.

Cillian traces my soft curves with his tongue, paying very close attention to the small diamond barbell, gracing my belly button. My back arches with need for more. His hands roam over my skin, setting my blood alight, making my core tighten with want and need. My hands grip his hair, holding him in place as he licks, sucks, and kisses every inch of my stomach.

Wrapping his arms around me, he forces me to sit up slightly so he can free me from my bra. With a small click of the clasp, it falls loose. The straps slide down my shoulders and free my tender-with-need breasts.

Reaching up, he pulls me free from the restraints of the thin, white lace material. He throws it over his shoulder, and it lands in a bundle on the floor beside my t-shirt. Ever so slowly, he peppers sweet delicious kisses around my now hardened buds.

"Cillian." His name, like a cry, falls from my lips. I need to feel him, his skin against mine.

Tugging on the black material of his Thin Lizzy t-shirt, I signal, I need it gone. Cillian sits back on his knees, and reaches around, doing that sexy one arm thing I've seen on T.V., he quickly rids himself of his shirt. I've seen Cillian's bare chest millions of times, but my God, it's exquisite. I make a mental note to explore each ridge with my tongue. Taking hold of the waistband of my leggings, he slowly and torturously peels them and my underwear down my legs. My breath hitches in my chest, causing Cillian's eyes to lock on mine. My nerves must show through my facial features because his movements halt.

"Snow... are you sure? If you're not ready, we can stop."

His bottom lip pulls between his teeth, something I learned he does when he is nervous. *Don't you dare stop!*

"Cillian, I promise you, I'm ready."

A majestic smile highlights his face. My chest fills with love and desire. I feel powerful, sexy, and wanted.

Pulling his mouth to mine, I repeat my earlier statement. "Make love to me, Cillian."

"For the rest of my life, Snow."

Chapter Ten

Amazed by Lonestar

Cillian

I'm minutes away from making love for the first time in my life. Sure, I've had sex more times than I can count — but this is not sex. This is her, my Snow.

The love of my life.

Sex is completely different. Sex is just basic human instinct, a mechanical movement with no strings attached. We all know how to do it, or at least we should. Making love, showing someone exactly how much they mean to you, is a whole different ball game. It's about slowing down, opening yourself up, mind, body and soul. It's putting your heart on the line and praying to every fucking God out there, they don't smash it into a thousand unfixable pieces.

With Rosie, it is not about the heights you reach with sex. It's about showing her the depths of our love. It is two souls connecting to form one. Sharing emotions and feelings. Feeling the raw and meaningful love.

Rosie's words hit me like a loaded gun to the chest. *Make love to me Cillian.*

Leaning forward, I cage Rosie beneath me and capture her lips with mine. Desperately seeking how to portray everything I feel for her into our kiss. My eyes never leave hers because there is not one single second of this, I'm willing to miss.

Roaming my hands over every inch of her skin, the heat radiating between us builds, it's strong enough to start a wildfire.

Breaking the contact, I kiss my way towards her exposed neck. A low throaty moan escapes from her lips as I suck on the sweet spot hidden behind her ear. Her body arches into mine, begging me to give her some release.

I hear you, darling.

Running my palms down her stomach towards her centre, her abdomen tightens beneath my touch. "Open those legs for me, Snow." My voice is both commanding yet loving.

She opens them, allowing me to run my fingers through the wetness forming between her legs. *Sweet Jesus.*

Her body bucks at my touch and my name from her lips, filling the surrounding air. "Cillian."

"It's okay baby, let go. I've got you," I whisper before taking her nipple into my mouth. Gently, I tug on the small pink bud while strumming her clit like my Gibson. It doesn't take long before her body spasms in my arms. The effect of her orgasm ripples through her, trembling like an earthquake.

"That's it, Snow, let go."

"Cillian... God, Cillian."

To me, Rosie has always been the most beautiful girl in the world, but right now she is on a whole nother level. She's stunningly breath-taking with the sheen of her orgasm displayed across her delicate skin. I'm lost in her eyes, amazed she is sharing this part of herself with me.

"I love you, Rosie Mulligan."

She runs her palm over my cheek, her eyes shining brighter than a mine full of diamonds. "I love you too, Cillian O'Shea."

Kissing her lips softly, I travel down her body, feathering tiny kisses along her now pink skin — courtesy of the past orgasm.

Once my face is positioned between her thighs, I look up to find her stare focused on me. "Is this okay?" Her head nods up and down, while she swallows back with anticipation. "I'm gonna need words, Snow."

"Yes."

Her hand's grip my hair as I bury myself in her soft centre. I run my tongue along her slit while gripping her hips to keep her still. Using the tip of my tongue, I spell out the letters of the three little words I need her to know. *I love you.*

Each stroke makes her buck beneath me. Thrusting two fingers deep into her core, I stroke her G spot until finally, she erupts all over my tongue.

She cries out in pleasure. "Cillian. Oh. My. God."

I stand off our makeshift bed and take my wallet from my back pocket. Pulling out a condom, I drop my jeans and boxers to the hardwood floor. Quickly, I cover my length with the latex rubber and lay back down beside her.

"Come here." I motion for her to climb up on top of me. Her legs straddle my waist, her hands roaming the length of my bare chest. I hold her gaze with mine. "We'll try it this way okay, that way, you'll have complete control over everything. If it hurts too much, let me know and we will stop."

"Okay." She bites down on her lower lip. *Jesus, is she trying to kill me?*

Lifting her hips slightly, I shift her until she's hovering over my tip. "Ready?"

Rosie nods her head in reply.

"Baby, I told you, I need words."

"I'm Ready, Cillian."

I lower her slowly over my length. Once my tip enters her opening, a struggling gasp leaves her mouth. I immediately still, the last thing I want to do is hurt her.

She takes slow steady breaths before proceeding to take another inch. Inch by torturous inch she takes me in, her inner walls moulding around my length.

Once I'm fully seated in her depths, she lets out a breath, sweat beads between her breasts, glistening against her snow-white skin.

"Can I move?" I hesitantly ask, fearful of hurting her more.

"Yes, Please."

I flip her over onto her back, my mouth intertwined with hers. I move at a steady pace, using slow gentle strokes.

Rosie's hands grip the flesh on my back, her nails digging into my skin with every pump of my hips. Nothing in this world could compare to this feeling. Each kiss, each touch, each thrust, connects our souls for eternity. I will never forget this moment. The moment Rosie made this hollow boy whole again.

"Never stop, Cillian. Please, never stop loving me," she cries out through her release.

I follow her over the edge, clinging to her body for dear life. Kissing her lips, I let her know I will love her till the end of time. "I won't Snow. Forever and always."

"Forever and always."

Rosie

We lay there, completely and utterly spent, sweat beading on our naked skin. Cillian's arm wraps tightly around me, while my head rests on his chest. The steady beat of his heart pounds beneath my ear, this… this is where I want to be.

Right here, forever.

I never want to leave, if I could, I would stay here in his arms for a lifetime. I lift my head from where it lays and entwine his lips with mine. Even this…

the simplest of touches, makes my breath hitch. As cliché as it sounds, he makes my body feel alive. The fluttering of a thousand butterflies erupt deep in my core with every brush of his lips.

What we just shared was so much more than sex, it was a deep-rooted connection—just two people who love each other fiercely. Every single emotion flowed between us. I know I could never experience something like that with anyone else. The chemistry between us made it so special, we didn't just share our bodies; we shared our minds and our souls.

Cillian breaks the kiss, his eyes roaming over my face, and with his free hand, he gently caresses my cheek. The way he is looking at me now is... it's everything. *The Allie and Noah kind of love.*

I know no matter what happens between us, I will never love anyone the way I love Cillian O'Shea. The broken boy with so much love to give. He thinks he is unfixable, undeserving, unwanted, but I plan to change that; even if it is the last thing I do. I will pick up all his broken pieces and mould them back together, taking extra care to blend the cracks until finally, he feels whole again. I'll show him that loving someone unconditionally, can heal even the deepest of scars.

"You are so beautiful, Snow. How did I get so lucky?" The intensity of his gaze sends shivers down my spine. "Thank you for loving me. I know I'm not good enough for you; but I promise you, baby, I'll do everything in my power to be the person you deserve. No more drinking. No more partying, I will be better, for you, for us."

It breaks my heart, knowing this is how he views himself. I wish he could see what I see, a loving brother and son, an amazing musician, a great friend and a kind, caring, romantic boyfriend.

"Cillian, I don't want you to change. Not for me. I love you for who you are now, flaws and all. Has your drinking got out of control? Yes. But I don't want you to stop for me. That is something you need to stop for yourself. Your demons won't leave until you face whatever makes them haunt you. Talk to me, let me help."

"It's hard, Snow, I want to, but I don't want to taint you. You are too pure and too precious, to be touched by my darkness."

Leaning up onto my elbow, I rest my head in my palm. "Luckily for you, I'm not afraid of the dark. Everybody is a little broken, it's through those cracks the light gets in. Let me in Cillian. Let me be your light."

The walls he has built fall before my eyes, each brick crumbling with the weight of my words.

Cillian lets out a heavy sigh. "Okay, but promise me, whatever I tell you, it stays between us. Not many people know, and I'd like to keep it that way."

"Promise."

He lays me back down, so my head is resting against his chest. His fingers gently play with the strands of my hair. I think he finds some comfort in the simple act. His breathing gets thicker, almost heavier, and I know the next words will be hard for him to express.

"Do you remember when my Da got arrested last year?"

I don't answer, he doesn't need me to. He needs me to just listen.

"Well, I had been out drinking with Ciaran and Cian at some party in town. I don't know where Conor was, probably hanging out with Bronagh. Anyway, Lily called my phone a few dozen times, but I didn't hear it over the noise at the party. Eventually, she got through to Ciaran and she was hysterical. My Da had come home from work, pissed out of his mind per usual. He was tearing the house apart, excusing my Ma of cheating or some shit. He was beating her black and blue. Lily, well... she tried to stop him, but he was completely out of control. Ciaran hadn't drunk anything, so he drove us home. We couldn't have been over ten, fifteen minutes max."

Cillian pauses for a minute, taking deep breaths. I can tell this is hard for him, his body's physically shaking beneath me. Running my hand over his chest, I silently let him know I'm here and it is okay.

He swallows, his Adam's apple bobbing in his throat. "When we got there, we heard Lily screaming. Ciaran kicked down the door, and there he was... my own fucking Da, hovering over my baby sister. He was pulling at her clothes, trying to tear them from her body. She was kicking and screaming, begging for him to stop, but it was like something inside him had snapped. I pulled him off her, thankfully before he could do whatever the hell he had intended to, but me, I saw red. I just kept hitting him, over, and over, and over again. If it wasn't for Cian, I would have killed him there and then. That son of a bitch had left my poor Ma unconscious and tried to... do whatever the hell he was doing to my sister."

He can't say it. But I have a feeling I know. Lily has been different since they arrested her Da.

"I wasn't there, Rosie. I was out partying instead of protecting them both. They needed me to protect them, and I wasn't there. Did you know that prick only got a three-year sentence? Three-fucking-years. They should have locked him up and thrown away the key. He deserves to rot in the place for the rest of his miserable life. But, instead, he'll get out while the rest of us have to live with a lifetime of abuse that he inflicted."

In all my life, I've never seen Cillian cry, but now, laying in my arms, he's sobbing uncontrollably. My own tears are streaming down my cheeks. Lily never told me, she has been living with that for a year and she never once let on. My heart is breaking for her, for Cillian and for their mam, Mary.

Looking up at the face of the broken boy I love, I caress his cheek. "Cillian, you can't blame yourself—not for your father's actions. It wasn't your fault, it was his. You did nothing wrong; you were only eighteen. It wasn't your job to protect them... it was his, and he failed. You need to let go of all this guilt; it's eating you alive."

"I know Ro, but I can't. For years we lived with a monster, and for all those years, he chipped away at us. Piece by piece, until finally all the pieces were scattered on the floor. Lily will never be the same after that night and Ma blames herself for not throwing him out sooner. Then there is me, and I am beyond fixing."

A part of me is glad he shared his demons, but the other part wishes I could take them away. As I lay there silently beside him, my heart breaks in two for him and for my best friend.

Right there, wrapped in his arms, I make a silent promise to myself. I will never let anyone hurt him or Lily again.

Chapter Eleven

Unless it's with You by Christina Aguilera

Rosie

The Present Day

If someone had asked me what I envisioned the morning of my wedding to be like, hiding in a hotel bathroom contemplating my life, my love and my losses, would have been the last answer I'd have given them.

How did I get here?

It was meant to be Cillian. Forever and always.

Nonetheless, here I am. Squeezed into a porcelain bathtub, wearing what most girls would describe as their dream dress, feeling irrevocably sorry for myself.

There is well over a half bottle of Prosecco flowing through my bloodstream and still, I couldn't care less.

The same question plays through my mind on repeat — what the hell am I doing here? I'm hiding from my soon-to-be husband, that's what! *Comical, if you were to ask me.*

Oh God, even the thought of him has hate crawling underneath my skin. Don't misunderstand, there was a time I actually thought I had some feelings for Sean.

Were they the heart racing, breath taking, all-consuming kind? No! They were more like, he is dependable, sensible, and doesn't hold the power to break my heart. He won't hurt me. Not in the way Cillian did.

I blame myself; I allowed this to happen. I... I gave up.

For years, I played tug of war with love and pain. Finally, I did what I had to do.

It was time; I had to let him go. So, I wrapped my shattered heart up, placed it in a box and marked it: Do not open. Ever! But what I failed to realize was, there were still pieces missing. Pieces that Cillian had claimed.

Now, here I am, minutes away from walking down the aisle into the arms of a man I feel nothing for. All because I need to protect the one who makes me feel everything. Even after everything we've been through, I'm still trying to keep his demons locked away for good, so they can't come back to haunt him. I made a deal with the devil, and now it's time to pay the price.

A loud thump ricochets against the bathroom door.

"Rosie, you in there? It's Lil. Can I come in?"

Oh, shit, she can't see me like this. I'm a complete disaster. My professionally applied makeup is rolling down my swollen face and my hair looks like a bird has been nesting in it. Oh, and let's not forget that fact, I'm stuck in a bathtub in a freaking wedding dress.

"I'm taking your silence as a yes!" Lily pushes the door open, just enough to squeeze herself inside. Quickly, she closes it behind her and flicks the lock in place. "Dear God and all that is holy! No offence Hun, but you look..."

"Beautiful, sexy, ever the blushing bride."

She sneers at my obvious sarcasm. "You know I love you to bits, but I'd never lie to you. You, my darling, are the definition of a hot mess."

Pushing the many layers of my Wang out of her way, she climbs into the bathtub beside me.

"Well thanks a million, that's exactly what a bride wants to hear on her wedding day," I sass.

Once she's squeezed in and facing me, she holds out her hand and motions for the Prosecco bottle. "Pass it over, if you're allowed to get drunk, so I am. Also, I'm sorry, Ro, you know I think you look beautiful all the time. But right this minute, you look like someone has dragged you through a hedge backwards kicking and screaming. What's wrong? Are you having second thoughts?"

Laughter bubbles from my lips, I don't know why though, there's nothing funny about this situation.

"You're joking right, more like twenty-second thoughts. I don't know if I can do this. I can't marry Sean. I don't love him."

Sadness fills her amber eyes while pity lines her pretty face. "Well, don't do it then. Let's make like Usain and bolt. I swear I'll cut a bitch if anyone tries to stop us."

Swigging from the Prosecco bottle, I can see a plan formulating in her devious mind. "We can take your honeymoon tickets and escape this place for a while. If you don't want to do this, then don't. This is your life, Rosie. It's past time you live it for you."

"I wish I could, but I can't, and you know that. He'll destroy him if I leave. I can't let him do that to Cillian. He spent years getting himself to where he is now, and he has worked too hard to lose it all over me. We both know, if I hightail it out of here, he'll lose everything. I can't watch his career go up in flames. I won't do that to him, Lil."

Lily releases a defeated sigh; she's the only one who knows the real reason I sold my soul to the devil. The same reason I need to go through with this sham of a wedding.

Him, everything I'm doing is always for him.

"Have you heard from him?" Her mumbled words pierce my already damaged heart.

"He texted a few times."

Reaching over for my phone that's sitting on the edge of the hand basin, I pull up the recent messages Cillian sent me. Each one is more painful to read than the last.

Charming: Please, Snow. I'm begging you... Please don't do this.

Charming: You don't belong to him, but you already know that. Mine, Snow. Forever and always, remember?

Charming: I'm sorry. Just ignore those messages. I'm drunk and I miss you.

Charming: I AM NOT GOING! I CAN'T WATCH YOUR DAD GIVE YOU AWAY TO SOMEONE WHO ISN'T ME... I JUST CAN'T!

Charming: Do you love him? Did you ever love me?

Charming: I'm sorry, Snow. All I want is for you to be happy. Your happiness is all that ever mattered to me. If this is what you want, I will respect that and let you live your life. I'm sorry it took so long for me to figure all my shit out. You know, Lily was right all those years ago — when she told me one day, I'd lose my chance. You are not mine, you're his now. I hope he showers you with all the love in this world. You deserve it all; and so much more. I'm sorry I couldn't love you the way you deserved. You'll always be my Snow White, but I guess you finally found your Prince Charming in someone who wasn't me. This is me letting you go.

I'm happy you found happily ever after. I'll love you always. Goodbye Rosie.

Tears free fall from my eyes, his broken heart attached to every word he wrote. I wish I could tell him why I'm marrying Sean. I wish I could turn back the clock. Back to a time where we were happy. Before everything turned into this fucking shit show. Back to the place where Cillian knew exactly how much I love him and always will.

Chapter Twelve

Wait for Me by Hermitage Green

Cillian

January 2014

It's been two months since Rosie, and I announced our relationship. Every spare moment I've had, I've spent with her.

Things with the band have really picked up and we're set to join Sinners — the biggest indie-rock band in the U.S — on the European leg of their world tour, in six months' time.

Life is finally looking up. Even my drinking has lessened to an occasional beer with the boys after a show. But, if I've learnt anything in life, it's that what goes up must always come down. So, as I stand here, frozen to the floor of Michael's office, I realize, this is it. The beginning of my downfall.

"Good evening, boys. I've some great news." Michael, Cian's father and 4Clovers band manager greets us with a slimy all-knowing smile.

It's no secret that Mr. Mulligan and I don't get along. Honestly, the only reason he puts up with me at all is that I write at least eighty per cent of the music. Our so-called business relationship was already less than ideal before Rosie announced our relationship at a family dinner a few weeks back.

But ever since that night, Michael has found every way possible to keep my time with his daughter to a minimum. Holding rehearsals three nights a week and filling our weekends with shows on Friday, Saturday, and Sunday nights. To say he was furious that she ditched that dinner meeting at Sean's house, would be the highest of understatements. And, in true Michael fashion, he's blaming my relationship with Rosie on why she has no interest in dating that pretentious asswipe.

Cian's patience runs thin as we wait for Michael to explain why we are here. "Out with it, old man."

"Patience, Cian. Haven't you heard the saying; good things come to those who wait?"

"Yes, I have, but I've also heard the one where time waits for no man. So, can you please get to the fucking point?"

"Well, as you all already know, my old college friend Rich gave your audition tape to the members of Sinners, and they've agreed 4Clover would be an excellent addition to their European tour that starts this coming September."

"Yes, we are aware. You've told us about this already." Cian's irritated tone cuts Michael off.

"If you would let me finish, you would know that I spoke to them last week, and they want you to open for their U.S tour, too."

Conor's eyes widen at that new information "Doesn't that start in February? That's like two weeks from now."

"Yes, Conor. Will that be a problem?"

Ciaran wraps his arm around his brother's shoulder. "Of course not, right, bro? We're ready for this, we've been ready for months."

Ciaran's enthusiasm seems to settle Conor somewhat, but from where I'm standing, I can see the panic painted across his stress filled face.

Ciaran and Cian high-five, shouting statements like "Fuck yeah," and "This is it! We're gonna be Rockstar's."

They're both fucking ecstatic, and why wouldn't they be. All our dreams are about to become a reality. Everything we have worked towards is finally coming to fruition. This is the big break we need, and we all know it. But I just can't get excited. Deep down, I know it's because I'll be leaving Rosie behind.

Gazing back at Conor, I see he's wearing, what I would say, is a similar expression to my own. As much as he wants this, a life on the road, playing music together for the world to hear; he doesn't want to leave Bronagh either. They've been together since they were thirteen years old. He thinks the sun rises and sets with her. Him leaving, will be difficult on them both, especially now that she's living with him.

I can't even begin to explain the emotions I'm feeling now. This is what I always dreamed of; playing on stage for thousands of people while the crowds chant our names. Music is what I was born to do; it runs through my veins. I know this tour will be the making of us as artists, but I just pray that Rosie will wait around for me to come back. I need her to be waiting.

"Okay, that's all. Go, celebrate. Share the news with your loved ones. Two weeks until the start of the rest of your lives begins."

I walk from the office, with Conor by my side, but Michael's dominant voice booms from behind me. "Cillian… could I have a word, please?"

Conor shoots me a sympathetic look, knowing full well, what this conversation will be about. "I'll wait for you out front."

Tapping him on the shoulder in thanks, I nod for him to wait, before turning back to face Michael. He gestures to the chair in front of his desk. "Take a seat, son."

Shoving my hands deep inside my jean pockets, I move to the far wall. "I'd rather stand, thanks."

I know this little chat will have nothing to do with the band or the world tour, it's about Rosie and our relationship. Walking around his desk, he perches himself against the edge, his stare glaring at me with fierce intimidation. Not going to work, old man.

"Do you love my daughter?" *Okay, Michael. I see we are getting straight to the point here.*

Looking him straight in the eye, I answer without hesitation. "Yes sir, I do."

His teeth drag across his lower lip while he folds his arms across his chest. He huffs out an exaggerated breath, his eyes never leave mine, not even to blink.

"Listen here, Cillian, if you love my daughter like you say you do... you will end things before this tour starts. Six months is a helluva long time for her to wait around for you. Rosie needs to focus on her end-of-year exams, she has her heart set on a design degree. One she will not obtain if she's worried about what you're doing, with who knows who, while she waits at home. How do you expect her to focus if her boyfriend is off gallivanting across the world?"

"Michael," I protest. "With all due respect, I would never do anything to make your daughter doubt me, or our relationship."

"That may be the case, but regardless of what you think, I know my daughter, and what's best for her. And, sitting at home waiting for some boy, is not it. I know you will do the right thing here. I'm sure you can understand where I am coming from. As Rosie's dad, I want what is best for my daughter, and at the moment, that is not you. You both need the time and space to grow as people. To become who you were born to be. And then, if in time, you both are meant to be, you can pick things back up. Don't be the guy who stands in the way of her future, all while you're living out your own dream. Let her go, Cillian. It's better if you do it now before you fuck it up like you always do."

Michael's words cut me deeper than I thought they would, but he has a point, I'm bound to fuck this up—it's what I do. Should I give her up, even just for now? Maybe Michael is right if I am on the road; having a relationship with Rosie will be difficult, impossible even.

"Look Cillian, I know you don't want to lose my daughter, and you won't. Give her the freedom she needs to reach her full potential. It's only six months, then you'll be back here, and you can pick up where you left off—it's what you both want. Rosie needs to explore life, not sit around pining for you. If you stay together, she will spend the whole summer missing you and not focusing on her art. All I'm asking is that you think about it, you have two weeks before we leave. Take a few days to decide. But, honestly, it will be better for both of you if you just let her go. At least for now."

My eyes sting, the tears fighting to break free. Can I do that? Break her heart for her own good? I don't think I can.

"I'll think about it."

That's all I get out before rushing out of his office; the heart in my chest, melting from the fucking inferno burning it to ash.

Rushing from the Mulligan house, my chest heaves as I gasp for the air that's being ripped from my lungs. Leaving Rosie is not an option. Is it?

I find Conor, sitting on the bench beside the water feature in Rosie's front garden. His head bent and a cigarette hanging from his lips. The poor fucker looks as broken as I feel.

Taking a seat beside him, I pull my cigarettes from my pocket.

"What's up?"

He raises the hand holding the lighter and flicks to light the one now against my lips. "Bronagh's pregnant!"

Well shit, that was the last thing I expected him to say. I knew they were pretty solid. But pregnant... no wonder he's stressed about leaving.

"I don't know what to do, man. We just found out last week. She's only six weeks along. How the fuck am I meant to pack up and leave her here to go through that alone? We had a plan, now all that's fucked."

I nod my head, unable to comfort him. "Does Ciaran know?"

"No, Bronagh wanted to wait until we had the first scan. You know, just to make sure everything was okay with the baby."

Conor turns to face me, his eyes filled with unshed tears. "Do you know, this morning, I was on cloud nine. I woke up to the love of my life in my arms and my baby growing in her stomach. And now, all my dreams are coming true and all I want to do is run the other way. How am I meant to juggle all this, Cillian? What the fuck am I to do here?"

I've no idea how to answer that? No fucking idea. I'm still trying to get my head around everything myself. Luckily, Conor doesn't wait for an answer, he's up on his feet before I can even muster up a half decent reply.

"Sorry man, I gotta go. I need to talk to Bronagh. Please, don't say anything to anyone about the baby, at least not yet. I need to figure this shit out."

"I won't." I stand, pulling him into one of our man hugs. "Everything will be alright, Conor. Bronagh loves you. You know that. Go, talk to her. Ring me later if you need me."

"Thanks, man, will do. Good luck with Ro."

I watch as he drives away then pull my phone from my pocket. I decide, if this is the last two weeks I have with Rosie, regardless of whether we break up or not, I'm making the most of them.

Me: Meeting's finished. Fancy a date night? X
   Snow: Yes, please. X
   Me: Cool, I'll pick you up in an hour. Wear something warm. Love you. X
   Snow: K, will do. Love you more. X
   Me: Not possible! X
   Snow: Yes possible. Xx

How will I ever let her go?

Chapter Thirteen

Dancing Under Red Skies by Dermot Kennedy

Cillian

Trying my best to enjoy my date with Rosie, I push down the unnerving feeling of losing her crawling its way up my throat.

Michael's earlier words are replaying on repeat in my mind. Setting her free, allowing her to grow and live her life to the fullest, is most definitely the better option, but I can't. If that makes me a selfish bastard, so be it. She is the one for me; I know it. I always have.

Rosie may be the light, but I am the darkness that allows her to shine. One would be nothing without the other. Letting her go would be the biggest regret of my life, so I plan to hold on to her with both hands.

Strolling hand in hand along Donabate beach, I realize, maybe Rosie won't want to wait for me. Six months is a helluva long time.

"Hey, are you okay? You have been extremely quiet all evening." Her brows furrow, as her baby-blues roam over my face.

How do I answer that? I'm not okay. I should be on a high, celebrating the fact 4Clover has finally been given the opportunity to become legendary. But, the terrifying thought of what that means for us is too much. Rosie knows me better than anyone else, she can read me like one of her romance novels. She's the only person who can see right through my bullshit, almost as if I'm transparent to her eyes, and her eyes only.

Lifting my hands, I gently cup her face in my palms. The wailing sound of the ocean waves crash around us as the salty, cold sea breeze pinches her exposed face, making her rosy red cheeks glow. I kiss the tip of her cold nose, and a breath-taking smile illuminates her face.

"As long as I have you, I'll be perfect."

How am I meant to tell her we only have two more weeks together? I'm not great with expressing my emotions, not without the security of my guitar. A melody dances through my head, while lyrics form what I want to say. Hopefully, I can convince Rosie we're strong enough to get through the time we'll have to spend apart. Storing my thoughts away, I savour the time we have left.

We continue along the wet sand for about a mile before settling on some large boulders to watch the sunset. The sky is beautiful this evening, a blend of blues, purples and pinks paint the horizon, as the sun fades beyond the shore. I pull Rosie a little closer, so her back rests against my chest. Nestling my face into the crock of her neck, I breathe in the scent that is distinctly her, as I shelter her from the cold January air.

It's this, in the tiny, quiet moments where our love for one another shines brightest.

"Can we stop and get a Scrumdiddlys, please?" The sheer excitement in her voice is infectious.

Taking my eyes off the road for a split second, I spy the hopeful smile spread across her gorgeous face. "Isn't it a bit cold for ice-cream?"

Rosie playfully slaps my chest. "How dare you? It's never too cold for ice-cream, Charming. Besides, everyone knows it's a cardinal sin to drive by Scrumdiddlys and not stop for their famous ice-cream. I was on their Instagram page the other day, and I swear I nearly licked the phone. They looked so delicious."

God, I would do just about anything to keep that smile on her face for a bit longer.

"If my princess wants an ice-cream, she shall have ice-cream."

Rosie's adorable squeal of laughter fills my car.

Please, don't break my heart, Snow. Your love is the only thing keeping it together.

It takes fifteen minutes to find a place to park, but finally one opens in front of the famous Irish ice-cream shop. The queue is halfway down the road, but the joy radiating off Rosie's face will be worth the wait.

Rosie

Cillian hasn't been himself all evening; he seems lost in thought. I've kept quiet all evening, but now we are back in his room he seems even more withdrawn, and I'm getting worried. I think it may have something to do with their upcoming tour. I overheard Cian and Da talking about it earlier today, and as much as it breaks my heart that he's leaving, he deserves this.

I want him to open up, but I'm not sure how to broach the subject, so I'm thankful when Cillian finally breaks the silence.

"Snow?" He calls, uncertainty lingering between us. "Baby, can I talk to you about something?"

We're laying together on his bed; my head resting on his chest while his fingertips twirl my hair. This has quickly become my favourite place to lay. Right where I can hear his steady heartbeat, so close together, our legs interlocked, barely any space between us. Lifting my head, I meet his gaze. Whatever he has to say is important, it's written all over his handsome, chiselled face.

Shimmying out from beneath me, he sits up, resting his back against his black leather headboard. "Come here," he pats his lap.

Quickly, I oblige, throwing my leg over his, straddling his waist in one swift motion. He hardens beneath me and let's just say it's rather distracting—but now is not the time for hanky panky. The serious tone in his voice is a testament to that.

Capturing his face in my palms, I search his face for answers. "What's wrong?"

He releases a heavy sigh and brushes my hair from my face, tucking it gently behind my ear. The intensity of his stare electrifies my skin, goose bumps are no match for the prickling heat travelling down my spine with just one look from him. Nobody ever looks at me the way he does, pure love and adoration radiates from his irises, making me feel precious.

"I need to tell you something." He blinks slowly, dragging a ragged breath into his lungs. "I am not quite sure how you'll take it."

Sadness floods his hazel eyes and my chest fights against the tightness caused by his struggle.

Trying to make this easier for him, I ask the question. "Is this about the tour? I heard Da and Cian chatting about it earlier. They said that you're leaving in two weeks."

"You know?" His eyes widen bigger than spaceships.

"Only since today, I was waiting for the right time to bring it up."

If it's possible, I feel some weight lift from his shoulders. Gripping my hips, he lifts me off his lap and crawls from the bed.

"Where are you going?"

Panic consumes me. Is he mad I didn't say anything sooner? Picking up his old, black acoustic guitar from the stand in the corner of the room, he walks silently back to the spot beside me on the bed.

"Snow, I'm not very good with this sort of thing. I thought maybe I could play you something I wrote. I want you to listen to the words carefully; and when I'm finished, we'll talk. Okay?"

My heart is beating a million miles a minute and my palms are so freaking sweaty. Shit, what if this is it? What if he wants to break up? Finding it difficult to form words, I nod my head yes instead. Never taking his eyes off me, Cillian begins softly picking the guitar strings. A soft, beautifully gripping melody floats through the air. His unique, deep and sorrowful voice pulls me under.

Each word that leaves his mouth has tears rushing from my eyes. Flowing down my cheeks, carrying the weight of every emotion; he pours his fears, his hopes and his love into each word; touching a place in my heart that only beats for him.

"When I'm gone, far away from your loving arms. Would you wait for me?

When nights get long, and I'm not there to hold you through the storm. Would you wait for me?

The road I take is one less travelled, and I'll be gone so long.

Do you think that we can make it? Do you even wanna try?

Forever isn't worth it, if you're not always mine.

No matter where I'm going, Whoever I might see, I need you to remember, my heart is where you'll be.

So, would you wait for me? While I chase my dreams? While I follow, to wherever they may lead.

Would you wait for me? Oh, I gotta know, because no matter where I'm going... you'll always be my home. So, baby, wait for me."

"What do you say, Snow? Will you wait for me?"

The intensity of his gaze ignites a fire inside me. Seconds pass by, while every scenario on how things will play out between us runs through my mind. Could we make this work? Can we possibly survive the distance this tour would create? Would our love withstand six months of separation? Each question makes way for twenty more.

Deep down, I know it doesn't matter how many questions I ask myself—my answer will always remain the same.

Yes, I will wait. I would wait forever and a day for Cillian O'Shea.

Loosening his grip around the neck of his guitar, I peel his fingertips away from the strings and take the guitar from his hold. Placing it gently on the floor beside the bed, I kneel in front of him on the soft comfort of his duvet. I take his hands in mine as his eyes dart around my face, searching for an answer.

"Charming, I've told you already, I'll love you forever and always. Of course, I'll wait. I would wait as long as you need me to. I promise you; I'm not going anywhere. I'm yours, remember."

He pulls me close, lifting me up onto his lap. My legs immediately wrap around his waist as his arms fold around mine, locking me into his tight embrace.

"You've no idea how happy that makes me. I thought once you heard I was leaving; you'd want to put the brakes on us too."

His hands travel under the thin material of my white t-shirt, the tips of his callous fingers brushing softly along my bare skin. "I know things are going to be tough while I'm away, but I know we can make it. Especially if we're both willing to commit fully. We can FaceTime every day, and we have a show in Dublin in May. So, I promise, I'll see you then."

He rambles on, making promise after promise. Excitement fills his face, making him look just like the little bright-eyed boy I once knew. He stresses over every detail, instead of going with the flow. Sometimes in life, we are all faced with things that are completely out of our control, we just need to let go and trust that whatever road we are on; will lead us to the place we are meant to be.

"We'll figure it out as we go. It'll be tough, and there might be some rocky times ahead, but I love you and a few thousand miles won't change that. Now, if you're finished with this little meltdown, this would be the perfect time for you to kiss me."

Raising the side of my mouth, I tease him with a sassy smile, lightening the mood a little.

"Meltdown, huh?" Cillian's hands travel higher, stopping, and toying with the sensitive spot underneath the band of my bra, right where I'm ticklish. His expression changes from dark and serious to pure devilment.

"Don't you dare!"

My eyes widen with realization. He pushes me backwards, pinning my hips to the bed with his body weight. Laughter free-falls from his lips, and before I know it, he is attacking my sides, causing me to squeal out.

"Cillian! I'm so getting you back for… Ahhh... Stop... Mercy, mercy."

"You think this is funny, Snow? Me, pouring my heart out to you."

His hands still as he leans forward, his face hovering above mine. A cheeky grin widens across his face, flashing off those amazing dimples. "Have you any idea how much I love you? How scared I was when I was faced with the possibility of losing you? I need you, Snow. Like I need air to breathe. I'm so fucking happy you are willing to give the long distance a try. I promise you; I'll do whatever it takes to make this work."

His words steal mine, so I do the one thing I can, to make him realize that I feel the same. Capturing his lips with mine, I kiss him as if my life depends on it. Pulling at the hem of his shirt, I slide it up his back. I need to feel his skin against mine.

Cillian's urgency matches my own, in a matter of seconds, he has it off and throws it somewhere across the room. Next to go is my top, followed quickly by my black leggings.

I send a quick thank you to my morning's self for having the foresight to wear matching underwear today. *And sexy matching underwear at that. High five to me!*

Cillian's eyes burn with desire as his eyes wander over my near naked form. "Fuck, are you trying to kill me?" His fingers trace over the sheer white bralette. "This is so-fucking-sexy. Did you wear it for me?"

An all-telling blush forms on my cheeks as I close my eyes, trying to push back the shyness his question evokes.

Cillian's tongue teases me through the barely-there material, and my eyes snap open.

He's staring back at me over the hood of his brow as he slowly licks at my now hardened buds. The net-lace of my bra is rough, yet sensual against my nipple, and I moan out in pleasure.

"Baby, as much as I love this bra, I need it off, now."

I lift my arms up so he can pull the material over my head. Gripping the back of my head with his hand, he pulls my hair gently, exposing my neck to him. He slowly runs his tongue across my jawline, leaving my body quaking for release. I feel completely at his mercy, chasing a rush only he can give. The temperature of the room rises with each nibble, lick, and suck. My body screams to be released from the building pressure between my legs.

"Cillian... please, I need more."

I pull at the button of his jeans, freeing him as quickly as possible. Suddenly, he hops from the bed, his jeans and boxers simultaneously landing on the floor with a soft thud. The sight before me has my mouth watering. He has abs for days, each set more lickable than the next. Before I can eye-fuck him any further he turns toward the door. Giving me a glorious view of his muscular shoulders and back. *Did someone call Justin Timberlake? Because Cillian is definitely bringing a sexy back!*

Quickly, he twists the key in the bedroom door, so we won't be interrupted by anyone. Picking his discarded wallet from the floor, he retrieves a small square foil packet.

"Now, where was I?"

Playing along with his game, I run my fingers slowly down the middle of my stomach, coming to a halt at the edge of my thong.

"Right about here."

His tongue peeks out of his mouth, running across his bottom lip.

"If you insist."

Oh, I definitely do.

Chapter Fourteen

Photograph by Ed Sheeran

Cillian

I've spent every waking moment of the last two weeks, wrapped up in all things, Rosie. Any chance we got; we'd disappear together. Savouring every second and making every minute count. We stocked up on memories — nights in the treehouse where Rosie would draw as I sang her songs, dinners and movies, and walks through the Phoenix park — all so we could survive the next six months without one another. But, even at that, two weeks was not enough.

4Clovers flight to fame is jetting off today, and the unbearable grip around my lungs has only tightened. Thoughts of leaving her cripple me, but this is what I was born to do. The need to make music flows through my veins, it's essential to my survival. I have an imperishable hunger to create something bigger than myself; something so magical, it touches the lives of people, marking the depths of their soul.

It's not a hobby; becoming anything other than a musician was never an option. This is my path—my purpose.

So, why does it feel like I need to lose someone I love, in order to do something I love?

Zipping up my suitcase, I scan my bedroom one last time. Rosie helped me pack last night before heading home for her family dinner with Cian.

Being the selfish bastard, I am, I forgot I wasn't the only person she was saying goodbye to.

Her and Cian have always been close. He protects her with his life, that's just the kind of man he is. Family means everything to him. And, as much as I wanted to spend my last night with her, she needed to say goodbye to her brother.

A gentle tap sounds from my door.

"Cillian, can I come in?" My Ma's voice travels through the old wooden door.

"Yeah, I'm just finished."

The door hinges squeak as she slowly enters the room. Her eyes scan over every detail before setting on me. A wide smile graces her pretty yet tired face. She shuffles over to my bed, takes a seat, and pats the space beside her.

"Come sit with me for a second."

Once I'm settled beside her, she takes my hand in hers.

Contrary to the shitty childhood Lily and I had, I could never fault my Ma. She is the strongest woman I've ever met. Yes, she was dealt a shitty hand, and an even shittier husband, but she worked her ass off to make sure we were provided for and loved by her.

"You know, this place won't be the same without you." Her eyes well up with unshed tears. "I'll really miss you when you're gone."

Wrapping my arm around her shoulder, I pull her in close. "It's okay, Ma. It's only for six months. I'll be back wrecking your head in no time." I kiss the crown of her auburn hair. "Besides, Lily will be here to keep you young and on your toes."

She lays her hand on my cheek and her eyes crinkle with a smile. "Look at you, so handsome. I always knew you were destined for greatness. From the time you were a little boy, you had this glow that shone so bright. Then you started to obsess over that guitar," she points to my black Gibson, "and that shine sparkled tenfold. God, I can still remember your face on that Christmas morning. It didn't matter to you in the slightest that I bought it from the charity shop. Or that there were strings missing. I watched you fall in love for a second time that morning, and the joy I felt being able to give that to you, was one of my best moments of parenthood."

I cover her hand with mine. "Love you, Ma."

"I love you too, darling. And I'm so sorry I let your Da dim your shine. You deserved better than him. Promise me you'll remember just how very special you are."

"Promise."

We sit for a few quiet moments, soaking up our goodbye.

"Ma?"

"Yes, sweetheart?"

"What did you mean when you said you watched me falling in love a second time that morning?"

She huffs out a soft chuckle. "Well, the first time I watched you fall in love was when you first laid eyes on little Rosie. Honestly, I never thought it would take you this long to make her yours. Wherever she was, you followed. She wasn't just the star in your sad eyes, she was the moon. A bright shining light in all that darkness you carry. Make sure you hold on to her, she's a rare gem."

Slipping her hand into her pocket, she pulls out a small Polaroid photo. "I was going through some old photographs last night, and I found this." She places it carefully in my palm. "I thought you might like to bring it with you."

Staring down at the photo, my eyes wander over every detail. A beautiful little girl in a white floaty sundress, her hair blowing in the breeze. Daffodils clutched tightly in her hands. Next to her, a little boy, pulling at his too-tight-tie and wearing a suit jacket that was about twelve sizes too big for his little body.

It's us, Rosie and I.

Lily took this photo on Rosie's vintage camera the day she held our pretend wedding.

Ma tips the photograph. "You always loved her. Even as young as you both were, I knew deep down, that girl right there held my baby boy's heart in her tiny hands."

She kisses my cheek before standing to leave me with my thoughts. "We're heading to Maggie's in ten, I'll let you get the rest of your stuff. I'll be downstairs if you need me."

The door closes behind her, and I pick up my phone to send Rosie a text, letting her know I'll be there soon.

Me: Be there in ten. Miss you. X

* * *

Rosie barrels down the driveway and jumps straight into my arms. Locking her legs around my waist, she swings her arms over my shoulders like a Koala bear on its favourite tree. Not that I'm complaining, if I could keep her perched here permanently, I would.

She buries her head in the crook of my neck. "Ugh, I'm gonna miss you so much."

Her sweet cherry-apple scent fills my nose. Breathing it deep into my lungs, I savour it. "I'll miss you, too."

"Excuse me, I know you two are having some kind of moment, but could you please tone it down.

I can't stomach much more of your cuteness. I've reached my limit for the day." Sticking two fingers in her mouth, Lily dramatically heaves at us.

Rosie untangles herself, sliding down my body until her toes tip the ground. Tightening my hold, I lock her against my chest. "Where do you think you're going?"

"Charming, as much as I would like you to carry me around all morning, it's impossible."

"Says who? The word itself is, I'm possible."

Leaning forward, I grip her thighs and attach her to my waist. "Get comfortable, Snow. You're not leaving my arms until I've to leave for my flight."

Rosie

Having everyone around, laughing, joking and reminiscing about old times is bittersweet. The boys are set to leave soon and the energy in the room lessens with every passing minute.

The underlying sorrow of their departure lingers in the surrounding air. Curled up in Cillian's lap, he circles my body with his left arm. Keeping me as close as possible. His free hand playfully twirls a strand of my hair, while his head, rests in the space between my shoulder and neck. I scan the open living-slash-kitchen area, taking in the expressions of everyone affected by the boy's soon-to-be departure.

Bronagh, like me, is curled up against Conor's side. Her eyes rimmed red from all the tears she shed. Conor has his hand protectively splayed across her stomach and they whisper quietly amongst themselves.

Ciaran is lounging back in the armchair, never taking his eyes off Lily. Everyone knows he has feelings for her. Well, everyone except Lily. Cian and Lily sit side by side on the floor playing an Xbox game, every now and then shouting profanities at one another.

Lily hates losing, and Cian loves pissing her off. For outsiders looking in, you'd think they were together, but knowing what I know, all they'll ever be is friends. Neither of them has ever wanted more.

Lastly, gathered around the kitchen table are all of our parents. They're in deep conversation about God knows what. It seems like forever since we were all under the one roof, and as dysfunctional as it may be, we're all family.

The bond the boys have built throughout the years has moulded us together.

Cillian whispering against my neck pulls me from my thoughts. "Can we go to your room?"

Standing quickly, I hold out my hand. "Let's go."

We hurry down the hall towards my room and the grandfather clock catches my eye. Eleven-fifteen. Only forty-five minutes until they leave.

Cillian pushes open my bedroom door and heads for my bed. Making himself comfy, he kicks off his army boots and pats his chest. "Come lay with me for a second?"

I crawl up beside him, resting my head against his chest. I tilt my head slightly; my eyes wander over every crevice of his chiselled face. The silence between us is deafening. Why is this so hard?

"Please, Snow. Don't look at me like that. This is hard enough already. If you keep giving me those sad doe-eyes, I'll never get on that fucking plane."

Blowing out a breath, I close my eyes and blink back the tears. "I'm sorry. I want you to go, I really do. You deserve this, you all do. I'm just already missing you."

He bends slightly, capturing my lips with his in a sweet yet passionate kiss. Pulling back, he dots my nose with a small peck. "I know, me too, but I'll be back before you know it. Six months is nothing when we've got a lifetime." He pushes up, leaning his back against my headboard.

Moving, I straddle his waist and cup his face in my palms. "I love you."

"I love you, too. Promise me, that when it gets hard and the distance seems too much, you'll remember that. Never doubt how much you mean to me. This love I feel for you, it runs deep in my veins, Snow. If I ever lost you, I'd have to cut myself open and let you bleed out. Whatever happens, please remember, it's you I'm coming home to."

He lifts my chin with his index finger, edging my lips towards his. Nothing but love shines from his hazel-eyes.

When his lips finally meet mine, I swear I can taste the next seventy years of my life.

Everything around me fades as I get lost in the tenderness of his mouth brushing against mine. This kiss removes the air from my lungs, feeds my soul and reassures me that no matter what happens, we're going to be okay.

✳ ✳ ✳

It's time.

The inevitable is upon us.

Hand in hand, we walk down the cobblestone drive. With every step, Cillian's hand squeezes a little tighter. All around us, our family and friends hug goodbye and the noose around my heart pulls tighter. Closing my eyes, I blink back the burning tears, but when the seven-seater taxicab comes into view, my breath lodges in my throat and the tears free fall.

My heart thunders in my chest with each step closer. *Breathe, Rosie. Just breathe.*

Cillian faces me, his gaze could burn down buildings. "Remember what I said — I'm coming back for you. I love you so fucking much. Hold on to that, don't forget. Forever."

"And always."

His lips meet mine with a hundred meanings.

I love you.

I miss you.

Goodbye.

Serval arms wrap around me as Cillian climbs into the taxi. And together, Bronagh, Lily and I watch as the most important men in our lives drive off into the sunset to follow their dreams.

Chapter fifteen

Faithfully by Journey

Cillian

May 2014

*T*o say I've been eagerly awaiting this day would be a Goddamn understatement.

We've been on the road for over three months; travelling from city to city, night after night, performing for hundreds and thousands of people.

Touring the U.S was everything I imagined it to be, but I'm exhausted, my joints are aching, and my throat feels as if I swallowed a handful of razor blades. Not to mention, I've been missing Rosie like hell. We FaceTime daily, sending thousands of messages in between but it's never enough to dull the distance between us. My phone bill for last month could rent a small apartment in Dublin City for fuck's sake. But hearing her voice and seeing her beautiful face — even if it's just through a phone screen — is worth every cent.

The first few weeks were the hardest. I found myself spiralling down a dodgy road, but with the help of Conor, I got through. He's the only other person who knows how difficult it is to leave your girl behind.

Tonight, none of that matters, it's the opening show for the European leg of the Sinners world tour and my girls twentieth birthday.

The roar from the crowd filling Dublin's 3arena is louder than any other venue we've played so far. It's still an hour until the show starts and they're already getting impatient.

4Clover. 4Clover. 4Clover.

Even though we're only the supporting band, tonight is different, tonight... We're home. These are our fans. Our supporters.

We landed in Dublin this morning, but I've yet to lay eyes on my Snow-White. There was no time between setup and sound check, but knowing she's coming to see me play has me flying higher than Afroman.

"Any news from Rosie?" Conor asks as we head towards the dressing room.

"Yeah, they were picking Lily up and heading straight here. Shouldn't be too long."

"Fuck man, I've haven't seen my fiancée in months. How the hell am I meant to play an entire set knowing she's standing in the wings waiting?"

"Fucked if I know," I respond. "At least we'll have a night with them before flying back to L.A.

Are you still planning on asking Bronagh to fly out to you in Vegas for your twenty-first?"

He releases a heavy sigh. "Yeah, she'll still be in her second trimester so she can fly out for the week we've off and I'll get to spend some time with her before the baby comes."

"Maybe I'll see if Rosie and Lily want to come too, that way Bronagh won't have to fly alone."

Conor throws his head back in laughter.

"What?"

"Don't pretend you're asking for Bronagh's sake. If you want her to come, just ask her. Knowing Bronagh she's already told the girls she's flying out. Rosie's probably wondering why you haven't offered."

"Shit. You're an asshole, you know that."

"And yet, you still love me."

✱ ✱ ✱

She's late.

Fuck, we go on stage in five and she's still not here.

Pulling my phone out of my back pocket, I read her last message.

Snow: I'm sorry, traffic is a nightmare. We'll be there soon. If I don't make it before you go on… break a leg. Love you.

"Boys, it's showtime." Michael pops his head into

our dressing room informing us it's time to head to the stage.

"What about the girls?" Ciaran stands, wiping his palms in his black, ripped jeans. He won't admit it, but he's dying to see Lily. Unlike Conor and I, he hasn't spoken to her since he left, and it's been wearing on him.

"Don't worry about them, I've left their passes at the door. They'll be here. Now, move your fucking asses and let's show theses fuckers what you are made off. We're on our home turf, this crowd is yours. The boys are back in town."

Rosie

"You should have let me drive," Lily complains from the back seat as I roll my eyes at her through the rear-view mirror.

"What difference would it have made? I'm not Moses. I can't part the sea of traffic."

"No, but you do drive like Miss Daisy. You need to be more aggressive. Drive like you're late for mass."

She rolls down the window and sticks her fiery-red head out. "Hey, asshole, move it. The light is green. We've got a show to see, and you and your eco-friendly Prius, are in the way."

Bronagh wipes the tears away with the sleeve of her top. I slap her thigh.

"Stop laughing, you're only encouraging her more."

"I'm sorry, but she's too much."

A cyclist swerves out in front of us and Lily's off again. "Yo, Lance Armstrong! Ever heard of hand signals, or has that too-tight-spandex cut the circulation to your non-existent brain off?"

"Get in the goddamn window."

Finally, she slumps back into the seat. "Rosie, why do you have to suck the fun out of my evening? And anyway, cyclists are a danger to mankind. Did you see the way his ass was eating that poor seat? Illegal if you ask me."

"We didn't ask you," Bronagh and I say in unison.

Thankfully, before she can take her road rage out on anyone else, the arena comes into view. Time to see my man.

✱ ✱ ✱

Standing in the side wings of the 3arena with Lily and Bronagh, as all our boys perform, is insane. The crowd goes nuts as Cian belts out song after song. It doesn't matter that I've seen 4Clover on stage more times than I can count, this is on a whole nother level.

There isn't an empty seat in the stands and the floor space is jam-packed. Cillian told me how different the stadium shows were. But I don't think it fully registered until this very moment.

It takes everything in me not to run out and wrap my arms around the man I've spent the last three and a half months without.

I stand there like a star-struck groupie as his fingers travel effortlessly across every fret. Sweat drips from his longer-than-normal hair, making his now transparent, white t-shirt mould against his skin. The devilously sinful muscles of his shoulders and back are on show for everyone to see. And, my God, he's stunning.

He's changed in the time he's been away. His once boyish features are nowhere to be seen. Stubble lines his sharp jawline forcing images of him between my legs to take over my every thought. He looks my way, smiling at me with his eyes as he shreds chord after chord and as much as I love watching him in his element, I can't wait for this show to be over.

Finally, after what feels like forever, Cian addresses the crowd. "DUBLIN!" The whole place erupts. "Thank you so much for that amazing welcome home. The last few months have been nothing less than fucking epic. We've travelled all over the U.S with Sinners, and not once did we play for a crowd as awesome as you lot. Thank you for such a warm welcome reception. We love you all."

Chants for one more song begins, and Cian breaks out in laughter. "Before we leave you, my boy Cillian here has something he wants to share."

Ear piercing screams ring through the arena as Cillian confidently walks towards centre stage. Cian hands him the microphone and then takes a seat behind the grand piano.

Cillian's deep, raspy voice reverberates through the arena as he greets the crowd. "Alright, Dublin. How are you doing? It sure is fucking great to be home."

Once again, the cheers and shouts drown him out.

"Thank you so much for being such a great audience. As you all know, I don't take centre stage often — we wouldn't want the main man to get a complex."

Lily, Bronagh and I laugh at how true that statement is.

"But tonight… I'm making an exception. You see, today is a very special day."

I feel the colour drain from my face.

"Today, the love of my life is celebrating her birthday." *What the fuck is he doing?* "For those of you that don't already know, I've been in love with this girl since I was seven years old. Not only has she stuck with me through all my shit, but she also loves me more for it." Panic settles in the pit of my stomach. He better not call me out there. *Oh God, I think I'm going to be sick.*

Looking at Bronagh and Lily, I wonder if they know what he's up to. But, both of them look as shocked as I feel. My eyes near bug out of my head when I see Conor pulling a chair across the stage. He places it right beside Cillian and my stomach lands in my shoes. Has he lost his mind? There's no way in hell I'm going out there in front of all those people.

"Would you guys like to help me sing happy birthday to my girl?" Cillian's eyes capture mine when he turns to face me. His stretched-out arm pointing in my direction. "Come on, Snow. Don't leave a guy hanging."

His face is full of mischief and all I can do is step towards him. *Dead, I'm going to kill him.*

The heat from the spotlight burns my skin as I make my way across the stage. Deafening hoots and hollers from the crowd, puncture my ears but Cillian is all I see. Each step I take brings us closer, I haven't seen him in months and instead of our reunion, being quiet and intimate, there are thirteen thousand people watching my every move. *Did I say he was dead?*

Stepping into his open arms, he engulfs my tiny frame. "Welcome home, Snow."

It takes me a second to realize he means me, back in his arms.

"Hi."

"Fuck, I missed you. Happy Birthday, Baby."

Guiding me into the chair, he kisses my forehead. His lips linger there, but not long enough. His eyes latch to mine with a promise. *Tonight.*

Giving me a wink, he turns to face the crowd. "Okay, everyone. I might need a bit of help singing this one. So, if you know it, sing along."

Soft notes flow from the piano as Cian's fingers dance across the keys. Cillian interlocks his fingers with mine, his eyes only focused on me and somehow the crowd fades away. His sorrowful voice floods the stadium, the natural raspy lilt I love so much delivering every word of Journey's Faithfully perfectly.

Every lyric, every chord, every beat of the drums, travels up my spine as tears fill my eyes. God, I love this man.

He pours everything he has into it as he sings about a music man who's on tour and how his heart is home with the woman he loves. That no matter where in the world he is, he will be forever hers, faithfully.

When the song comes to an end, I throw myself into his arms. "I love you, Cillian O'Shea."

"Forever and always, Rosie Mulligan."

His lips crash onto mine and we get lost in each other. I know right there, at that moment, there is nothing that could ever tear us apart.

If only I'd have known how wrong I was.

Chapter Sixteen

Arsonist's Lullaby by Hozier

Cillian

June 2016

I knew this day was coming, but what I never anticipated was how we were going to deal with it. His release was imminent. But, yet, we weren't prepared.

Hopefully, three years in a cell has given him enough sense to stay the fuck away, because I swear if he comes within one hundred feet of my Ma or sister, I'm burying him six-feet deep.

It only takes one look at my tough-as-nails sister, to rattle my cage. She's rocking back and forward in the corner, her body shaking as tears stream down her face. I haven't seen Lily cry like this since we were kids, but now, she is inconsolable.

Rosie sits beside her, arms wrapped around Lily's waist as she whispers whatever the hell she can think of, to calm her down.

"Ciaran, I need Ciaran." The only words Lily has spoken since we received the call from Mountjoy prison. Where the fuck, is he? I called him twenty minutes ago.

"He's on the way, Lily." Rosie pulls her tighter, tucking her against her chest. "He's coming, I promise."

Pushing up off the couch, I kick the coffee table with a full force boot. Fuck this. I head for the wooden drink cabinet in the corner of the room and rummage through it for something, anything, to dull the unbearable urge I've got to punch someone.

Pulling out a bottle of Absolut vodka, I slump into the nearest armchair. It's not whiskey, but it will do.

After tearing off the plastic seal, I twist the lid off and throw the small silver cap across the sitting.

"Son, you need to calm down."

"Ma, with all due respect, don't fucking tell me to calm down. That man you called your husband, was released from Mount-joy prison this morning. The same man who beat you, and us, for years. The same fucking man who tried to sexually assault my little sister. How in God's name do you expect me to calm down?"

Rage courses through my veins, seconds away from bubbling over. The thunderous beat of my heart accelerates with every breath I take. Closing my eyes briefly, I try to gain some sort of control. When that doesn't work, I raise the bottle in my hand and rest it against my lips once more, allowing the vodka to hit my tongue before burning its way down the back of my throat.

"Did you forget, it was us who got him locked up? Don't think for one second, he won't come back here. Technically, this is still his fucking house." I know this is not my Ma's fault, but I can't help but feel some anger towards her. When I offered to take them away from this place and move her to somewhere new, she refused. Telling me, this was her home, and she wasn't leaving.

"Cillian, your Ma is right. You need to calm down and drinking that shit won't help."

Turning to face Rosie, I level her with a don't-give-me-shit, glare. The last thing I need right now is her and her self-righteous preaching. If I want to have a drink, I'll have one.

"Rosie, just shut up. This has nothing to do with you. What the hell are you even doing here?" Harsh I know, but I can't deal with her here, she should never see me like this. If I've to push her away with hurtful words, I will. I'll do whatever it takes to get her to go home, at least she'll be safe there.

Horror flashes across her beautiful face. In the two years we've been together, I've never spoken to her like that.

Suddenly, her shoulders straighten. "Fuck you, Cillian. If you want to bury your demons in a bottle of vodka, go right ahead. But, don't think for one second, you have the right to speak to me like that because you don't, not now, or ever for that matter. I'm here because I love you. I'm here because I love your sister. And you can push me away all you like, but I'm not going fucking anywhere."

The doorbell chimes, sending the already hostile room into complete silence. Four sets of eyes narrow in on the main door. Slowly, I make my way to it, picking up the wooden hurling stick on the way. Just in case. Looking back over my shoulder, I ask for some unspoken permission to open the door. When Ma nods her head, I grip the handle with a shaky hand and twist the knob. Ready, just in case it's my so-called father standing on the other side.

"Jesus, Cillian. Put the hurl down. Who do you think you are, Cu Chulainn?" *Ciaran, Thank-fucking-Christ.*

Lily barrels across the room as if it's on fire, jumping straight into my best friend's arms. "You came?"

"I told you, Lilybug, no matter what. If you need me... I'll be here, anytime. Day or night."

Leaving them to it, I walk back over to the couch, ignoring the daggers coming my way from Rosie's eyes. I lift the bottle again, giving exactly zero fucks.

Rosie

As the night progresses, so does Cillian's temper. With every swig he takes from the bottle, all the years of resentment he carries, finally, come to ahead.

He paces the room like a mad-man and knowing him the way I do, he's losing control.

Watching him now is like seeing a storm brewing beyond the horizon. And although you know what's coming, there is nothing you can do to stop the ineluctable destruction it will cause. He is one step away from demolition, and there is nothing anyone can do to stop him.

Cillian drops the bottle on the table and grabs his car keys. "Fuck this shit."

"Where are you going? You can't drive like that, you're pissed."

Stalking across the room, his anger radiates from his pores. He stops inches from my face, his six-foot-two frame towering over me and asserting his dominance. "I'm not waiting here like some kind of sitting duck, for that son of a bitch to show up. And whether you think this is a good idea or not, I'm going to find him. He needs to know that he can't hurt my family, not anymore. I'm not the same kid he used to slap around. I'm a fucking grown man who won't hesitate when it comes to putting his pathetic ass down."

Placing my palm against his cheek, I plead with my eyes. "Please, don't do this."

Cillian turns his head breaking our connection, his gaze focuses on the floor. "There is nothing you can say that will change my mind. I need to do this, Snow."

Ciaran rises from the armchair with Lily still tangled up in his arms. Placing her back on the chair, he whispers something to her, and she nods her head in understanding.

Lily is the strongest person I know, she takes no prisoners with her tough cookie attitude, but that's gone now, and in its place is a broken, fragile little girl. As her best friend, I know her usual sarcastic self is a form of defence. She hides behind that tough exterior because it keeps her safe and guarded, but with the news of her Da's release her walls are crumbling down.

Ciaran steps to Cillian. "If you are determined to do this, I'm coming with you. And before you get any ideas, I'm driving. Rosie's right you can't get behind the wheel like that. I'm not prepared to lose someone else because some drunk dickhead got behind the wheel."

Cillian's face drops to the floor and he hands Ciaran the keys in defeat. "Fine, just don't try to stop me. This needs to end tonight."

Ciaran knew those words would work. But, that's a story for another day.

Cillian takes my face in his palms. "Please, stop worrying. I'll be fine. Stay here and look after Lil, I'll be back shortly."

He presses his lips to my forehead, but I pull away. I can't pretend I'm okay with this suicide mission, but I know deep down Cillian won't rest until he faces his demons head-on. And, unfortunately, those demons are in the shape of his father. Trying to stop him is futile and will only lead to further pain.

"Look at me, Snow." He tilts my chin. "I know it might not seem like it right now, but I do love you."

He's out the door before I can reply.

✻ ✻ ✻

For hours, I wait for Cillian to come home.

It's a little after two a.m. when Lily decides she wants to go to bed so I give up and join her.

Together, we snuggle up and pull comfort from one another. I must have fallen asleep because the next thing I know, Cillian's arms are lifting me from Lily's bed, pulling me from my slumber. "Where are you taking me?"

"My bed. Where you belong."

He seems calmer now, and a lot more sober than he was when he left. *What time is it?*

"What about Lil? I don't want to leave her alone. She's not doing so well."

He pushes open the adjoining bathroom door between his and Lily's room and lays me gently on his bed. "Don't worry, she's fine. Ciaran is going to stay with her."

Pulling back the covers, he lifts me underneath them and tucks me in. "I'm just going to take a quick shower. I'll be right back."

He flicks on the bedside lamp and the light illuminates his face. My stomach flips as I take in his ragged appearance.

Dried blood stains his white t-shirt and cuts mar his swollen knuckles. Not to mention, the split in his bottom lip. *Jesus, Cillian. What did you do?*

I jump from the bed and run my fingers over the slight bruise forming under his left eye. "What the hell happened?"

Wrapping his fingers around my wrist, he pulls my hand from his face and kisses my open palm. "Not tonight. I promise I'll tell you everything tomorrow. I need to wash this off. Just please, get back into bed, I'll be right back."

His eyes beg me, letting me know he needs me to just be there for him.

"Okay, but tomorrow, you tell me what happened. No excuses, Cillian."

"Tomorrow, I promise."

After Cillian takes his shower, he climbs into bed behind me. His arm wraps around my waist and he pulls me closer to his chest. His hand travels under the thin material of my t-shirt, tracing the skin of my stomach. Sleep pulls me under as Cillian softly sings me to sleep.

A loud thumping forces my eyes open. *Is someone at the door?* Checking the small alarm clock next to Cillian's bed, I see it's only six-forty-five.

Quickly, Cillian unravels himself from around me and climbs from the bed. "I'll be right back."

He pulls on a pair of tracksuit bottoms and heads for the door but the churning in the pit of my stomach makes me follow.

We're halfway down the stairs when I see Lily and Ciaran standing at the now open front door. Vomit rushes up my oesophagus at the I take in the two uniformed police officers.

What the fuck happened last night?

The room spins as they step towards Cillian.

"Cillian O'Shea, you are under arrest for the attempted murder of Mr. Damien O'Shea."

Chapter Seventeen
Way Down We Go by KALEO

Rosie

The world around me moves in slow motion.

Everyone around me is panicking, but there is no sound. I am stuck, frozen to the ground beneath my feet. My body is nothing but an unmovable shell, helplessly watching the other part of my soul get carted out the door in handcuffs.

A silent scream rips from my throat as I crash to the ground. My entire world is crumbling around me, and all I can do is stare blankly as the aftermath of storm Cillian takes place. I've never felt more helpless than I do now.

Two policemen escort Cillian out of the house and force him into the back of their squad car. Mary questions one of the uniformed Garda, her hands wave in all directions and her mouth moves at lightning speed. All I can hear are the sirens, wailing with the continuous flash of the red and blue lights.

Cillian's eyes capture mine through the back window of the car. The glass stops me from hearing his words. But I see them mouthed from his lips. "I love you, Snow. I'm so sorry."

Salty tears flood my cheeks as bile bubbles in my throat. I force it down. Not now, I need to stay calm. Cillian needs me. I need to get him out of this. Desperately, I try to control my breathing, taking deep breaths in through my nose, then releasing them slowly out through my mouth. It isn't until the police car descends the driveway; I break.

A wave of nausea surges through my body as I bolt towards the hedges that line the property and spew my guts all over Mary's geraniums.

Ciaran's hand runs along my spine. "It will be okay, Rosie."

I turn around so fast, almost knocking him over. "Okay... nothing about this is okay, Ciaran. My boyfriend just got fucking arrested for trying to kill his Da. How can you tell me it will be okay?"

I know this has nothing to do with Ciaran, but at the minute, I don't care.

"What the hell happened last night?"

He was there. He knows exactly what happened. And, so help me God, he will tell me so I can fix this.

"There's not much to tell, Ro. As Cillian suspected, Damien was at The Golden Barrel. When we got there, he was paralytic drunk. The barman said he'd been there for hours. Cillian told him to leave town and never come back, then shit kicked off. Words were exchanged, and Damien swung for Cillian. Clocked him straight in the eye. Then Cillian lost it, he just kept hitting him. Over and over, until finally, I managed to drag his ass out of there. But Rosie, he was bad when we left. Cillian didn't hold back. In all the years we've been friends, I've never seen him lose control like that. If I didn't get Cillian out of there when I did, he would have killed him."

✻ ✻ ✻

I barge through the front door of my house, a woman on a mission, heading straight to the one person I know, who has the contacts to get Cillian home.

Mary spent the past hour on the phone to the Gardai station, trying to get information on her son's arrest. But they won't tell her anything. Cillian is not a minor; he doesn't need a parent present. And by law, they're not obligated to tell her shit.

What Cillian needs is a good Solicitor, and I happen to know one of those.

"Da," I scream at the top of my lungs. "Da, are you here?"

Michael's office door swings open, his eyes furrowed in concern. "Rosalie, what's the matter? Why do you sound so panicked?"

"Cillian's been arrested. He needs help... your help. Please, daddy, you need to call Mr. Morgan. He needs to help him."

Motioning me into his office, he closes the door and turns to face me. "Rosalie, darling, you need to slow down. Tell me exactly what happened?"

To the best of my ability, I relay the events of yesterday and this morning, everything I know — which isn't exactly much. Once I'm finished, Da releases a frustrated breath.

"Okay Rosie, I'll see what I can do." He massages his temples and closes his eyes. I can almost see the wheels spinning in this head. "This is a mess, Rosalie. I hope you finally see; you deserve better. That boy's proving to be more trouble than he's worth. Cillian could go down for a long time. If I can get him out of this, it must be under my conditions. I do not want you to be involved with him anymore. Do you understand?"

It's no secret that my Da has been trying to put a wedge between Cillian and me for years. I'm not shocked in the slightest, I knew coming here would give him the ammo he needed, but I didn't have a choice. Cillian needs my help and if the cost of his freedom is me, so be it.

"I understand."

Dread and regret grip my chest as I sink lower into the chair in front of his desk. I have to keep reminding myself why I am here — about to throw away the one person I love most in the world. Digging my fingers into the edge of the chair, I plant my feet to the floor to ground myself a little.

With a deep breath, I lift my head up and face the devil I know. "I'll do whatever it takes, as long as you promise me, whatever bullshit charges he's facing, will be dropped. And... When he gets out, I need to know he will never have to deal with his father again."

Michael drums his fingertips against his desk, calculating and contemplating how exactly he plans on ruining my life. "Okay, I will make this whole mess disappear. But..." *always a fucking but.* "In return, you will break up with Cillian O'Shea, effective immediately. We both know Mr. Morgan wants you to marry his son before he hands his company over to him. A marriage that will be mutually beneficial to both families. Anyhow, he believes you are what Sean needs and I happen to agree. You're a strong woman with a powerful background."

I bite my tongue. What I think doesn't matter. If this is what it takes to get Cillian out of that cell — I'll do it.

"If you are compliant to your end of this deal, Patrick Morgan will have Cillian released by the end of the day. But, if you refuse to play ball, he will have him locked back up quicker than you can say, I do."

It comes as no surprise that my Da would use this situation for his own gain, he's a money-hungry, power-crazed lunatic. If I marry Sean, he becomes more powerful. Patrick Morgan is a very wealthy man with more contacts in the music industry than my Da could dream off. He could expand his label and artist, generating more money.

For him, me marrying Sean is a win-win.

A little voice in the back of my head tells me not to do this. But I force it back, Cillian needs me. I'm doing this for him. He deserves a better life than one behind bars. I'm sorry, Cillian.

Swallowing the lump in my throat I hold my hand out for him to shake. "You have a deal."

"Great, I'll call Patrick now. Oh, and Rosalie?"

"Yes, Da?"

"This stays between us, if anybody so much as gets a sniff of this, all deals are off. Are we clear?"

I breathe back the tears. Forgive me Cillian, I did this for you. "Crystal."

Cillian

If I could relive last night, all over again — I wouldn't change a thing.

That son-of-a-bitch deserved every punch I landed. And, to be completely honest, he's lucky I left him breathing at all.

For years, he not only physically abused his wife and kids, but he also destroyed us mentally. Bruises may fade with time, but the mental scars, they're a lot harder to shake. Those fuckers hold on tight and cripple us. They enable us from having any resemblance to a normal life. I won't lie and say I wasn't edging towards a fight when I went looking for him. But I didn't strike first. I told him to leave, to go as far away as he could from my family, and he didn't listen. No, instead he started mouthing off like he always does. And when I didn't shut up and listen like I used to do, he lashed out. Just like I expected he would. Only this time, I was prepared. I'm not the same little boy he used to lash with a belt or lock under the stairs. I'm a grown man, one who can kick the shit out of his deadbeat father.

Last night, I gave him a dose of his own medicine, it's safe to say, it didn't go down well. Instead of taking it like a man, he took the pussy way out and called the Garda.

"Fucking wanker."

I've been locked in this cell for far too long and this steel frame bed is anything but comfortable. I can understand how people lose their minds in prison, there's nothing in here, even remotely exciting. The three walls are painted a lifeless shade of grey and the final wall holds a large cast door, which shockingly, is also grey. There's exactly three pieces of furniture — all of which are bolted to the floor — a bed, a table, and a chair.

Laying back on the bed, I close my eyes and allow my thoughts to wander. Before I know it, Rosie's beautiful face comes into view. For as long as I live, I will never forget the look on her face this morning. Fear, heartbreak, anger, confusion; each one was etched across her face. I should have told her what happened last night. At least then, she would have been prepared. There was nothing I could do to stop her from crumbling this morning.

Right before my eyes, she shattered. And there wasn't a goddamn thing I could do to comfort her.

Knowing it was me who caused her that pain kills me. I never wanted my darkness to touch her, and in the beginning, that's why I kept her at a distance. I knew one day she would end up caught in the crossfire of my demons. Today was that day. Now, I have no idea if she'll ever look at me the same again.

A loud creak fills the cell as the large grey cast door is pried open. My eyes snap open when a shadowed figure, looms over me.

"Cillian O'Shea. You're free to go." It's the same Garda who arrested me this morning. "We have dropped all charges."

Sitting up, I swing my legs off the metal cot. "Sorry, could you repeat that?"

"If I were you, kid, I wouldn't question it."

"But, what about my Da?"

Shoving his hands into his pockets, he sways on the balls of his feet. "Look, all you need to know is, we don't take too kindly to men who abuse their families. Your father violated his parole conditions, he's going back to prison. Don't look a gift horse in the mouth, Son. Today's your lucky day."

I hear what he's saying, but somehow, it's not sitting right. There's no way I'm just walking out of here — no questions asked. An unsettling feeling forms in my stomach and no matter how hard I try to shift it; it only grows bigger with every passing second.

After an hour of signing release forms, I'm finally free to leave, but the second I step out into the open air and see Patrick Morgan—Sean's father and the country's most sought after solicitor—that unnerving feeling spreads to an all-out ache.

Rosie. What the fuck did you do?

Chapter Eighteen

Let's Hurt Tonight by One Republic

Rosie

I'm a terrible person.

I've been avoiding Cillian like the plague since they released him because I have no idea how to let him go.

How do you break the heart of the person who's holding yours?

I know this is something I need to do in order for him to have his freedom, but the selfish part of me can't comprehend a life without him. Then, I remember, music is Cillian's lifeline. Without it, he wouldn't survive. But, me, he can lose. It will hurt at first, but, in time, he'll be okay. Knowing that doesn't make this any easier though. I never thought I'd have to give him up, and if I'm honest with myself, I don't know if I can.

My phone beeps for the millionth time this evening. Cillian has sent text after text, begging me to answer his calls, but this one is different.

Charming: Please, Snow. Give me ten minutes. Meet me here. Please. *google/maps/meetmehere*

Staring at the message for longer than I should, I decide he needs an explanation. I can't let him think I don't care.

Me: Okay.

Once I'm in my car, I plug my phone in and connect it to the built-in GPS. Clicking on the link Cillian sent me, I head his way.

Fifteen minutes pass before I come to a halt outside a large set of electronic gates. The long driveway behind them is sheltered by an archway of trees, but in the distance, I can just about make out a gorgeous house. *It's beautiful, but who lives here?*

The gates open automatically, allowing me to follow up the gravel laneway. Then, there he is. My broken boy. He's sitting on the front step with his head hung low. His eyes trained on whatever he holds in his hands, but when I get out of my car, he quickly shoves it into the pocket of his black jeans. Out of my sight.

"Hey." For such a small word it carries so much pain. Cillian's not an idiot, he knows something is wrong.

"Thanks for coming."

I want to tell him, for him, I'd run to hell and back, but I can't, not anymore. Probably because when I went to hell for him, the devil held me captive.

Taking small careful steps towards him, my heart beats double time in my chest.

"Hi."

Cillian lifts his hands towards my face, then carefully brushes my hair behind my ear. "You look beautiful."

My lips curl with a small sad smile. His fingers trace along my jawline until finally, they stop beneath my chin. He tilts my head up, locking his tired eyes onto mine. It's too much when he looks at me like this and I can't escape the turmoil brewing beneath my skin. A lone tear falls free, sliding down my cheek without warning. Cillian leans forward, kissing the tear from my face before pulling me tightly to his chest. His arms cover me like a protective shield, and I break, sobbing uncontrollably against his chest.

I can't do this. This is too hard.

"Rosie, darling." His voice breaks with the weight of his emotion. "Can you please look at me?"

Lifting my chin, I step from his arms, but he places his hands on my shoulders keeping me from pulling away further.

"Snow, whatever it is you came here to say... please don't. At least not until I show you why I asked you to come here."

Unable to form words, I nod my head in agreement. It's the least I can do. Using the hand he has placed on my shoulder, he turns me to face the house. I thought it was beautiful when I was driving in, but I was wrong… this place is breath taking. It's a two-story, sandstone, modern farmhouse—just like the one in my sketchpad.

Cillian pulls me back against his chest so my back rests against his front. His strong arms circle my waist, and he interlocks his fingers with mine—leaving them to rest on my stomach. His warm breath lingers against the exposed skin of my neck, sending the best kind of shivers down my spine. When he brushes his soft lips over the sensitive spot behind my ear, that all too familiar ache of need erupts in my stomach. Next, he nibbles on my earlobe and the sacred place between my thighs tightens.

Stop, Cillian. Please. You're making this so much harder.

Finally, he whispers, "Welcome home, Snow."

Wait, what did he just say?

Cillian

Rosie stills in my arms and I know bringing her here was a bad-fucking-idea. Whatever Rosie came here to tell me, this… this house is not going to fix it.

I don't know what I was thinking. I can't cover an internal bleed with a plaster. Nothing can fix this, not even the eighteen-carat, diamond engagement ring I shoved in my pocket when she arrived.

We're broken, and we both know it. It's practically radiating from her pores. Every time I touch her, she flinches, I'm losing her, she's slipping from my grasp and there is nothing, not one-fucking-thing, I can do to stop it. But that won't stop me from fighting with everything I've got. I promised her forever and always and I'm not ready for that to end. Not yet.

Slowly, she turns in my arms, blinking back her unshed tears. "Did... did you buy this house?"

Her nostrils flare, but not with anger. No, her heavy breaths are holding back the dam of emotion behind those sad blue-eyes. My mouth dries as I swallow back my own impending heartbreak.

"No. I didn't buy it. I... uhh, I had it built." Taking her face in my palms, I kiss the tip of her nose. "I found the plans in your sketchpad. I tried to keep it as close to your drawing as possible, but the architect said we had to change a few minor things for it to be structurally sound. The interior layout is the same though."

I'm rambling, but I can't help it. Deep down, I know I'm trying to make her stay. I built this house for her. "This is your forever home."

Like glass, she breaks, collapsing in my arms before lashing out and slapping her palms against my chest.

"Why Cillian," she sobs. "Why now? Why today?"

"Rosie. Rosie, stop."

Grabbing hold of her wrist, I still her flailing arms. She sinks to her knees against the gravel and raises her hands to shield her eyes. Falling down beside her, I wrap her in my arms as she rocks back and forth. She heaves for air in between sobs and there is nothing I can do or say to make her calm down.

"Look at me, Snow. Please, baby, please."

Her eyes finally lock on mine and my heart shatters just like she did, because right there, in her blue irises, is nothing but goodbye.

"No. No, Rosie. Don't. Please, don't do this."

"We can't, Cillian. It's... it's too late. I'm so, so sorry. I had to... I had to do something. He, we... I'm sorry. It's over."

She pushes herself up onto her feet and I follow. She can't do this. She can't walk away. Clutching at straws, I throw out the last thing I can think of to make her stay. I capture her face in my palms and her hands immediately cover mine. Together, we hold on for dear life.

"You promised me. Forever and always."

Her eyes close, holding back the inevitable tsunami. "Listen to me, Cillian. I will always, always love you. That will never change. What this means is, I love you so much, I'm willing to walk away so you can be free. Eventually, you can learn to be happy again, maybe even fall in love. All I ever want is for you to have the life you deserve; and deep down, we both know, we will never have that together. They will never allow us to be happy, Charming."

"I love you, Rosie. Nothing they can do or say could ever change that."

"But, that's where you're wrong. Everything you did, changes things. You gave me no choice when you lost control. I get that you had to face your demons, I do. I've spent my whole life trying to save you, pulling you out of the dark so you can be free of your chains. But, us, staying together is only making it worse. I know you love me, but, sometimes, love isn't enough."

"Yes, it is. It's more than enough. We can get through this. Please, don't do this, don't let them decide our fate. I promise you; I don't need anything in this world. Only you."

Wiping her wet eyes in her jumper, she tries to gain composure. "That's just it, Cillian, I did this for you. What kind of life did you expect us to have when you're behind bars? Did you even think for a second what your actions would do to us? This is not my fault. I had two options, lose you to prison, or set you free. I choose the latter because I love you enough to walk away. The damage was already done. You set the wheels in motion, I just picked which road they'd take. It's over, Cillian. They won. They were always going to win."

She kisses my closed eyelids. "I'll always love you, don't ever forget that." She frees herself from my hold. "Goodbye, Charming."

She heads for her car, and I stand there, hopelessly watching the love of my life walk away. It can't end like this. We can't end like this.

"Rosie, wait!"

I grab her by her elbow, spinning her into my arms. My lips crash against hers. I pour my heart, my soul, and all my love into this kiss. Because if this is the last chance my lips get to touch hers, I need to make sure she never forgets what forever tastes like.

Pulling back, I push the hair from her eyes. "Never goodbye, Snow. Only for now."

Chapter Nineteen

Lost on You by Lewis Capaldi

Rosie

*E*veryone always tries to explain what heartbreak feels like, but for me, it isn't an emotion; it is a sound. A sound so silent, it doesn't reach my ears. Instead, it grabs a hold of my being, penetrating the depths of my soul. A devastating echo that cuts so deep, it paralyzes me. A gut-wrenching scream suppressed in my lungs, leaving me gasping for my next breath. Nothing I do can make me escape it, it plays on repeat, constantly reminding me my heart is in a thousand irreparable pieces.

Last night was the worst night of my life. I barely slept a wink, because every time I closed my eyes, Cillian's face haunted my dreams. I'll never forget the way he looked as I walked away — so broken and defeated. For years, we fought so hard to stay together, and naively, I thought we'd beaten all the odds. I shouldn't blame Cillian, but a small part of me does. He struck out without thinking about the consequences. Not once did he stop and think about how his actions could affect everyone around him. Then there's the other part of me; the one that thinks he was right last night. Could our love be enough? In my attempt at saving him, I forgot how hard it would be to live without him.

There must be another way we can wade through this messy situation, and come out on top?

Why should I give it all up? Him, us, and the life we planned together? Honestly, I don't know if I can. Am I willing to put everything on the line so we can be together?

I need to talk to him, tell him everything. Maybe then, we could come up with a better solution. There needs to be a way we can be together.

I refuse to believe otherwise.

Pushing back the soft lavender duvet, I drag my lifeless body from my bed. Lifting my hand, I pinch the top of my nose—right between my brows—and blink back the aftereffects of last night's emotional migraine.

My haggard reflection in the floor-length mirror catches my attention. My eyes, swollen red from all the tears I shed and yesterday's mascara stain's my face, leaving thin black lines along my puffy cheeks. I feel worse than I look, which is like shit. Cillian's t-shirt covers my aching body. Last night, I needed to wrap myself in his scent. Eventually, after my tear ducts dried up, I fell asleep with my nose nestled against the cotton material. His woodsy aftershave bringing me both heartache and comfort.

I head for the dresser on the opposite side of the room, where I purposely left my phone last night — all so I wouldn't call him. Picking it up, I unlock it and stare at his goofy face staring back at me from my home screen. I love this photo; It is all the gang. Cillian and me in the centre, surrounded by Bronagh, Conor, Cian, Ciaran, and Lily. We took it in Las Vegas, back when we were still young and carefree. Lily, Bronagh, and I flew out to meet them on tour, so we could celebrate the twin's twenty-first birthday. That was the last time we all were together, happy in one place. Everything with Bronagh happened shortly after that trip and Conor was never the same.

Pushing the memories back, I pull up Cillian's number and my finger hovers over his name. *Call him.* Pressing call, I wait for him to pick up. It rings and rings going straight to voicemail. I hang up without leaving a message and try again. *Pick up. Pick up.*

After the fourth attempt, I decided to call Lily. Maybe she knows where he is.

"Speak to me," she greets after the first ring.

"Hey, are you still at home? I'm looking for Cillian." My voice breaks when I say his name. "He's... he's not answering his phone."

"Eh, no. I'm on my way to work, but he wasn't home when I left. I thought he spent the night with you?" She questions.

Shit! When I don't reply right away, Lily's Spidey senses kick in. "Did something happen? Last I heard from him was yesterday, he was heading over to the house to meet you."

The house. Our house. Fighting back the urge to break down, I hold the phone from my ear and slow my breathing with a few deep breaths.

"Rosie. Are you still there?"

"Yeah, sorry." It takes everything in me to push the next words out, but with a bit of force, I manage. "We broke up."

"Motherfuck...!" Her scream pierces my eardrum. "Sorry! Sorry, I spilt my coffee all over my lap. Did you say you broke up with my brother? Because I know for a fact, that was not his intention when he left the house yesterday."

"Things here, they kind of went to shit. Da forced my hand. I need to find Cillian and apologize. It's a long story, but I promise, I'll explain later."

"I'll hold you to that. Now, go find my brother. Check the house, he's more than likely still there. Call me later and tell me how it went."

"Will do. Thanks, Lil."

"Anytime, Ro. Love you."

Concern lines her voice. As tough as she is, Lily loves as fiercely. If you are in her bubble, she will do everything in her power to protect you.

"Love you, too."

Grabbing my makeup wipes from my dresser, I clean my face as best I can. I throw my long black hair into a messy bun, then pull a pair of leggings and one of the many hoodies I stole from Cillian from the wardrobe.

Time to save my relationship.

Cillian

Slowly, I peel my heavy eyes open. The room is dimly lit, which does fuck-all to help my blurred vision. Rubbing my eyes, I blink away the sandpaper scratching against my eyelids. *Fuck me, my head is splitting.* The potent smell of whiskey assaults my senses, making my delicate stomach churn like a carton of gone off milk. I run my tongue over my teeth, cringing at the sediment stuck to them. Gathering some moisture in my drier-than-the-Sahara mouth, I swallow back the bitter aftertaste of last night.

I lay still for a moment, trying to clear my foggy head. Using my fingers, I rub them in a circular motion over my throbbing temples while also begging the room to stop spinning. I need to stop drinking. This wouldn't be the first—or even the second time, I have woken up with no recollection of the night before. There's a giant black hole where my memories should be. *Fuck, I drank way more than I intended to.*

In the distance, the faint sound of Rosie's personal ringtone echoes through the near-empty hall of our house. Or should I say, my house?

I try to drag my less than responsive body out of bed. But with limbs like spaghetti, it takes far longer than it should. Swinging my dehydrated ass over the edge, I rest my feet against the cold floorboards. Leaning forward, I cradle my forehead in my hands, rubbing my tired eyes with the heel of my palms.

Everything that went down with Rosie yesterday, knocked me severely off kilter. After she left, I dragged my pathetic self to The Golden Barrel. I needed to rid myself of her and the devastation ingrained into her heartbroken face.

Blowing out an exaggerated breath, I place my hands on my thighs and push myself up from the mattress. But an unfamiliar high pitch voice coming from the open doorway, causes me to freeze in place.

"Oh, hey! You're finally awake. I made myself some coffee. I hope that's okay?"

Who? The. Fuck. Is. She?

My head turns so fast, it almost disconnects from my shoulders. One look at the less-than-half dressed bleach blonde and regret wraps around my throat, squeezing off my air supply. *What the fuck did I do?*

Leaning against the doorway with two cups of coffee in her hand, is a chick I have never met before — well, at least not before last night. Searching my mind, I try to recall every detail of last night, but come up empty. Rosie's face floods my mind. *Whatever chance you had at winning her back, is gone now. How could I be such an eejit?*

"Are you okay? You're a little green." *Thanks, Captain Obvious, and no I'm not okay. I'm the furthest thing from o-fucking-kay.*

I glance back at blondie; her hair is piled on the top of her head in one of those knot things and she's wearing nothing but the t-shirt I had on yesterday. She looks nothing like the girl I love. Bile rises, burning whatever lining is left in my stomach. The excessively fake-tanned Oompa Loompa steps towards me, last night's make-up still baked on her face. *She'll need a chisel to take it off.*

This girl is the definition of a band bunny, and I'm the world's biggest fucking asshole for bringing her here. To Rosie's dream house. *What the fuck was I thinking?*

Drinking got me into many sticky situations throughout the years, but this... this takes the whole tin of biscuits.

Holding up my hand, I stop her in her pursuit. "You..." my breath hitches as panic floods my veins. "You need to leave. Now!"

Rushing around the bedroom, I pick up her discarded clothes and hold them out to her at arm's length. Logically, I know this is not her fault, but I don't care. She needs to leave. I just made the biggest mistake of my life and her standing here is a reminder of how much Rosie is better off without me and my alcoholic ways. There is no way I can win her back, not after this. The nameless girl places the coffee on the locker beside the bed and I fling the clothes into her open arms. Thankfully, she takes them without arguing.

When she doesn't make an effort to get dressed, I lose it. "Leave, now. This is her house. You shouldn't be here. I shouldn't have brought you here. You need to go."

She holds up her hand. "Fine, I'm going. Let me get dressed first."

I should apologize for shouting at her, but she's not my concern. Rosie, how am I going to explain this to her? I know she broke it off yesterday, but she still deserves better than me sticking my dick in the nearest bimbo. *Fucked, I'm so fucked.*

"Yeah, okay. I'll call you a cab."

Five minutes later, wannabe barbie appears, looking at least somewhat more covered than she did this morning. Silently, I lead her down the spiral staircase, and towards the front door. I open the front door motioning for her to get the fuck out.

"Last night was fun, you should call me if you want a repeat. I left my number on the dresser."

I open my mouth to reply but the words lodge in my throat because standing in the now open doorway with her hand raised, ready to knock is the girl who broke my heart. *Rosie.*

Nothing could ever have prepared me for the horror on her face. Her bloodshot eyes are wide with shock and her open mouth is almost hitting the ground. She blinks, once, twice then closes her mouth and shakes her head.

"I'm sorry... I, eh... I didn't mean to," she motions between me and the blonde, whose name I still can't remember. The next word to leave her mouth is laced in venom. "Interrupt." Turning on her heel, she hurries towards her car.

Taking off after her, I grip her elbow. "Rosie. Wait, please."

She spins in place, tears freely escaping her ocean eyes. She stabs my chest with her finger. "Don't. Do not try to explain away what I just saw. Hours, Cillian. We broke up only hours ago, and already you're sticking your cock in an overly plucked chicken."

"I'm sorry, Snow. I was drunk and upset and I..."

"Really? You're going to stand there and blame alcohol. Fuck you, Cillian. I've been by your side through everything. Every-single-thing. Do not disrespect me further by placing blame on what got us into this situation in the first place."

Beating me away, she slams her palms into my chest.

"Stop, Rosie. I'm sorry. Please, hear me out."

Her body stills in my arms, but when she looks at me with eyes full of hate, I almost collapse. This is it, her last straw. I fucked it up, just like I always do. The realisation hits me harder than a left hook from Rocky Balboa.

Grasping at straws, I capture her face in my palms. "I love you, Rosie."

"There is a fine line between love and hate, Cillian. And you just crossed it."

She pulls away, and the knife of regret digs deeper as I watch the best thing that has ever happened to me get into her car and drive away.

Chapter Twenty

Joke's on You by Charlotte Lawrence

Rosie

Running from the house that was meant to be our home, the tears stream from my eyes. How could he? How could someone who mere hours ago, whispered promises of forever, have someone else warming his bed?

The anguish bubbling in my stomach is seconds away from boiling over. The minute he opened that door, every dream, every promise, every I love you, burst into flames.

I grip my shirt trying to dull the excruciating ache in my chest. The pain resembling ten thousand knives piercing my damaged heart. Tears blur my vision, as I lock myself in the confines of my car and take off before Cillian can stop me. Pulling out of the driveway, I head to the one place where I can let go — my studio.

After I graduated from NCAD last year, Cillian co-signed with me on a business loan so I could purchase a space for my interior design business. Enchanted Forest Design is my safe place, I worked my ass off for my design degree and thankfully business is booming.

I keep the front space free for clients and meetings, but I also have a backroom where all the magic happens. It's my own personal art studio, where I make custom pieces for my high paying clientele. It's the perfect place for me to lose myself for a few hours. I need to clear my head and erase the images of him with her from the forefront of my mind.

On the drive, I replay the scene I just witnessed over and over. The look on her smug face. The guilt reflecting in his eyes. The shock I felt at the sight of him with another woman. Hurt crawls under my skin. Do I even have the right to act like this? I broke up with him. We weren't together anymore, but still, I feel betrayed. It's only been hours. How could he move on so quickly? And as for her, she must have known he was attached, everyone knew. We've been the topic of every magazine since he publicly announced our relationship on my twentieth birthday — two years ago.

The headlines were endless. *Cillian's Childhood Sweetheart, The Girl Behind the Guitarist, The Queen of 4Clover.*

She saw her opportunity, and she took it, not caring who she would hurt in the process. Between the events from yesterday with my Da, and what just transpired, I'm done. I am past hurt and beyond broken, something in my chest snapped when that door opened. Hurt, anger and resentment took over my every thought. I never thought Cillian could hurt me, but then again, I didn't think I would ever hurt him either.

I'm aware Cillian isn't one hundred per cent to blame for my heartbreak, I played a massive part in the lead up to our downfall but tell that to my shattered heart. Yes, it was my gun that held us hostage, but Cillian was the one to pull the trigger. If I thought I was heartbroken this morning, I was sorely mistaken. There are no words to describe the utter devastation I'm feeling right now.

Paint splatters across my cheek as I take out my anguish on the cotton hemp. A whirlwind of thoughts thunder through my mind.

Music blasts through the speakers, as I attack the canvas with my paintbrush, releasing the onslaught of emotions residing under my crawling skin. A scream bursts from my core, travelling up my chest and filling my lungs before escaping into the room.

Picking up the half-finished painting, I fling it across the room, hitting the shelf full of art supplies. Paint tins fall to the ground, bursting open and ruining the natural oak flooring. But I don't care. I'm done fucking caring.

Strong, unfamiliar arms wrap around me, covering me like a blanket. It isn't until his Hugo Boss aftershave hits my nostrils; I recognize who it is. I struggle against his tight grip.

"Sean, let me go."

His arms loosen but he doesn't release me. "It's okay," he whispers. "I've got you."

Defeated, my body breaks in his arms, and I collapse against his chest. Turning to face him, I look into his aquamarine eyes.

"What... What are you doing here?"

"I was across the street locking up the office when I heard you scream. I wanted to make sure you were okay."

"Well, you've checked. And I'm fine. You can leave now."

I wiggle from his arms, stepping out from his personal space. Sean closes the gap as quickly as I made it, he lifts my chin with his fingertips and narrows his eyes on mine.

"Forgive me for intruding, but you don't look fine to me. What did he do this time?"

I hate that he immediately thought of Cillian, and what's worse is, he's right.

"It doesn't matter, Sean. Nothing fucking matters."

His fingers trace my jawline, then he cradles my cheek in his palm. "That's where you're wrong, Rosalie. You matter."

The intensity in his eyes unlocks something inside me. And for a split second, I wonder what it would be like if I had never fallen in love with the broken boy who's hell-bent on destroying everything around him.

The events of this morning tear through my mind; that girl leaving what was meant to be our forever home scorches my lungs, pulling me under and leaving me to drown in a sea of self-destruction. Before I can think about the consequences, my lips crash against Sean's with rapid fury. I need to forget. I need an escape.

"Rosalie." My name falls from Sean's lips as he grips my hips drawing me in closer.

The little voice in the back of my mind screams this is a bad idea. But I can't find the strength to pull away. Cillian's actions made me feel worthless and replaceable. I'm done with being the nice girl, the one who would give it all up to save someone who never really wanted to be saved. I'm so tired of getting my heart trampled on by someone who doesn't appreciate me. Sean's hands travel under my shirt, lifting it higher until finally, he pulls it over my head and discards it on the floor.

I don't stop him. I don't tell him no. Instead, I lose himself in his touch. He lifts me off the ground and I wrap my legs around his waist.

Walking across the room, he deposits me on the workbench while peppering my neck with kisses. I can't help but compare his every caress to Cillian.

His hands are smooth as they run along my rib cage, not calloused from years of playing the guitar.

His face is clean shaved as his kisses down my chest, not rough like Cillian's three-day-old stubble.

Sean pulls at the waistband of my leggings, dipping his fingers under the thin black material as I close my eyes and allow the nothingness I'm feeling to drag me under. And then, the realisation hits me, nobody will ever compare to the hazel-eyed man who owns me, heart and soul.

Sean dips his hand below the seam of my underwear, tracing small teasing circles along my clit.

"Fuck, Rosalie. You have no idea how long I've wanted to do this."

His voice, nothing like the melodic rasp I've spent many nights listening to, as Cillian lulled me to sleep. I can't do this. This is not who I am; I'm not a revengeful person. And, as much as I am furious with Cillian right now, I can't erase him with someone else. I can't let my heartbreak drive me into the arms of someone I don't belong to.

"Stop. Stop. I can't,"

I push against Sean's chest. "We can't do this."

"Jesus, Rosie. Are you serious?"

"As serious as a heart attack. I can't do this, Sean."

He looks furious but I couldn't care less. This is my body and if I don't want to share it with him, I won't.

Picking my discarded t-shirt off the floor, I put it back on.

"You know what? You're pathetic. When are you going to realize this is happening? Or did you forget that you signed your life away to keep your Prince Charming from a life behind bars?"

He steps forward, his face inches away from mine. "You're mine now, Rosalie. If, and when I want to touch you… I will. Sooner or later, you are going to be my wife. So, you better get used to my hands on your skin."

I swallow but keep my eyes locked on him. I will not be intimidated.

"You came in here and used my vulnerability against me. This never should've happened. It was a mistake."

"Keep telling yourself that. You want me. Admit it."

"Fuck you, Sean."

His hand grips my elbow, applying just enough pressure to leave a bruise.

"Oh, you will be doing just that. And when I finally have you beneath me, I guarantee you, Cillian O'Shea will be the furthest thing from your mind."

Tearing my arm from his grasp, I rise to my tippy toes. "I will never want you, and this arrangement," I motion between us, "is just that… an arrangement. So, carry on living your life, Sean because I will never truly belong to you. Did you honestly think, you could ride in here on your Shetland pony and convince me you were my knight in aluminium foil? I'm being forced into marrying you, but you can bet all your daddy's money, I will never, ever be yours. You weren't, nor will ever be, my choice. You might hold my future in the palm of your dirty, seedy hands but you will never hold the one thing Cillian does… my heart."

Walking towards the door, I stop and pull it open. "Now, get the fuck out of my shop."

Shoving his hands into his suit trouser pockets, he stomps towards the door. He stops inches from my face, glaring at me, warning me this isn't over.

"See you real soon, Rosalie."

Chapter Twenty-One

Back to You by Selena Gomez

Rosie

The Present

So, there you have it. Those final nails that closed the casket on mine and Cillian's relationship.

I always thought it was crazy how one simple decision could change the direction of someone's life—or in this case, two lives. In the span of two days, Cillian and I tore down everything we spent years building. There was no going back. Choices were made and the consequences cost us a once-in-a-lifetime love.

It may not seem like a huge deal now, but to my twenty-two-year-old self, it was soul-crushing. For weeks on end, I cried myself to sleep, until my exhausted eyes leaked out every tear. Inside, I was a wreck, fundamentally depriving my body of basic human needs. I couldn't eat or sleep... I was barely functioning.

Our last conversation haunted me for weeks, taunting my every thought. If it wasn't for Lily dragging me from my bed on more than one occasion — unwilling to allow me to wallow in self-pity — I would have lost my business too. I had clients to meet, and houses to remodel. Enchanted Forest Design was all I had left, and after everything, I wasn't willing to let that go too.

Cillian tried for months to mend what we'd broken, he showed up night after night, begging me to forgive him, but it was no use.

Even if I could get over the betrayal, there was still my impending marriage to Sean. I tried everything I could think of to get out of that arrangement, but each time I was shot down with threats towards Cillian, and the future he was building. Even after everything, I still loved him and now, I know I will never experience that same kind of soul-claiming love again.

Cillian is my soulmate, my twin flame, and no matter how hard I try to convince myself; I'll never be able to let him go, not fully. He resides in the deepest crevices of my heart, in a special place created just for him.

Our break-up affected everyone, Cian and Cillian's bromance suffered the most. Cian refused to speak to Cillian for weeks until finally, I had enough of his constant bickering; so, I sat him down and explained, it was my fault. I was the one who ended things. It took them some time to get back to a good place but, thankfully they're working on it.

As time passed, I was expected to accompany Sean to business events. We had to make our relationship believable, even if the last place I wanted to be was by his side. We became the IT couple of every gala, ball, and business function, but behind closed doors, we barely spoke.

I moved in with Lily and avoided him as best I could. It didn't upset me to find out he was sowing his seed in half of Dublin, because I honestly didn't care what he did. Sean never meant anything to me, he was a means to an end. Cillian's ticket to freedom.

Without Cillian, my life became colourless and the only thing keeping me going was watching him strive.

In the last few years, 4Clover has taken the world by storm. Cillian wrote some of the best material of his career in the months after our demise. You could feel his pain behind every lyric, and each song, more gut-wrenching than the former. They all held raw, real untouchable emotion, only reachable by those who live with demons.

4Clover were at a peak in their career — taking home not one, but two Grammys last year. They are still not showing signs of slowing down, and daddy dearest took every opportunity to remind me just how easily he could take it all away. With one click of his fingers, he could ruin everything Cillian had spent his life working towards. So, I abided by his rules, keeping my mouth shut and my distance from the only man I've ever loved.

Don't get me wrong, there were plenty of times, where we tip-toed around each other, and our feelings. Sharing stolen glances across crowded rooms but I was always careful not to be alone with him for any length of time. In my weakest moments, I avoided him at all costs, because I knew, one look and my resolve would shatter. Plenty of words were left unspoken between us, but I convinced myself it was for the best.

Things got better when 4Clover left for their second tour, six months without having to bottle up all of my emotions. It also made fake-dating Sean ten times easier, Cillian couldn't question our strange non-relationship, but when he did see us together, the look on his face broke my heart.

Eventually, things became somewhat more bearable, Cillian finally began to date again, and as much as it killed me to watch from the side-lines, I was happy that he was happy.

I watched from a distance as models and actresses, paraded through his life — each one prettier than the last, but never lasting more than a few weeks. And, even though there were days, I wanted to scream from the rooftops, that it was all a lie, a ploy to keep him safe… I never did, because, to love someone the way I love Cillian O'Shea, you must love them unconditionally. And if that meant giving up my happiness in exchange for his freedom, so be it.

So, I grieved for him at a distance, and that grief never went away. Some say the price of love is loss, and losing Cillian was a price I had to pay.

I spent years looking for a way out, but every time I got close to freedom, my so-called father would shoot me down. Then, on my twenty-fifth birthday, Sean sent me a parcel with an ostentatious engagement ring and a congratulations card. Before I knew it, my wedding was set for the following October. The engagement party was planned, invites were sent, and there was nothing I could do to stop it.

Chapter Twenty-Two

Power Over Me by Dermot Kennedy

Cillian

August 2019

*L*oosening the black-tie that's wrapped around my neck like a noose, I unbutton the top button of my white dress shirt and ease the suffocating feeling this penguin suit brings.

What the fuck was I thinking? This is her engagement party. I shouldn't be here.

I clutch the near-empty tumbler between my palms, rolling it back and forth, watching closely as the ice cubes clink against the Waterford crystal. Time for a top-up. Lifting the glass to my lips, I drain the last drop of top-shelf whiskey then hold it out to the barman, signalling for another.

It's been three years since Rosie left me, but my feelings for her never changed. They're still very present. If anything, they grew stronger with time and distance.

Rosie Mulligan will always be the greatest love of my life. Nothing, nor no one, will ever fill the giant hole in my heart that is shaped like her. Deep down, I know if I can't have her in this lifetime, I will wait for her in the next. My forever and always girl.

While I sit, awaiting my next fix, I spin on the barstool and look out across the crowded ballroom. I can't help but wonder: what the hell happened to the Rosie I knew? She would never want something as extravagant as this pretentious party.

Yes, she always loved details, but not this over the top, rich bitch shit. She's more delicate, she loves lace and wildflowers, not chandeliers and ice sculptors. She prefers flawed beauty not perfection at first glance. *Maybe she has changed?*

Out of the corner of my eye, a flash of silver grabs my attention. Turning on the stool, I scan the growing crowd until my eyes lock on her. The bride to be. Her onyx black hair is pinned delicately at the nape of her neck in some kind of purposely messy bun. Small loose tresses linger around her face, gently kissing her cheeks. She's wearing more makeup than I am used to seeing on her porcelain face — her ever-shining blue eyes are framed with heavy black lashes and her lips are painted a kissable shade of ruby red. She is a picture of beauty.

There is nothing I wouldn't give, to have the chance to hold her in my arms again, but I can't. She's not mine, not anymore.

Taking several laboured breaths, I desperately try to calm my beating heart. I don't just see her, I feel her, in the very depths of my being. The need to kiss her burns under my skin with the heat of a thousand suns. I would give anything, everything I've got, to taste her lips. Just once more.

Tracing her every curve with my eyes, I devour her from a distance. The silk material of her dress moulds her body to perfection. The deep V in the front exposing her collarbone, and barely covering her breasts. Jesus Christ, I wish I could run my tongue over that patch of exposed skin. As if she can feel my gaze on her skin, she looks up. Her eyes latch on mine, and the hundreds of people around us, fade.

Stop pretending, Snow. We both know your fairy tale ends with me.

Sean slides in beside her, wrapping his arm possessively around her waist. She stills, almost weary of his touch. I watch closely as she plasters on a fake smile and turns to face him. *What are you hiding?* Sean's hand tightens around her waist as he bends to whisper in her ear. To anyone passing, it would look like a happy couple having a loving moment, but if they knew Rosie the way I do, they'd see she is uncomfortable. Her lips are pierced together, and her eyes crinkled with disgust.

Something is not right with this whole set up, and I plan to find out what.

Don't get too comfortable, Snow. I'm coming for you.

Ciaran drops onto the stool beside me and orders a drink from the free bar. "Hey man, how are you holding up?"

"Honestly... not great. I don't know what possessed me to come here tonight. I should have never accepted that invitation."

Raising my glass, I knock back the amber liquid, letting it work its magic. His eyes follow my line of sight until they land on Rosie and Lily.

"If I were in your shoes, I'd have done the same."

He nods his head towards the dancefloor, where the girls have been dancing most of the evening. "Have you spoken to her?"

Running my finger along the rim of my glass, I shake my head. "No."

"Are you going to talk to her?" He questions with a raised brow.

The scene I witnessed earlier replays through my mind. She's not happy. Not like I thought she was. "Yeah. I've just been biding my time until I can get her alone. I don't think she would appreciate an audience when she hears what I have to say."

Ciaran releases an uncertain breath. "Are you sure that's a good idea, man? She's getting married. Isn't it time you start to let her go?"

I know he means well; he's seen me pine for Rosie from a distance for years, and if anyone understands how I feel, it's him.

"Let me ask you something? If roles were reversed and this was Lily's engagement party… would you just let her go."

His eyes flick toward my sister, then to his hand; he traces the small ladybug, tattooed on the underside of his ring finger. His eyes narrow, deep in thought. "Not a fucking chance."

"That's what I thought."

Rosie

Naked.

That's how I feel with the weight of Cillian's stare burning through my dress. All night long, his eyes follow my every move. Reminding me that in this game of love, we both lost.

His hazel eyes are dangerous, inflicting emotions inside me that I've kept buried for so long. Even in a room full of people, he's all I see. The invisible thread between us, is no longer avoidable, not when he's so close. Needing a reprieve from this fake party, and all the equally as fake people, I shout over the Ed Sheeran song that's blasting through the overhead speakers. "I'm going to the bathroom. I'll be right back; I just need a minute."

Lily searches my face. She's been my saving grace all evening, she knows this is the last place on earth I'd rather be, but being the best friend, she is, she does everything in her power to make it bearable. "Do you want me to come with you?"

"No, I'm fine. Go get us some drinks, I'll be right back."

Her lips lift in a sad smile. "Okay, call me if you need me."

"I'll be fine." *I'm fine... Always a lie.*

"You can do this. A few more hours and you can go home, put your feet up and devour a glass — okay bottle, or two — of wine." As far as self-pep-talks ago, this one has been pretty shit, but I just don't have the energy to care.

I've been hiding in the bathroom for way longer than I should. Tonight, has been exhausting. If one more person congratulates me on the engagement I never wanted, I think I might lose it.

After splashing some water on my face, I top up my lipstick and fix my fake smile into place. A few more hours. Just a few more hours.

Suddenly, the bathroom door flies open with a loud thud. Standing there, in all this six-foot-four glory is none other than, Cillian O'Shea. I drink him in like a dry martini; his slightly dishevelled, tailored suit hugs him in all the right places, igniting sinful thoughts I've spent years suppressing.

"What? Err... erm."

The words lodge in my throat. I need a drink. A tall glass of him. *Nope, we are not going there.*

Kicking the door closed behind him, he flicks the lock with one twist of his wrist. "We need to talk."

His eyes roam over my skin as need, want, and desire shines from their depths. It's been far too long since someone looked at me with such reckless abandonment. And fuck me, I missed it.

He closes the distance between us with two large strides, forcing me to step backwards and my ass to meet the edge of the bathroom counter. Placing his hands on either side of my body, he cages me in. *Is it just me, or is it hot in here?*

He's so close, his breath mingles with mine. "Tell me, Snow... How is it, every time I see you, you're even more beautiful than the last?"

I don't answer, I can't. Visions of the last time we were this close, erupt in my mind. The tension between us is palpable and building with every passing millisecond. An involuntary shiver courses through my body. How is it possible I'm craving his touch more than my next breath?

As if he read my thoughts, Cillian's fingers brush against my cheek. "I missed you, so fucking much."

Closing my eyes, I drag in a deep breath. Cillian's earthy cologne assaults my senses. *Hello, willpower? Now would be a perfect time for you to show up.*

"What... What do you want, Cillian?"

Like always, when I am around him, my resolve breaks, and, this... this facade I've been hiding behind seems pointless. Nobody else affects me the way he does. Just one touch and I'm ready to throw the last few years away. This, us... it can't happen. No matter how badly I want him, I can't. We can't.

"Seriously, Snow. You already know what I want. It's the same thing I've always wanted."

Tilting my chin, he captures every ounce of my attention. His intense hazel eyes are dangerous, resurrecting emotions I thought I had buried.

I'm torn between the urge to run or losing myself in his touch, I'm frozen in the palms of his hands. Cillian drags his tongue across his bottom lip, then pulls it between his teeth.

"You."

One word. One word that shook me to my core.

"Cillian…" His lips crash against mine, silencing my next thought. His hands roam my body like I'm his first meal after a hunger strike.

It's explosive and needy.

Demanding and aggressive.

The bristles of his unshaven stubble scratch against my face as I grip his hair and pull him closer. I need him closer. Together, our tongues dance to the beat of our untameable chemistry. This kiss says it all. Speaking every word, we had left unsaid.

I'll never have enough.
I'll never stop wanting you.
I will always need you.

Chapter Twenty-Three

Bitter Love by Pia Mia

Rosie

*T*his is wrong.

We need to stop.

This is my engagement party.

Does this still count as cheating?

I'm getting married to another man. No, no... you don't love Sean. It's not real, it has never been real. Its forever been, and always will be, Cillian.

I need this, his touch. I need it more than my next breath.

We're magnetic, the pull between us drawing our bodies closer with ferocious intensity. The force so strong it obliterates every drop of my self-control.

His tongue travels along the sensitive skin of my neck sparking a thousand fireworks, and when he drags my earlobe between his teeth, those fireworks erupt into an all-out explosion. His fingers trail up my arms as he licks, bites, and kisses my neck.

Every touch provides a glorious high, one that is unmatched by anything I've ever experienced before. It's purely Cillian and the effect he has on me.

I direly want this.

I desperately need him.

Fully and completely, in every possible way.

Cillian O'Shea is intoxicating, like my own personal morphine, and it's been far too long since I've had my fix. Too long since I've allowed myself to overdose on the undeniable sparks between us.

There's nobody in the world who can light my body on fire the way he does. Every single look, touch, and caress has my body bursting into flames.

"Rosie, baby, I need this dress off right now."

My thighs clench with the ever-growing need pooling between my legs. This is the side of Cillian I crave. The alpha male who knows exactly what he wants.

Freeing myself from the thin straps that hold my dress in place, the silk material falls to my waist. My nipples harden under his hungry gaze.

With a throaty groan, he buries his head in between my aching breast. "Fucking beautiful."

My head falls back as I cry out his name. "Cillian."

His unshaved stubble tortures every nerve ending, and I grip his hair, steadying myself for my inevitable fall.

"I missed you, Snow. So goddamn much."

He sucks my left nipple, lightly grazing it with his teeth.

"Oh. My. God." Pleasure courses through me, building to an explosive crescendo in my core.

"Did you," *kiss* "miss," *suck* "my mouth," *lick* "on you, baby?"

"Yes! Yes, so much."

He switches to the opposite bud, paying it the same amount of attention, and I almost spontaneously combust.

He leaves no inch of me untouched.

My body.

My mind.

My soul.

Finally, his mouth crashes against mine, hard and claiming. I drown in the dominance every swipe of his tongue demands. With his eyes, he speaks the words we left unsaid.

I am yours.

You are mine.

We are forever.

Pulling away, he spins me to face the mirror. Our reflections stare back at me through the aluminium glass. The top half of my body is entirely naked and flushed pink from Cillian's touch.

Desire burns in his hazel eyes, and when he chews on his bottom lip, wetness gathers between my thighs.

I follow his every move, his roaming hand caresses my skin while the other gently tugs my hair, forcing my neck to elongate.

His lips hover over my throbbing pulse, his whiskey-infused breath sending shivers down my spine. "Look at us, Snow. Look in this mirror, and tell me... who belongs by your side?"

"You. It's always been you."

"That's right, Rosie. Nobody else makes you feel like this. Reckless with lust. Fuelled by desire. Only me."

"Touch me."

His fingers pinch my nipples, and my body instantly responds. "I'm going to do more than touch you. I'm going to fuck you. I plan on burying myself between your silky thighs while you will watch your sweet delicious tits bounce with every thrust. Can you do that, Snow? Can you stare at our reflection while I make you come so hard; you'll never forget it's my name that should forever fall from your lips?"

I nod my head, far too turned on to form words.

"I need words, baby. Tell me... what do you want?"

"Fuck me, Charming. I want you to fuck me."

Cillian pushes my dress down until it lands around my feet. "Jesus, you've been naked under that dress all night?"

A devilish grin curls on my lips. "There's nothing sexy about a VPL, Cillian."

"Guess not. Spread those legs, baby."

I do as I'm told, enjoying every moment of his demanding side.

Cillian drops to his knees. "Put your hands on the mirror."

I lean forward and Cillian runs his tongue along the inside of my thigh until finally, he's exactly where I need him. Circling my clit, he moves in slow, torturous strokes. My walls clench with every sweep of his tongue.

"More."

He flattens his tongue, hitting all my sensitive spots simultaneously. The sensation builds like a song. Starting slowly, building, building, until finally, I reach my peak, exploding all over his tongue. He doesn't stop, lapping me up until I'm a wilted mess, clinging on to the edge of the counter to stay upright.

Standing, Cillian frees his length, pulls a condom from his wallet and quickly shields himself. There's something extremely sexy about this scene. Me completely naked, the afterglow of my orgasm flush on my skin, and him, still fully covered by his deliciously sinful suit.

His hands grip my hips, as he dots kisses along my spine. In one, swift motion, he seats himself in my centre. "God, I missed you, Rosie."

I fall forward, my back arching as he pumps in and out of me with reckless abandonment. My legs shake uncontrollably, begging for that explosive release. A sheen of sweat covers my burning-with-need skin. I'm a hot mess, one who has forgotten how to form a complete sentence. "There! Yes, right there. Oh, my God!"

Reaching back with my right arm, I hook it around his neck and flatten my back against his chest. In the mirror, I watch as our bodies move together in perfect sync.

"So beautiful." Cillian's hand slides down my stomach, dipping between my legs. He circles my clit, once, twice, three times and suddenly my inner walls tighten, gripping his hard length. It starts in my core, travelling down my legs and throughout every nerve ending. "That's it, Snow. Cum for me. Cum all over my dick."

"Fuck."

Cillian's eyes watch me intently and the pressure rises in my core, then, just like a volcano, we both erupt together, exploding like hot molten lava.

Cillian places a gentle, loving kiss between my shoulder blades. "I love you, I never stopped loving you."

Like a bucket of cold water over my head, I freeze. The reality of what we just did washes over me, leaving me drowning in regret. *What did we just do? How did I let this happen? We can't.*

As if he can sense my sudden shift in mood, Cillian steps from behind me and quickly disposes of the condom.

Picking my dress off the floor, I slip it back over my body, allowing the thin material to hide some of my vulnerability.

Cillian paces the bathroom, his hands buried in his messy brown hair. "Shit. You're still going to marry him, aren't you? Even after," he points to the sinks. "Fuck, Rosie."

He drags his hands down his face, rubbing his eyes with the heel of his palms, before finally, settling them in prayer position underneath his chin. Closing his eyes, he tilts his head towards the ceiling.

I hate this. I never wanted to make him feel this way. I wish he knew how much this hurts me, or how I would do whatever it takes to make him happy. Including, marrying someone else, all so I can keep him safe.

His prominent Adam's apple gulps back his emotion, then he takes four steps, closing the physical distance between us.

Gently, he cups my face between his palms, and I almost break when I see the tears sliding down his cheeks. "Don't! I'm begging you. I'll get down on my fucking knees if you want me to. Please, Snow. Please don't marry him."

Looking into the eyes of the only person I've ever loved — the only person I'll ever love — my heart cracks. I wish I could tell him the truth. I wish he knew that the only reason I'm doing this, is for him.

The sour taste — of the words I need to say — lingers on my tongue. He can never know the reasoning behind my fake marriage because if he did, he would try to stop me. No matter what he'd lose in the process. I need him to let me go, so I do the only thing I can think of... I lie.

"I'm sorry, Cillian. I'm marrying Sean because I love him. This," I gesture between us. "shouldn't have happened. I don't... I don't love," The words lodge in my throat. "I don't love you, not any... more."

He's too close.

Needing to create space between us before I break and do something irrational, I push his hand from my face and head for the door. He grips my elbow, spinning me back to face him, leaving his devastatingly handsome face, only inches from mine. The hurt swarms in the pools of his hazel eyes, and I hate myself for causing it.

"Don't bullshit me. You will always love me. Want to know how I know? Because somehow, we found each other in this crazy, beautiful, fucked up world and we just fit together; like two pieces of the same puzzle."

His fingers brush against my tear-stained cheek. "So, forgive me if I don't believe a word out of your pretty, little mouth. Your body just told me everything I need to know. If you want to continue lying to yourself, go right ahead. But, I'm done, Rosie. I can't keep doing this, it's killing me slowly."

He releases me from his hold and walks away. The bathroom door slams behind him, shattering the very last piece of my already broken heart.

Taking a moment to make myself somewhat presentable, I clip my messed hair back into place.

How did I get here? Most days I hardly recognise myself. When did I become this horrible person?

The answer smacks me in the face. The day I signed away my happy ever after, condemning myself to a lifetime of misery. I made my bed that day, now, I'm just lying in it.

Lifeless from defeat.

The bathroom door swings open and my bleak future fills the doorway. Sean strides towards me with angry footsteps, closing the distance between us in second. "What the fuck was O'Shea doing in here?" His hands grip my shoulders, and he glares at me with rage-filled eyes.

Shoving him off, I turn to face the mirror. "Oh, I see you've taken your dick out of the nearest bimbo long enough to care about what, or who I'm doing."

His face boils red as he bites down on his bottom lip. "Don't get started with me, Rosalie. This is our engagement party, and here you are... whoring yourself out in a public restroom. How the fuck, do you think that makes me look?"

Honestly, Sean, I don't care.

"You have zero right. Don't pretend like you weren't off getting your cock sucked by one of your side pieces only moments ago. Do you think I'm stupid? Talk about double standards."

I've enough of him and his crap for one evening. I push past him; but he grabs my arm with unbearable pressure, halting me in my tracks. Turning my head in his direction, I breathe slowly, fighting back the tears from the burning pain coursing up my arm.

"Let go of me."

A smug smirk curls on his face, he gets off on moments of power. "Remember, I have the power here, Rosalie. One phone call and your precious Rockstar will be escorted out of this party in cuffs. Did you know he's quite the hothead? I reckon I could easily provoke him in front of all our well-respected guests. What do you think, fiancée? Would you like me to add another assault to his list of charges?"

I keep quiet, there's no point poking the bear.

"That's what I thought. Now, keep those legs of yours closed and we won't have a problem. Understood."

I swallow down my anger, fearful of his threats. "Understood."

Sean drops my arm from his grip and heads for the door. "Good. Now go and get me a drink, I'm parched."

Plastering on my fakest smile, I do as I'm told. I can't continue like this.

I need to find a way out of this marriage... but how?

Chapter Twenty-Four

The Time I Met the Devil by Brave Giant

Cillian

*I*n the weeks after Rosie's engagement party, I spiralled even further into my ever-growing pity party. I slipped so far down the rabbit hole, nothing nor no one could drag me out. Submerging myself in whiskey and women, I became a hollow shell of the man I longed to be. Losing Rosie—a second time—stole my hope of us ever getting our happy ending. We were without a doubt, over.

Searching for some kind of proverbial band-aid, I tried everything to hold the broken pieces together, but nothing worked.

Night after night, I confided in my guitar, bleeding my emotions into every chord. Bottle after bottle, I attempted to drown her out, to no avail.

It was useless.

Rosie will forever be tattooed on my soul; her love left a mark that no amount of time can heal. And whether we are together or apart, we remain timeless because when you love someone soul-deep, it can never be erased.

When Ciaran suggested we take a few days away from Ireland, I jumped at the chance. I needed to get away, clear my head, and force myself to pack Rosie away in the back of my mind. But what the sly bastard forgot to mention was that Sean was coming with us.

He also forgot to inform me it was for Sean's bachelor party.

How Ciaran thought this was a good idea is beyond me? It took everything in me, not to turn around and walk away, but somehow here I am. On a private flight to L.A. with my three best friends and my worst nightmare.

Taking a seat beside my ex-best friend, I lower my voice, not wanting to give Sean the satisfaction of my discomfort.

"What the fuck, Ciaran? How did you ever think this would be a good idea? Have you lost your mind? I'll be lucky if I make it through these few days without committing murder."

"Relax," he whispers, "Daddy Mulligan wants us to schmooze this asshole and think about it this way: if he's here with us, he's not with Rosie."

Genuinely confused, my brow line creases. "What the fuck are you talking about? Why do we care what Michael wants?"

Leaning closer, he talks in hush tones. "It's not the time nor the place," his gaze flicks in Sean's direction, "to get into the details. Once we're back in Ireland, I will explain everything. Until then, control your temper and pretend you like the guy. Do you think you can handle that?"

I have no idea what the hell he's talking about. Since when is Michael Sean's bitch? Is there more to the story than I'm aware of?

"Do you trust me?" Ciaran questions.

"With my life."

"Then play nice. Hopefully, this will all be over in no time."

I still have no clue what the hell is going on, but for now, I'll do what I'm told.

Thankfully, we land in L.A. without a hitch, and all in one piece. After an eleven-hour flight, all I want to do was sleep, but Ciaran has a different plan.

Apparently, he's booked a VIP table along the strip, at one of the most prestigious gentlemen clubs Los Angeles has to offer, The Doll House. I'm in no mood to go out on a binge session. I'm already struggling to be cautious with my alcohol, but the more time I spend in Sean's company the more irritated I become and the desire I've got to reach for a bottle grows tenfold. I have a feeling tonight will be a long night, and I need to keep my wits about me.

I don't know what is going on between Rosie and Sean, but what I do know is I don't trust that gobshite as far as I could throw him.

Something about their relationship doesn't sit right with me, but Rosie has told me countless times that she loves Sean, maybe it's time I start believing her.

* * *

This cunt is getting on my last nerve. I swear to Christ, if he manhandles one more dancer, he'll be getting pushed down the aisle in a wheelchair.

Ever since Cian ran out after that dancer chick, Sean has been waving his asshole flag high, knowing full well if Cian seen him disrespecting his sister the way he has been, he'd be a dead man walking. It's taking every ounce of strength I have, not to knock him into next week. A growl escapes my mouth alerting Ciaran to my struggle.

Grabbing hold of my shoulder, he holds my seeding body onto the chair. "Easy, Tyson. Don't do anything you will regret."

Through gritted teeth, I spit out a reply. "That asshole is marrying the girl I love, and he's spent the entire night mauling every woman who walks past."

Doing nothing to hide the smug smirk playing on his lips, Sean pulls a passing dancer into his lap. "Do you have a problem, O'Shea?"

"You're my problem. What would your wife-to-be say if she could see you now, grinding your limp dick on every woman within reach?"

"Do you really think I care what my fiancée would say?" He taunts. "Maybe if she was better in bed, I wouldn't have to look somewhere else. You did a piss-poor job at teaching Rosalie how to suck a cock."

That's it. I've had enough of his shit. Nobody speaks about Rosie that way.

Leaping across the table, I knock down all the glasses and bottles in the process. The girl in his lap scurries off as I grab hold of Sean by the collar of his shirt, lifting him from the chair.

Shoving him against the nearby wall, my hand grips his neck, just enough to make him uncomfortable. "Do you want to repeat that?"

Conor stands, "Cillian." My name falls from his lips in warning, but right this second, zero fucks are given.

I'm not concerned about the consequences; I've had enough of this prick's antics. All night, I have held my tongue while he continuously disrespects Rosie, and now, I'm done playing the mute. Someone needs to take Sean down a peg or twenty.

Ciaran's hand lands on my shoulder. "This is a bad idea, man." He pulls, trying to get me to release my hold.

Rolling my shoulder, I brush him off, Sean has had this coming for years. He's been a constant thorn in my side since we were kids, always trying his darndest to sabotage our group — and all because he never fit into our dynamic. He's always been a jealous asshole.

Sean's hands tear at my wrists as he fights to fill his lungs with his next breath. "What's wrong, bigshot? Cat got your tongue?" Loosening my grip, I give him the opportunity to reply. "I'm waiting."

"Fuck you, O'Shea."

Cutting off his pointless words, I apply more pressure.

"When," he chokes out, "will you realize... I won."

I release the death grip around his neck, and he drags a much-needed breath into his lungs. "What the fuck are you talking about, Morgan?" Caging him in, I make it so he can't run. "I wasn't aware this was a competition."

Billy brave bollox steps forward so we're now, nose to nose. "All my life, I've stood on the outskirts while you four assholes became town royalty. Everybody fucking loves the good ole boys of 4Clover. Well, I'm sick and tired of being stuck in your shadow, while you take everything you want."

Is this guy for real?

"Newsflash, it's not my fault you haven't got a note in your egotistical head. We worked our asses off to get where we are today, talent doesn't grow on trees, Morgan. You have to work for it."

His nostrils flare as he squares his shoulders. "You still don't get it. You took her from me, the girl I was going to marry. You slept with her, then threw her away like a dirty dishcloth. And, do you know what? Your drunken ass probably doesn't even remember. You took my happiness, so I took yours."

"Who the fuck, are you talking about?"

"Roisin Daly. You slept with her the night of our debs, ruining our five-year relationship. You took the only person I ever loved. Karma is a bitch, O'Shea. How does it feel knowing that the girl you planned to spend your life with, will be on her knees sucking my cock?"

Swinging hard and fast, I launch my fist into his gut, and he slides down the wall, clutching his stomach. Rage floods my veins. How dare he use Rosie as a pawn in his personal vendetta.

"Get the fuck up."

Standing at full height, he spits in my face. "That all you got, Rockstar?"

A smug smile creeps across his face and I want nothing more than to knock it off him. I raise my left hand, hitting him with an uppercut to his chin causing his head to fling back. Before he can recover, I deliver a right hook to his nose and blood rushes from his nostrils.

Conor pulls me back. "Cillian, stop. This is what he wants."

The twins restrain my arms behind my back, stopping me from beating this gobshite to a pulp.

Ciaran grips my wrists. "He is provoking you. Calm the fuck down."

Staring down at Sean's body hunched on the floor, and I realize how badly I just fucked up. Even bloody and bruised, the prick is laughing his ass off. The twins are right. This was all part of his plan, and like a good little boy, I played right into his hands.

I don't know what he was trying to achieve by riling me up, but I can guarantee whatever it is, his little scuffle just made things worse. Once again. I've fucked everything up. He knew exactly how to push my buttons; he used my love for Rosie as a weapon. Deep down, I know Rosie has made her choice, I've tried everything to make her leave him.

I've begged, fucked and pleaded and still, she chooses him.

I'm tired of coming across like the pathetic, asshole ex. I need to let her go.

For good.

Chapter Twenty-Five
What If I Never Get Over You by Lady Antebellum

Cillian

*F*or days, I've been mulling over everything that transpired between Sean and I. Granted, punching him in his smug face was probably not the best move, but let's face it, he deserved it. The chap is a world class bellend.

After deciding not to fly back to Ireland with Conor, Ciaran and Sean, I stayed in Los Angeles for a few days, needing the time and space to clear my head. Not that it did me much good.

Rosie's wedding is fast approaching and I'm sinking deeper, becoming an even bigger miserable bastard than my usual broody self.

I'm not entirely convinced Sean and Rosie's relationship is legit, but there is sweet fuck all I can do about it. All I know is, if I were in Sean's shoes, there isn't a chance in hell I'd be behaving the way he did the other night—especially if I was about to marry the love of my life.

In the past few days, I've talked myself in and out of every possible scenario pertaining to Rosie and her so-called relationship with Morgan but I'm still no closer to figuring out what in God's name she sees in him.

I can't wrap my head around it. Why would she want to spend the rest of her life with someone who treats her like she's the dirt on the bottom of his stuffy Italian leather shoes?

It makes zero fucking sense.

Pulling my phone from my pocket, I scroll through my contacts until I find her number. My finger hovers over her name as I contemplate whether this is a good idea.

Fuck it, I'm calling her.

The foreign dial tone rings through the tiny speaker as I fight back the bundle of anxiety settling in my solar plexuses.

"Cillian? Is everything okay?" Rosie's sweet voice floods the line.

Closing my eyes, I savour it. Fuck, I miss her so much.

"Hey, Snow. How are you?"

An awkward silence lingers until finally, she replies. "Could you not call me that?"

A sharp pain pierces my heart. "That's what I've always called you."

"I know, it's just... Never mind. Is there something you need? I'm kind of in the middle of something."

"No, sorry. I'll let you..." I can't say it. Letting her go has been the hardest challenge of my life. I'm just about to hang up when she reaches out.

"Cillian, wait. I'm sorry, this is just hard. I never know what to say to you."

"I miss you," I say before I can stop myself.

"Don't... don't say things like that, Cillian. It's not fair."

"Why not? It's the truth, Snow."

"Because I'm getting married in a few weeks."

Pacing up and down the kitchen of Conor and Ciaran Los Angeles apartment with the phone pressed tightly to my ear, I feel it, the distance between us.

"Why?" I ask.

"Why, what?"

"Why are you marrying him?"

"Cillian! You need to stop, please. I can't keep doing this with you. Whatever issue you have with Sean, you need to let it go. Did you know you broke his nose?"

Good, the Muppet deserved it.

"Look, I know this is hard for you, but it's past time for you to let me go. Goodbye, Cillian."

Firing my phone across the kitchen, it smashes into several pieces. I slump into one of the breakfast bar stools and rest my head against the counter.

I'm due to fly back home today but honestly, I have no more interest than the man on the moon.

***

"What time are you flying out at? Cian asks between spoonsful of his cereal.

Barely lifting my head from the counter, I let him know my plans. "I'm leaving in an hour; the flights at ten. Are you sure you're not coming?"

"Yeah, I'm sure, I want to spend as much time as I can with Croí before I have to head back for my brotherly wedding duties."

Muttering under my breath, I curse Rosie and her fucking wedding.

"What?"

Lifting my head, I look my best friend in the eye. "What does Rosie see in him, Cian? Seriously, can you tell me? Because I'm at a fucking loss here!"

I hate this, the look of pity shining in his storm blue eyes.

"I don't know, mate. If it's any consolation, I wish she chose you."

Standing, I push myself off the counter and run my hand through my messy brown hair.

"Well, she didn't. She chose someone who has no respect for her; he treats her like dirt, Cian. I don't think I can go to that wedding. I can't sit there and watch her walk down the aisle into the arms of someone else."

"Have you tried talking to her?"

"I'm done trying, I can't keep fighting for someone who doesn't want saving."

My head hangs in defeat. Cian wraps his arms around me in a man hug and he pats me on the back in an effort at comforting me. Shaking him off, I head for the door.

"I'm going to go pack. Say hello to little Croí for me."

"Will do," he replies. "I'll see you in a few weeks."

Raising my hand, I flip him off as I leave the room. I love that asshole to bits, but I needed to do something to take back my man card.

Rosie

All the fight has seeped from my body, leaving me holding up my white flag in surrender. They won. I spent years on this battle and now, my time has run out. The wedding is a week away, and I'm no closer to a solution; and to make matters worse, Cillian hasn't spoken a single syllable to me since that phone call a few weeks ago.

After collecting my new nephew from Dublin airport arrivals, we head back to Cian's house where everyone greets Ella and Croí — Cillian included. Ella seems like a great girl and judging by the many phone conversations I've had with my brother over the last couple of weeks, Cian has finally landed head over heels in love.

I'm happy for him, even if I can't ever have what he has. Fingers crossed everything works out for them both.

About an hour passes before I notice Cian and my Da sneak off to Cian's home office. Curiosity gets the better of me, so I follow.

Leaning up against the wooden doorframe, I strain my ears to hear the conversation.

A few choice words are thrown around, resulting in my Da storming from the office — leaving the door slightly ajar — and rushing right past me and out the front door.

Tapping on the large oak door, I enter the office to find Cian pacing the floor, his tattooed hands tugging his black hair.

"Hey, Bro. Are you doing okay?"

He lifts his head, his eyes full of torment. "Honestly, no I'm not. How could he do that to me, Ro? They needed me... and I wasn't there. And all for what? So, he could line his pockets."

Cian moves to the edge of his desk, leaning against it for support. Moving to the spot beside him, I wrap my arm around him in a comforting gesture.

"I'm sorry, Cian. I know all about Da and his games, trust me on that. He will do anything for more money or power — even use his own children as pawns in his sick little games."

He turns to face me, searching my face for an explanation. "Sean?"

I nod my head in response.

"Will you go ahead with the wedding?"

"Honestly, I don't know?"

I spent the next hour telling Cian everything from the beginning. All the years of blackmail, just to keep Cillian out of prison. I tell him about the facade that is my engagement—just a business transaction between our Da and Mr. Morgan.

"Jesus Christ, Rosie. Why didn't you come to me? I would have helped you."

"I couldn't, Cian. Da had threatened me into silence. Every time I got close to sorting this mess out, Cillian would do something stupid. Only adding more fuel to the already blazing fire. Yes, they were all small offences, but together, on top of the attempted murder charge, he would've never seen the light of day again. His happiness always meant more to me than my own."

Cian looks at me with sad eyes, finding Ella has really softened his usual intense demeanour. "Do you love Cillian?"

"Of course, I do, I've always loved him."

"Then we need to do everything we can to stop Da. It might take a while, but I will gather as much information as I can. He can't get away with this. He has gone too far. Sham-Rock Records is part mine, between the rest of the band and I, we own sixty-five per cent. There's got to be a way to force him out. If I cut off his funds, he can't pay his connections. I'll have Lily do some digging and see what she can find. There must be something to incriminate him. Anything at all we can use as leverage."

He pulls me in close to his chest, wrapping me in a brotherly hug. "Don't worry, Ringa Rosie. We'll fix this. I promise."

Kissing me on the forehead, he stands to leave.

"I have to go check on El and Croí. Don't worry, I'll do whatever it takes to ensure your happiness."

"Okay, thanks Cian"

"That's what big brothers are for. Now, go get some sleep. I'll call you in the morning."

I spend the rest of the night tossing and turning in Cian's spare bed. Silly questions play on repeat in my mind.

Can love really conquer all? Is everything fair in love and war?

Cian's promise sparked hope I thought I'd lost. His support gave me a promise for the future, one I don't dread with every single breath.

When the morning light fills my bedroom, the new day brings a new lease of life. For the first time in a long time, the feeling of happiness bubbles in my chest.

Reaching into my handbag, I pull out the photo I keep in the zip pocket.

It's a photograph of Cillian and me on my Twentieth birthday, the two of us on stage after he sang me the Journey song.

We were so happy back then, blissfully in love.

Looking down at his handsome face, I make a promise to him, and to myself.

Don't give up on us just yet.

Chapter Twenty-Six

What Have I Done by Dermot Kennedy

Rosie

Lifting my defeated body out of the bathtub, I drag myself and my ridiculous dress towards the vanity table. "I suppose I better make myself presentable."

Slumping down into the chair, I face the mirror and begin fixing the disaster that is my face.

Placing her hand on my shoulder, Lily's gaze catches mine through the mirror. "Are you sure about this, Ro?"

Lily and I, spent weeks searching through my Da's files, searching for something, anything we could use as leverage, but it was no use. Michael has all his dealings locked up tighter than the Buckingham Palace. I've accepted that there is no way out of this.

I'm marrying Sean today.

Whether I like it or not.

"I don't have a choice, Lil. I have to do this."

"Do you want me to take him out?" She arches her brows while giving me her best Maleficent face. "You know I love true crime. I'm an expert at how not to get caught."

"Ha. Thanks, but no thanks. Keeping one O'Shea out of prison is enough. I don't want you to get arrested too."

A loud knock booms against the door. "Rosie, darling, it's Mam. Can I come in?"

Dragging in a deep breath, I fix on my best smile and lift myself from the chair. Heading toward the door, I flick the lock and pull it open, revealing my Ma who looks as beautiful as ever, just like a modern-day Grace Kelly.

The last few weeks have been tough on her, she's been staying at Cian's house ever since she found out my Da hid the knowledge of her beautiful grandson.

Little does she know that the same man is forcing her daughter into a loveless marriage, to her, I am over the moon with my relationship with Sean and if I have my way, she'll never know any different. She doesn't deserve to have her heart broken by another betrayal inflicted by her monster of a husband. And, although there is no love lost between Maggie Mulligan and Sean—she's never said it, but I know she's always been #TeamCillian—she puts up with his pretentious ass because she believes I'm happy.

Cupping my cheeks in the palm of her hands, my Ma's gaze searches my face with concern. "You look beautiful, darling." She drops her hands and heads to the two-seater love seat in the corner. "Lilyanna, be a dear and pass me that bottle of Prosecco."

Lily's head falls back as her laughter ripples through the room. Picking up the half drank bottle she passes it to my Ma. "Maggie, I like your style."

Lifting the green glass bottle to her lips, my Ma swigs back a more than generous gulp then glares at me with a look only a mother can muster. "Now, Rosie... care to explain to me why you're marrying someone you have zero feelings towards."

My eyes become saucers as I stand there with my mouth hanging open in shock. "Who? What? When?"

Her statement has stolen my ability to form a coherent sentence.

"Your brother. Last week, after I left your father, he told me everything. I'm so sorry, darling. If I had known, I never would have let this happen. I genuinely thought you were happy with Sean." She releases a disappointed breath. "After everything that happened between you and Cillian, I thought you were trying to move past it. Love and heartache can be very tricky emotions to manoeuvre, and I knew deep down you would never love anyone the way you did Cillian, but I honestly believed you were moving on with Sean. Never for a second, did I think you were coerced into it."

Wiping her teary eyes with a tissue she took from the glass table; she looks at me with a sad smile. "I'm sorry, Ringa Rosie."

Lily and I squeeze onto either side of her on the love seat and wrap her up in a group hug. We stay like that for a moment, before finally, my mother pats our knees with her hands, making us sit back. Picking her new Louis Vuitton Neverfull handbag from the floor, she takes out a large, thick, brown envelope and hands it to me.

My brow line creases. "What's this?"

A smug smile graces her elegant face as she taps the cover of the envelope in my hands. "That my beautiful daughter is your freedom. Every single dodgy dealing your father has ever made, you name it, it's in there. Fraud, bribery, off-shore bank accounts, the whole nine yards."

As I sit there in shock, Lily pounces of the chair and pulls my Ma to her feet. "Maggie Mulligan, you are a legend. Can I kiss you? Who am I kidding? Of course, I can. C'mere, you big ride."

Ma's laughter bounces off the walls while Lily covers her face in kisses. Pulling page after page out of the envelope, my mouth hits the floor. *Where did she get all this?*

"How?" Finally, my voice decides to join the party.

"I have been married to your father for thirty years. I know all his secret hiding spots, every password and every key code. He is a creature of habit, and luckily, I know him better than the back of my hand. The information was there, you just need the right person to find it. When Cian told me what was going on, I knew I had to stop it. I'm your mother, it's my job to protect you, even if it's at the hands of your own father. And, don't worry, I've made several copies of those documents, you have him by the balls. There is no way he can retaliate without landing himself in it."

"So, what now? How do we go about this?"

A self-congratulatory look covers my mother's face as the corner of her mouth twists with mischief. "Follow my lead, ladies. Mamma Mulligan's got a plan."

✱ ✱ ✱

The string quartet begins to play the opening bars of Canon in D as the doors open to the large room where the ceremony is being held.

I watch from the side as Lily begins a slow pace up the long aisle. The room is decorated just like the wedding scene in that Twilight movie, and if this was my real wedding, I would love it, but it's not.

My stomach flips like a piece of paper caught in a gale-force wind. Releasing a nervous breath, I convince myself I can do this.

From my hidden spot behind the door, I see Cian, Ella, Croí and all the members of 4Clover seated on the left-hand side — all, except for Cillian.

Over to the right, standing beside the priest is Sean, next to him acting as a groomsman, is his Dad, Patrick Morgan.

Once Lily reaches the top, she takes her position and nods her head, signalling for me to start my descent down the white rose covered aisle.

Originally, I was supposed to walk myself down the aisle, but after talking through my Ma's plan's I asked her to accompany me.

Linking her arm through mine, we face the guests. "Are you ready, Sweetheart?"

Pushing my shoulders back, I stand taller. "As I'll ever be."

"Okay, darling. Let's do this."

Taking a deep breath, I place one foot in front of the other, holding my head up high as I make my way past the guests. Ma's arm tightens around mine, right where our elbows meet, making me look in her direction. Our eyes lock, and she mouths, *'You can do this, I'm right here.'*

She gives me one of her reassuring smiles and I gather the confidence I need to execute our plan. We reach the altar within a few steps and the smile on Sean's face disgusts me. He thinks he has won.

Think again asshole.

"Ladies and Gentlemen, we gather here today to celebrate the joining of Rosalie Margaret Mulligan and Sean Patrick Morgan. Before we begin, does anybody have any objections to the union of these two people," the priest pauses, but the room remains silent. "Okay. Let's begin."

Looking back at my mother, she gives me a slight nod of her head urging me to speak up.

My gaze locks on Sean as I clear my throat. "Actually, I object."

Guests gasp at my statement, but the beaming smile on my brother's face spurs me on. Holding my hand out towards Lily, she hands me the brown envelope containing the copies of all the documents my mother found. I pull out the pages, one by one and pass them out to Sean, his father Patrick, and finally, my Da.

Sean grips my elbow and whispers under his breath. "Rosalie, what the fuck are you doing?"

"What is all this, Rosalie? My father questions. "Couldn't you wait until after the ceremony to pass out these silly papers?"

Turning to face him, I level him with a glare. "No, I could not. You see Daddy, I'm not marrying Sean. Not now nor ever."

Gathering the many layers of my wedding dress, I get ready to make my exit. "Now if you would excuse me. I need to go find the love of my life."

Sean's grip on my arm tightens, forcing me to a halt. "You're not going anywhere," he barks. "Did you forget about our little arrangement?"

Before I have time to reply, Lily, my mother, and three very intimidating Rockstars appear at my side.

Cian ice-cold eyes are blazing with rage. "Morgan, I suggest you remove your hand from my sister before I remove your head from your body."

Sean drops my arm and then looks around the room in a panic.

Ma steps forward, focusing on the three confused men. "You lot should really read over those papers before I call the authorities to come and arrest each one of you."

Sean's eyes scan the page and they double in size when he realises what he is holding. "You fucking bitc..."

Lily's hand connects to the side of his face, cutting him off and shocking everyone in the room into silence. Ciaran wraps his arms around her waist, stopping her from lashing out again but when Sean spits in her face, all hell breaks loose.

Ciaran moves Lily over to the side, then spins around, connecting his fist to Sean's nose, knocking him out cold. His limp body hits the ground with a loud thud, leaving the poor priest standing in shock.

My father and Patrick Morgan rush to the nearest exit only to be blocked by Conor. You're not getting out of this one, Da. Handing me the keys to his jeep, Ciaran urges me to leave with the promise of sorting out Michael and Patrick. "Go, Rosie, we'll handle things here."

Lifting the hem of my dress, I thank him with a silent nod and take off running; I pay no heed to the shocked stares coming from guests because none of them matter. The only thing I am focused on is how fast I can get to Cillian.

I hope you're ready, Charming because Snow White's about to storm into your castle.

Cillian

I thought I could do this.

If she was happy nothing else mattered, right?

Wrong! So, fucking wrong.

How the hell am I meant to sit back and watch the only woman I've ever loved, marry someone else?

Today, she's walking down that aisle and it won't be me standing at the other end.

It won't be my ring on her finger.

I could ask myself where it all went wrong? How did something as soul claiming as our love for one another end in flames? But the answer will always be the same.

Loving her was paradise.

Losing her was inevitable.

Staggering around my empty as fuck house in a Tux meant to be worn to a wedding I never wanted to attend, I clutch my — second bottle of the day — Jameson Gold Reserve tightly in my hand.

I decided I can't do it. I can't go.

So, instead, I do what I always do. I'll drown it out, the memories of her, of us, all of it, with the only thing that never leaves me… my whiskey.

I fucking hate this house; once upon a time, it was my future. Now, it's just a consistent reminder of all the ways I fucked up.

After that first tour, I poured every penny I made into these foundations. I was a twenty-two-year-old with stars in his eyes and the woman of his dreams in his arms. Together, we were madly in love with forever insight. I built this house for her.

For us. For the family, we planned to have one day.

But, all in the span of one day, everything I dreamed of came crashing down with the force of a bulldozer. Any hopes of Rosie and I getting our happily ever after was scattered amongst the rubble.

I had handed her my heart on a silver platter, but what I didn't realize was, what I actually gave her was the power to destroy me.

In her hands was a loaded gun, and I just sat back and watched as she pulled the trigger.

Slowly, I make my way up the spiral staircase and into my master bedroom. My steps faulting along the way, courtesy of all the alcohol I've consumed. Lifting the bottle to my lips, I allow the amber liquid to chase the pain away.

Rosie is getting married.
Rosie is getting married.
Rosie is getting married.

Those four words replay over and over. The same four words stuck on repeat. Each fucking syllable twisting the proverbial knife in a little further.

Taking a seat on the edge of my king-sized bed, I slide open the drawer of my oak bedside locker. My fingers grip around the box I'm searching for. Pulling it out, I stare down at the delicate red-jewelled apple-shaped ring box. I had spent months designing this with one of the top jewellers in the world. Sending email after email, making phone call after phone call just to get it absolutely perfect.

Drawing in a sharp breath, I undo the solid gold clasp and then flip the top half of the apple back. Suddenly, every drop of air escapes my lungs, leaving me breathless.

It's been so long since I allowed myself to look inside this box and now, I remember why.

Sitting there, perched on the red satin cushion, is the platinum eighteen-carat, diamond-encrusted engagement ring. The sapphire gemstone in the centre glistens as the overhead light hits it. This ring was designed especially for her.

My Snow White.

Tears fill my eyes, and I let them fall. I never got a chance to give her this ring. Being the stupid fucker, I was, I tried waiting for the perfect time. I wanted the moment to be just right. But, as it happens, that moment never fucking came.

And now, she's with him.

Sean-fucking-Morgan.

The same asshole who tried for years to come between us. He waited, lurking in the shadows for me to fuck up. And when I eventually did, he was there ready to cushion her fall.

Rearing my arm back, I fire the ring box with full force across the room. It smashes against the large mirror doors of my sliding wardrobe.

Anger replaces my sadness, building beneath the surface of my skin like a volcano. Suddenly, I erupt. Smashing everything in my way. The glass lamp, the framed photo of her that sits next to it, nothing is safe. I tear through the room as a man possessed. Trashing everything in my wake.

I'm on a path to destruction, tearing apart everything I lay my eyes on. I don't want it. I don't want fucking anything if it's not her.

In a matter of hours, the love of my life, the other half of my soul, will belong to someone else.

Mrs. Rosie Morgan.

My chest heaves as the uncontrollable sobs tear their way out.

I lost her.

Bending forward, I pick up the ring off the floor and roll the platinum band between my fingers. I clutch it in my palm, holding it over my shattered heart.

It wasn't meant to be like this.

She never belonged to him.

She was mine.

Forever and always.

Finally, I break. Falling to the floor, I wrap my arms around my legs and rock back and forth. The tears streaming from my bloodshot eyes.

I cry.

I cry for her.

For me.

For us and everything, we could have and should have been.

My body shakes uncontrollably as pain ricochets through my chest. It's actually over.

We're done.

It's there, full of too much whiskey and broken-hearted I decided, I'm done too.

I don't want this life. None of it. Nothing fucking matters if she's not by my side.

Reaching for the half-full bottle, I bring it to my lips and drain every single drop. My head no longer feels attached to my body as the alcohol flushes through my veins. My limbs become numb as the room around me fades.

I'm done with it all, this life, the pain, the heartbreak and most of all the shattering reality of a life without her love.

I promised you forever and always.
Goodbye, Snow.

Chapter Twenty-Seven

Don't Give Up on Me by Andy Grammer

Rosie

*T*he drive to Cillian's feels like it's taking forever, but when the familiar Roth Iron gates come into view, I push harder on the accelerator, desperately trying to reach my destination. *Please be here, please be here.*

Pulling up to the entrance, I put Ciaran's ridiculously big Ford Ranger into park, and jump from the jeep. Racing over to the key code, I press the buzzer, once, twice, no answer.

Peering through the gates, I look for any sign that Cillian is home. Spying his new Audi parked out the front, I sigh with relief. I ring the buzzer one more time before deciding to enter the code manually.

Entering his birthday, I am greeted with a red light.

Shit. Try again.

Lily's birthday. Red light.

Come on Cillian, what the hell is the code?

Suddenly, a date enters my mind. The eighth of November 2013, the day I gave Cillian, all of me. Punching the numbers in, I pray for a green light.

Bingo.

Slowly, the gates open. I haven't got the patience to wait, so I squeeze myself through the small opening, tearing the lace detail of my dress.

Sorry Vera, but desperate times.

Pulling off my high heels, I gather the long train of my dress in my hands and take off up the long driveway like I'm competing in the Women's Mini Marathon.

I reach the door in no time, slightly out of breath but still breathing.

Who knew wedding dresses were so heavy?

Entering the same code into the keypad by the door, I twist the handle and thankfully, it opens.

The first thing to hit me when I enter the hallway is the smell. The potent scent of whiskey wafts through the air.

Jesus Cillian, what were you drinking?

My stomach churns as the distinct odour of vomit fills my nose, lifting my hand, I cover my mouth and swallow my gag.

Following the smell, I rush up the spiral staircase and into Cillian's bedroom. The sight that greets me forces me to my knees. The room is a mess, broken glass lines the floor and the full-length mirror is shattered into a thousand pieces. But none of that matters because Cillian's lifeless body is face down in a pool of vomit.

"No, no, no, no, no."

I crawl towards him, not caring if I get cut by the shards of glass that litter the floor.

Shaking his limp form, I beg him to wake up. "Cillian! Baby, please wake up. Baby, please... Please wake up."

Shit Cillian, what did you do?

Scanning the area, I search for his phone and luckily, it's within reach. I grab it, and with shaky fingers dial 911.

"Hello, what's your emergency?"

"Help, I need help! He's unconscious and there is vomit everywhere. Help me, please, help me."

"Miss, please try to calm down. Can you tell me your location?"

Blowing out a few breaths, I control my racing heart and rattle of Cillian's address as quickly as I can.

"Okay, now, I want you to put him in the recovery position and monitor him the best you can. Do you think you can do that?"

"Yes."

"The paramedics will be with you shortly."

Dropping the phone to the floor, I'm not sure if she is still on the line and honestly, I don't care.

Rolling Cillian onto his side — just like the lady directed me too — I lay beside him and wrap my arms around his waist. I'm covered in vomit, but I don't give a fuck.

Pushing his hair off his face, I beg him to wake up.

"Come on, Cillian. Open those hazel eyes. You can't leave me. I'm here, please don't leave me." I can barely see through the stream of tears, but my eyes never leave him. "Don't give up on me, Charming. Please, don't give up."

"WAKE UP, GODDAMMIT!"

I'm not sure how long it will take before the ambulance arrives, but when they do, the paramedics push me out of the way so they can work on Cillian. Putting him on oxygen, they speak to each other in medical jargon. They mention a few medical terms I don't understand before lifting him onto a stretcher, carting him down to the awaiting ambulance.

Panic grips me, threatening to pull me under. "What's happening? Will he be okay?"

"His pulse is weak and his oxygen levels are low. I'm uncertain but by the looks of it, he was unconscious when he vomited, resulting in the contents of his stomach ending up in the lower respiratory tract because he couldn't protect his airway. This is a potentially very serious condition. We are taking him to St. James Hospital for further assessment. Unfortunately, you can't ride with us because we need the space to work on him. Have you got someone you can call to take you to the hospital?"

Feeling helpless, I nod my head yes. "My brother, I'll call my brother."

I realize that this situation is completely out of my control. I just need to let the paramedics do their job.

"Please look after him. I need him."

"We will do our best."

Rushing back to Ciaran's jeep, I connect my phone to Bluetooth and call my brother. "Hey Ro, everything okay? Did you find him?"

"Cian." My voice breaks. "I need you."

"Rosie, what's wrong? Where are you?"

Forcing back the tears free, I drag in several breaths. "Cian... he was barely breathing... paramedics... vomit, so much vomit... Hospital."

"Rosie, calm down. I can't understand you. Where are you?"

"I'm at Cillian's. They took him... to the... the hospital."

Frantically, I try to form a coherent sentence, but my wildly beating heat steals my breath. "I need to go... I need to get there. He's on his own."

"Rosie, stay where you are. I'm coming okay, I'm on the way. Don't you fucking dare drive? I'm coming."

Vaguely, I hear the commotion in the background, followed by Cian roaring at someone to get the fucking car.

"Don't hang up, Rosie, stay on the phone. We're on the way. Don't hang up."

"I'm scared, Cian," I sob. "He wouldn't wake up. Why wouldn't he wake up?"

"It's okay, Ro. He will be okay."

"Promise me, Cian. Promise me he will be alright. Promise me, Goddammit!"

"I promise, Rosie. I promise he will be okay."

We both know his promise means shit, he didn't see him. He didn't hold Cillian's near lifeless body in his hands. A pang of anguish, grips hold of all my internal organs as the image of Cillian laying there helplessly, slaughters my mind.

"I need him, Cian. I can't live this life without him."

"You won't have to Ro. You won't have to."

* * *

Together, we all sit waiting—not too patiently—for news on Cillian. Thankfully, the hospital staff found us a quiet room away from prying eyes. The last thing we need right now is some fan taking a picture of one of the band members and alerting the media. This is a private matter, and if the paparazzi get wind of Cillian's overdose, things could get very messy. Not that, that even matters right this minute.

It's been two long excruciating hours since they rushed Cillian to A & E, and still no word from the team who are looking after him.

I hate this, the waiting, the not knowing if he is okay. I pace back and forth the small room as the walls feel like they're caving in on me.

My stomach flips with nervous energy while I look around at all the people I love gathered together. Each one loves Cillian in a different way. Mary loves him the way a mother loves a son. Lily loves him the way a sister loves a brother. Cian, Ciaran and Conor all love him as a friend. Then there is me, I can't put into words how much I love Cillian. He is the only love I've ever known.

He was my first everything, the broken boy who taught me how to love with my whole heart, my complete soul. He's my once in a lifetime, all-consuming love.

As I circle the room for the millionth time, I send a silent prayer to whoever is listening, begging for a chance to tell Cillian how much he means to me.

"Ro, maybe you should try to sit down. You're wearing a hole in the lino," Cian jokes in a poor attempt to lift my mood.

"Just shut up, you're not funny. Where are the doctors? Why haven't we been informed on what the hell is going on?"

Irritation crawls under my skin. Pulling at the ridiculous skirt of the wedding dress, I mutter to myself. "Fuck this dress."

Mary stands, pulling me into a motherly hug bringing me some comfort. It should be me consoling her. Cillian is her son.

"Rosie, sweetheart, I know it's tough, but you need to calm down. He is in the best hands here. The doctors will do whatever they need to. I'm sure they will inform us as soon as they are able. Why don't you take a seat and I'll go find you something to change into? You can't be comfortable in that gown."

I nod my head yes, too caught up in my head to form words. How is she handling this so well? He could have died. He still might. We have no idea what the outcome will be? Mary walks me to a nearby plastic chair, easing my defeated body down onto it. My leg bounces with the anticipation of what's to come.

"I'll be right back, darling. I'll see if anyone knows anything too."

* * *

I'm curled up in a ball with my head resting on my brother's lap. Thankfully, Mary was successful in her hunt for a change of clothes, a lovely nurse named Danielle gave her some scrubs for me to wear. I couldn't wait to get that dress off me. If I never agreed to that wedding, Cillian wouldn't be here.

This is my fault.

Maybe if we stayed together, I could have helped him overcome his drinking. I thought he was getting better. As far as I was aware, he only drank occasionally.

The door of the waiting room opens, and all eyes swing to the older gentlemen wearing a white lab coat. He must be Cillian's Doctor. "Good Evening, my name is Dr Bannon. I'm the doctor looking after Mr O'Shea. I'm sorry to have kept you all waiting. Which one of you is his next of kin? Perhaps we could speak in private about his condition?"

I'm eternally grateful when Mary replies. "Hello, Dr Bannon. I'm Mary, Cillian's mother. You can speak freely here. Everyone in this room is family."

The doctor hesitates momentarily before delivering the news on Cillian's condition. "As you wish. You are all aware when Cillian arrived he had a staggering amount of alcohol in his system. His blood alcohol concentration was one of the highest I've encountered in all my years practising medicine. It was well above 0.40, which is unfortunately life-threatening."

We all sit in silence, waiting on the doctor to continue. "When he was admitted, he was unconscious and although he was still breathing, he was in respiratory failure. His lungs were not functioning as they should which means there was not enough oxygen getting to his brain and other vital organs. The combination of this and the fact that he was intoxicated meant that he was essentially in a coma. We believe he was more than likely unconscious when he threw up. His gag reflex was ineffective, and consequently gastric contents entered his lungs."

"What does that mean?" Mary questions.

"It means Cillian is likely developing a serious lung infection called aspiration pneumonia, it is still early days, but the signs are there. We have also performed gastric lavage, commonly known as stomach pumping and thankfully, we were able to remove any remaining alcohol from his stomach before it gets into his bloodstream. We have had to put a tube down into his lungs to help him breathe so we can maintain his oxygen levels and we have given him some strong antibiotics to help fight the infection that is developing in his lungs."

"What now?" Conor asks.

"Well for the moment, we wait. We have done everything we can. The rest is up to him. At the moment, he is stable but still critical. The next 48 hours will help us determine our next step."

"Okay, can we see him?" I question.

"Yes, but I'll ask that you keep it to two at a time."

"Of course," Lily agrees.

"Have you any more questions?"

"No, that is all, Doc." Cian stands, walking the doctor to the door. "Thank you for all your help."

Mary offers me to go see him first, but I decline, letting the rest go first because once I enter that room, I'm not leaving.

Not until Cillian wakes up.

Chapter Twenty-Eight

Praying by Kesha

Rosie

*A*rising from my slumber, I hear loud voices outside of Cillian's hospital room. *What the hell is going on out there?*

Reaching up to the back of my stiff neck with my hand, I roll my head in a circular motion while rubbing out the creek I've gotten from sleeping on this plastic chair. I stand up, stretching my arms over my head, desperate to rid myself of my aching muscles.

Releasing an exhausted breath followed by a yawn, I realize I've never been so tired in all my life. The last few weeks have really taken their toll on me and now with everything that happened in the last forty-eight hours — I've barely slept a wink. I have been keeping my eye on Cillian, praying, hoping, wishing, for him to be okay.

My eyes wander to his sleeping form laying there on the small hospital bed. He looks so peaceful, his dark eyelashes brushing against his hollowed cheeks. The past few days have been unbearably hard. I've tried accepting the powerlessness that my love for Cillian brings because, at the end of the day, I'm just glad he's here.

The helpless, endless ball of anxiety is draining me both physically and mentally, but I can't bear the thought of leaving him, even for a short period of time. *What if he wakes up and I'm not here?*

Watching his almost lifeless body brings a vulnerable pain I've never experienced before, I know it's always difficult to see the ones we love so defeated, but when that person is the other half of your existence, it's a whole different ball game. It's alarming, scary and confusing and I've all but driven myself insane with worry.

Fortunately, Cillian's condition has improved dramatically since they admitted him. His oxygen requirement has come down and his lung function has improved. With the help of antibiotics, the doctors were able to stop the infection developing in his lungs before it progressed into something more serious. Yesterday, he woke up enough to breathe by himself, and after a few routine tests, they decided to extubate him. The Doctor said it could take a few days for the sedation to wear of fully, but we're hopeful that he will be okay.

Running my palm along the few-day-old stubble lining his chiseled jaw, the hair prickles my skin.

"Good morning, Charming. Are you going to wake up today? I need to see those gorgeous eyes."

The nurse has encouraged all of us to keep talking to him because patients are more likely to respond when they're surrounded by the positivity of their visitors. "Let him know he has something to wake up for," she said.

My brother's raised voice echoes through the paper-thin walls, making me freeze my movements as I strain to hear what is going on. "Not a fucking chance are you getting within reaching distance of my sister. You're lucky I haven't buried you six-feet under after everything you've done to our family."

"Son, please." *Da? What is he doing here?*

Bending forward, I brush my lips against the skin of Cillian's cheek. "I'll be right back; I'm just going to see what's happening outside."

Striding towards the door, my anger builds with every step. How dare he show his face around here? Does he not realise this is partly his fault? He pushed too far with his silly games. He should count himself lucky he is not already behind bars.

We nearly lost Cillian; He is my main concern. My Da can go rot in hell for all I care. Gripping the handle with a shaky hand, I twist the silver knob and pull open the door with force, locking eyes with the man I once called my father.

"I'd like you to leave." The words fall from my mouth without a hint of emotion.

The sight of him makes me sick, he's ruined so many lives with his selfish games. I'm done, he no longer has any power over me.

Michael takes a step forward, etching nearer to me. "Rosalie, please, sweetheart, I came to apologise."

Cian moves his large frame in front of me, blocking me from my father's pleading eyes.

"It's okay, Cian," I whisper, stepping around his protective stance.

My so-called father's eyes bore into mine. "I'm sorry about Cillian."

"Just stop." I hold up my hand. "I never want to hear his name leave your lie-filled mouth again."

Looking around the hallway, I wave my hand at our surroundings. "This... this is all your fault. All of this is on YOU," I point to his chest. "Cillian was getting better until you ruined everything with your twisted little games." I release a heavy sigh before continuing. "Why? Why couldn't you let us be happy?" Tears gather in my eyes, moments away from falling. "Cillian was all I ever wanted, my once in a lifetime love. Did you get a kick out of taking that from me?" *Silence.* "Do you feel more powerful knowing you destroyed your daughter's happiness?" *Nothing.* "Answer me, Goddammit!"

Cian wraps his arm around my shoulder, giving me the support, he knows I need.

When my father refuses to answer, Cian gives him a piece of his mind. "You destroyed our family.

You played both of your children like chess pawns. You dictated our every move for your own benefit."

Cian releases me from his hold and steps towards our father with a murderous glare in his storm-blue eyes. "You robbed me of countless years with my son. You stole memories I can never get back. You banished my sister into a loveless relationship, and for what? Power, money, greed, well, Da... which was it? You don't deserve my mother and I'm glad she finally left your pathetic ass." His words are filled with venomous hate. "Oh, and another thing... the label's gone."

My father's eyes become wide when Cian's words finally register. He's been unaware of the moves Cian has been making the past few weeks — ever since we had that little chat in his office, the day he arrived back from L.A.

"What do you mean the label's gone? It can't be. I never agreed to that."

"Oh, he speaks," I say, doing nothing to hide the sarcasm in my tone.

Cian steps closer, towering over my father with his intimidatingly large frame. "You didn't have to agree. After I found out you kept my son hidden from me for six years of his life, I decided I'd had enough of you and your lies. So, the rest of the band and I sought some legal advice."

The grey hue on my father's face is almost comical.

"See, daddy dearest, as it turns out, you only own thirty-five percent of Sham-Rock Recordz. I own twenty-five, Cillian owns ten, and the twins own twenty between them. You paid for your shares using their money. So, collectively, all four of 4Clover own sixty-five percent of the label which makes you," Cian points to my Da. "the minority shareholder."

My father's face turns a paler shade of grey at Cian revelation. He didn't know we knew his little secret. For years, he has been embezzling money from his own son and his friends, bad move, Daddy.

Clutching at straws, he starts throwing out pointless facts. "I still own thirty-five percent, you can't kick me out, I have rights."

Cian comes to stand by my side, and together we create a united front. "We are not kicking you out. We are just moving our shares to a new label. Oh, and we are taking the clients with us. They're only there because of us, so they are leaving to join our new label—Vitamin C Records. It's over Da, face it, you lost everything. Your wife, your kids and now your business. Nobody will ever work with you again, not when they find out you've been stealing from your artists. You're done in the music business."

Running his fingers through his grey hair, his facade begins to crumble. "You can't do this to me, your own father. Rosalie, tell him this is absurd."

"No can do. If I were you, I would count my lucky stars we didn't have you arrested. You deserve much more than what we dished you, and if it were solely up to me you would never see the light of day again. Take what you have left and leave us all alone. I never want to see your face again."

"You should listen to her," Cian tells him, stepping right into his face, their noses touching from their close proximity. "If I ever see you near any of us — Ma included — I will be heading straight down to the police station to turn you in. You have twenty-four hours to make yourself scarce, or I will have you locked up in no time. Understood?"

"Understood."

Before he can make a speedy exit, I grip his elbow and plaster on my fakest smile. "Oh, and Da, pass that message along to Patrick and Sean too, one sniff of trouble and you will all go down faster than a lead balloon."

Our father lowers his head, shoving his hands into his pocket. He turns and walks away. He knows we aren't bluffing, and thankfully, he has enough sense to walk out of our lives in order to save his own ass. *Good riddance to bad rubbish.*

Cian takes my hand, squeezing it tight. "It's over," he says before pulling me into a brotherly hug.

Together we walk back into Cillian's room. Finally, we're able to put my Da behind us. Taking the seat beside Cillian's bed, I cover his hand with mine. The twitch of his finger causes me to jump from the chair. "Cian, he just moved."

"Cillian, can you hear me, baby? Wake up."

Standing above him, I search his face for any movement. His eyelashes flicker with every word I speak. My heart pounds loudly in my chest as my stomach fills with hope. "Come on, Charming. Open those eyes."

"Snow." His special nickname for me escapes his lips in an airy breath, one I would have missed if I wasn't paying attention.

"That's right, baby, I'm right here."

Chapter Twenty-Nine

This Year's Love by David Gray

Cillian

A bright white light shines through the thin layer of skin shielding my eyes and no matter how hard I try to open them, they won't budge. They're welded shut by a heaviness my exhausted body cannot shake.

A continuous beeping rings in my ears, the sound magnified by my heightened senses. The pulsation of the steady beat is like someone's holding a megaphone to the side of my head.

Beep, beep, beep.

Beep, beep, beep.

Raised voices echo in the distance.

Where the fuck am I?

Staining my ears, I seek validation on who is nearby, but it's no use.

The constant beeping is drowning them out.

Making another attempt at pulling my body from its heavy slumber, I blink rapidly but still, my eyes refuse to open.

Why can't I open my eyes?

I try to call out, but the words get caught in my dry throat. Water, I need water.

Okay, Cillian. Think. What's the last thing you remember? Why can't I remember?

Suddenly the memories come crashing in, hitting me with a force that would rival a tsunami. The events that took place pulling me under, the images flooding my brain.

Rosie. Wedding day. Whiskey. More whiskey. Rosie, Sean. Married. Rosie. Engagement ring. Broken glass. My Rosie. Whiskey. Shattered mirror. Shattered heart. Whiskey. Blackness.

The beeping becomes frantic.

Beep, beep, beep, beep.

Beep, beep, beep, beep.

Stop, breathe Cillian. In, out. In, out.

It's only then, I fully realize that the monotonous beeping is my heart.

Fuck, Cillian, what did you do?

Focusing on my physical body, I mentally scan myself from head to toe. Nothing hurts, well besides the throbbing in my skull and the pressure I feel across my chest.

I try to move my limbs without success. *Nothing.*

A loud creak captures my attention. *A door?* Footsteps shuffle across the floor. Two. *There are two people.*

I focus on the surrounding sounds, a chair scraping against the floor then a heavy sigh, someone sitting down, followed by sniffling.

A scent I'm more than familiar with fills my nostrils. Fresh flowers on a spring day with a hint of cherry red apples. *Rosie.*

The warmth of her hand covers mine and I try to reach for her, but my efforts are futile. My body is not cooperating.

Suddenly, her body jumps away from mine. "Cian, he just moved."

Her voice is like music to my ears. "Come on, Charming. Open those eyes."

"Snow," I eventually force out that one syllable using up more strength than I possess.

"That's right, Charming. I'm right here." The love that's evident in her soft voice gives me a new lease on life. I pry my eyes open, my vision blurred but I can still make her out, the light to my darkness.

"Cian, go get the nurse, he's waking."

She looks over her shoulder, but I don't hear his reply because all my scenes are solely focused on her. The raven-haired beauty in front of me. Slowly my vision sharpens, and the hospital room becomes clearer.

"Welcome back, Charming."

The smile on her face is almost blinding as I drink her in, her long dark hair is pulled back from her face with a hair tie. Her face, void of any makeup and the blackness around her sea-blue eyes is new.

She looks exhausted but still as beautiful as she has ever been.

Lifting my weighted head up off the pillow, my body struggles to sit forward.

"Careful, do you need a drink?"

I nod my head at her question, my throat feels like I swallowed a mouthful of sand. Rosie works at fixing the pillows behind me, supporting my weak body in its new upright position. I watch her closely as she fills the small glass on the table beside me with the large jug of water. She adds a straw before holding the glass up to my lips, encouraging me to take small careful sips.

For some reason, my eyes wander to the hand holding the glass. I don't know what possessed me to look, but as my eyes scan her fingers, my heart fills with hope. They're bare, empty of any jewellery. *No rings.* Does that mean she didn't marry Sean?

Her eyes follow mine and she realizes what I'm staring at. Our eyes flick up, now focused on each other.

"I didn't marry Sean."

Those four words fill my body with relief. We stay silent for a moment, living in the moment. Her eyes tell me a story of their own. They hold so much: sorrow, regret, concern but most of all love.

After taking a few small sips of water, I force out the question I need the answer to. "Why not?"

Rosie never takes her eyes off me. "I didn't love him. I never did. There is a lot about mine and

Sean's relationship you don't know. I promise I'll tell you everything, but for now, I just need you to get better, okay."

She runs her palm over the stubble on my chin and even in my current condition, her touch affects me. The electric current that sparks between her skin and mine is undeniable.

"You nearly died."

Silent tears slip from her eyes making me feel like an asshole for being the one who caused them. Leaning further into her touch, I close my eyes. "I'm sorry, Snow."

She rests her forehead against mine, our lashes kissing with every blink. I would give anything to hold her, to pull her close and never let her go. There is too much-unspoken truth between us and now is not the time to drag up the past, so instead, I just breathe her in. Just like that, an Aha moment hits me.

I need help.

If I want Rosie in my life forever, I need to evict the demons from my mind. I need to quit the clutch that keeps them at bay and rid them for good. My habit has become an addiction. I've become dependent on alcohol to numb the pain, the loneliness, the heartache but... the high is only ever temporary.

I have wasted so many years chasing away my demons by drowning them out with a bottle of poison, but the reality is they were the ones chasing me.

I'm fully aware that alcohol is not the answer, but for a long time, it made me forget the questions.

I'm done, done running from the past.

Now, looking into the eyes of the only girl I've ever loved, I want to fight for her, for us, for the future I promised her when she was just nineteen years old. The future where she is the one standing by my side, but first, I need to get help. I need to become the man she deserves, not some twenty-six-year-old alcoholic.

"Snow?"

She kisses the tip of my nose, just like old times and pulls back so she can see my face. "Yes, Charming?"

I let the tears behind my eyes fall. "I need help. I can't keep living like this. I'm becoming him. I promised myself I would never be like him and I'm doing a fine job at proving myself wrong."

Overcome with emotion, I hate who I am right now. A drunk and a coward. It's time to save myself before I drown.

Rosie lifts her hand, wiping the tears streaking my cheeks. "It's okay, baby. I'll organize it. Once you're well enough, we will get you the help you need. I promise."

I kiss her palm letting her know I appreciate her and everything she's doing for me.

"Sorry to interrupt this magical moment, but the Doc here wants to see sleeping beauty," Cian states after he barrels through the door with the doctor behind him.

"Cillian, nice you see finally awake? How are you feeling?" The doctor asks, reading the file at the end of my bed.

Stealing a look at the girl beside me, I can only come up with one answer. "I'm doing pretty fucking good Doc, best I've felt in years."

✱ ✱ ✱

I can't take my eyes off her.

Rosie is curled up onto the armchair beside my bed, her hands held together in a prayer position resting under her cheek and acting as a pillow.

I know she can't be comfortable sleeping like that, but still, even after eight days, she refuses to leave my side.

Rosie has spent every minute here, tending to my every need. She had Lily bring her a few things so she could shower and change, but other than that, she's been right where she belongs — by my side.

We've spent the last few days tiptoeing around everything. Every time I would bring us up, she would tell me it's not the time, or that I needed to focus on getting better. But today, I'm not letting her avoid the inevitable talk we need to have.

I still have no idea why she didn't marry Sean. I tried to ask Lily, but she told me it wasn't her story to tell.

Rolling over onto my side, I take her all in, in all the years she hasn't changed one single bit. Her hair is still the darkest shade of black, making her skin appear whiter somehow. Her pouty lips are slightly open, still holding that natural luscious shade of red. I watch as her long black lashes flicker with every rise and fall of her breath. Reaching forward, I sweep the fallen strands of hair — stuck to her cheek — back behind her ear. So beautiful.

Laying there, I rehearse everything I want to say to her when she wakes. I want to tell her I still love her. I still need her. That I still dream of the life we once planned. The house, the kids, fuck, even the dogs, I want it all, but only with her.

Fighting against the — medication-induced — tiredness that makes my eyes heavy, I sit up in the bed because there is no dream I could conjure that would compare to the vision before me.

I still don't understand why she is here, why she never married that dickhead Morgan, but I sure as hell want to find out. I always knew there was something more to it than what she led everyone to believe.

Today, I want answers.

I need them.

Before long, her eyes flicker open. Stretching her arms above her head, her crystal blue irises fixate on my face. "Hey, sorry I must have dozed off."

"No worries, Snow. You must be exhausted; you've been sleeping on that chair for days."

"I'm okay, it's not too bad."

She's not fooling anyone; I can see the pain in her face every time she rolls her neck.

"You're a terrible liar."

Silence fills the room, but we keep eye contact. That has been happening quite regularly over the past few days, the heaviness of our unspoken truths lingering in the air between us.

Rosie stands, "I'm going to go get coffee. Do you want anything?"

I'm getting frustrated with her obvious avoidance. "You know, you can't keep avoiding me, Ro. We need to talk about this at some point."

She stills before exiting the room then spins to face me. "I know that, Cillian. I guess I'm just terrified I won't like what I hear." Blowing out a breath, she pulls at the hem of her t-shirt.

"Yeah, well ditto on that but I can't say I'm not curious as to why you are here and not married to Morgan."

Pain shows behind her ocean eyes as her body visibly stiffens at my words. She squeezes her eyes tight before walking back towards the bed, dropping her handbag to the floor. There is a fire raging behind her gaze. Good, at least she's fucking talking.

"Really, Cillian. You honestly believe I would choose Sean over you?"

Sitting up in the bed, I hone in on her. "Newsflash, Snow. You did, for years you chose him over me. Don't expect me to think differently. Haven't you heard? Actions speak louder than words."

"Don't be a wanker, Cillian. It doesn't suit you."

"You're right, I'm sorry. I'm just confused. The last time we spoke you told me you didn't love me anymore."

"I don't love you any more. I also don't love you any less. I love you the same as I always have—with every cell in my body."

Reaching for my hand, she covers it with her own. "I never stopped loving you, not for one second. Even after witnessing that girl leaving what was meant to be our home, I still loved you. I also hated you, but never enough to stop the pain that came from the love I felt."

I will forever regret that day, the day my entire world crumbled at my feet. The day I lost Rosie for good.

"The only reason it hurt the way it did, was the heart in my chest—that only beats for you—shattered. We shattered that day," she explains brushing the tears from under her eyes.

"That's where you are wrong, Snow. I didn't break us that day. You did. Did you forget you were the one who came to our home and tore the soul right out of my body? I regret my actions after that, but don't place all the blame on me. I thought we were done. You left. I'm not excusing what I did because it was fucked up. But I was heartbroken, Rosie. I dealt with it the only way I could. I'm sorry, and if I could take it back I would."

Squeezing her hand tighter, I wish I could comfort her more, but the machine wires I'm hooked to aren't exactly accommodating.

Rosie lowers her head, her eyes cast to the floor. "I need to tell you something about that day... actually, about all of it."

Scooting over as much as the thin bed will allow, I make space for her to climb in beside me.

"Come here," I say, lifting my arm so she can fit against my chest.

She hesitates for a second, scanning the space for any wires. Finally, she kicks off her shoes and nestles against me, resting her head against my pec as I wrap my arm around her tiny frame.

"Comfy?"

She draws in a deep breath and closes her eyes, basking in the togetherness of us. "Extremely."

A small smile curls on my lips.

"Good, now start from the beginning."

Chapter Thirty

The Reason by Hoobastank

Rosie

"When they took you away in that police car, I felt helpless and I didn't know what to do. They arrested you for attempt murder, Cillian. I was physically sick and frankly, terrified. I thought I'd never see you again. I had to do something, anything I could to get you out of that place. So, I ran... I rushed home, begging, pleading with my Da to do whatever he could," I explain. "I didn't know who else to contact. I knew he had the connections to get you out. What I didn't know was the price your freedom would cost me. Cost us."

"Sean?" he asks, his hands gently stroking my hair.

"Yeah, I had to agree to leave you and marry Sean."

The tears are streaming from my eyes, soaking the cotton of Cillian's t-shirt.

"I didn't even hesitate. I agreed to his conditions in a heartbeat, your life, your freedom, it was worth it. I couldn't let you rot in there Cillian; you didn't deserve that life. I loved you too much to watch you lose everything over a worthless human being like your father."

"So, you're telling me, after all these years, the reason you were with Sean was to protect me from prison? Rosie, that is beyond ridiculous. Why didn't you say something? Fuck, I would have hired a lawyer. We could have figured it out. You didn't need to do that."

He thinks it's simple. Love conquers all. Yes, we could have fought, but we wouldn't have won. Not without the right ammunition—which we now have thanks to my mother.

"It wasn't that simple, Cillian. He had so much hanging over your head. You would have lost everything; I couldn't do that to you. I wouldn't. I thought maybe with time, I could figure out a way to get out of the deal I made with him." I pause, looking up at him through my now wet lashes. I gently brush my fingers back and forth over his stomach, the feel of his skin bringing me comfort. "But the more time passed, the worse things became. You were all at the peak of your career. Temptations surrounded you, your drinking had got out of control. You were free-falling and there was nothing I could do to catch you. Then, eventually, you were getting better, until the stupid engagement. I firmly believe my Da pulled that just to get you to submit to your poison. Once you stayed drinking, he could control you. It gave him power over you."

"I'm sorry, Snow. I had no idea. I swear to you. If I did, I would have put a stop to it somehow."

He bends forward, kissing the top of my head. The arm that's wrapped around me pulls me in closer than I thought possible. "So, then what? How did you get out of it? The marriage I mean?"

"Well, after the engagement party I was determined to put an end to the charade... Lily and I started digging into the label's records, searching for anything that would incriminate my Da, Sean, and his father. Then everything happened with Cian and Ella, which put a spanner in the works. We found a lot of emails from her, spanning the six years they spent apart, but nothing we could use as viable leverage to take my Da down. I was stuck at a crossroad not knowing which way to turn."

Pushing myself up, I turn to face him. I need to see his face, his eyes, all of him.

"I had given up; I had accepted that I had to go through with it. The only way out was to marry Sean—spend four years with him—then file for divorce. The morning of the wedding I locked myself in the hotel room bathroom. I knew I was making a big mistake, but I couldn't see a way out. Cian was looking for anything he could find to use and when he came up empty, he approached my mam. Right before the ceremony, she arrived with a file full of dodgy dealings implicating my Da to no end. She had found a way out and I took it with both hands. I ran from there as fast as I could and went straight to you. That's when I found you."

Images from that day rush to the forefront of my mind, bringing with them a whole meagre of emotions. Pushing them back, I focus on the present. He's here, and he's alive, that's all that matters.

Cillian lifts his hand, taking hold of my cheek. His soft touch wiping away my falling tears. "I'm sorry you had to see me like that, baby."

Scooting forward, I rest my forehead against his. Our breaths intertwine in the small space between us.

"Cillian, I was so scared, when I found you like that, I... I thought you were dead. I thought I lost you. Seeing you there lifeless was the worst moment of my life."

"Please don't cry, sweetheart. It's okay, I'm okay. I'm so, so sorry you had to witness that."

"If something happened to you, Cillian, I wouldn't have been able to live with myself."

"Don't. Don't you dare blame yourself? This is all on me, Rosie. I have a problem; one I will sort the minute they release me from this place. I should have sought help years ago, but I was a stubborn asshole with a huge grudge. I know now in order to be the man you need me to be — the man I need to be for myself — I have to get some professional help," he chokes out battling his own tears. "I don't know whether you want to start again, but I swear to you, Rosie, if you give us another chance, I will not waste it."

"Of course, I want that."

Pulling back, I hold his face between my palms. "Cillian O'Shea, your existence in my life has given me some of my most life-altering moments. You have been part of my most painful times, but you have given me all the happiest ones too. You were my biggest heartbreak, but you are also my greatest love of all time. There is nowhere in this universe I would rather be, than right by your side. We will do this together, the way we should have done all along. I love you, Charming."

"I love you too, Snow."

Finally, our lips meet, in this one kiss I find my home, I find my hope and most importantly, I find my love.

Cillian

"Well, well, well... What do we have here?" Lily questions when she strolls into the hospital room and finds Rosie fast asleep in my arms.

She's exhausted from sleeping at the hospital, but she refuses to go home. Glancing down at the raven-haired beauty that holds my heart, there's nothing I can do to stop the smile that lights my face.

Just the sight of Rosie back in my arms again is something worth living for. I hold her a little tighter. My nose nestled in her messy hair as the scent of her apple shampoo invades my senses. My mind is still reeling from everything she just told me. I don't know what she was thinking, keeping all that from me. It took everything in me to hold back the anger I feel towards Michael. *How could he do that to his own daughter?*

When she recounted everything that went down, I had to bite my tongue and force myself to just listen. The last thing Rosie needed was for me to explode into one of my rages. So, I stayed calm while she got it all out. Even though underneath my calm demeanour, my blood was boiling. I knew losing my temper wouldn't give us back all the years we lost.

I'm quickly learning that life is short, and we need to hold on to the time we have left instead of fighting over what if's? I'm just happy we are finally back on track. Even if we still have a long road ahead, I know we're finally walking that road together.

I never understood the hatred Michael directed at me over the years. I know he never liked my family. In his eyes, we were beneath him. He never approved of the friendship between Maggie and my Ma, but they were always inseparable — much like their daughters.

Many times, over the years, Ma would say Lily and Rosie were exactly like her and her Mary were when they were younger. I think he always felt threatened by how close they are.

"It's good to see a smile on your ugly face, it's been far too long, you're getting frown lines," Lily jokes pulling a chair closer to my bed. "How are you feeling?"

"Honestly, I'm feeling shit, my body is still recovering. Thankfully, I'm over the worst. The last few days have been tough, but I'm getting there."

I search my sister's eyes and when her gaze meets mine, I hold it. "I'm sorry Lil, I shouldn't have put you through this. I thought I was getting better, then everything became too much. I thought I could drown out the hurt and the pain, but all I did was cause more for the people I love most."

She fidgets with the sleeve of her top. "Cillian, if I have learnt anything from going to therapy over the years, it's that no matter how fast you run from your demons, they will always catch up with you. The only way you can rid yourself of the things that haunt you is to face them head-on."

The sadness behind her amber eyes that guts me. "I have arranged to visit Da in prison," she says, completely shocking me. "I need to forgive him. It doesn't mean I will forget, but I know, in order to be free and move on with my life—I have to let it go. I'm doing this for myself and nobody else. Maybe you should do the same?"

Could I ever forgive the man who raised me? He put us through hell for years, all the beatings, and verbal abuse we encountered, all because in his eyes we could do nothing to his satisfaction.

I know now he was an addict, one who had no willpower to get help, to become better. That's the difference between us. I don't want to be like him; I don't want to live a life so full of hate that it becomes the only thing that feeds my soul.

For a long time, I thrived on the anger inside me. No more, from now on I'm choosing happiness.

"Yeah, maybe you're right. I need to face him. Tell him how much he destroyed me, let him see that I am better than the man he was meant to be. I'll let him know I forgive him for his addiction, but I can never forget the things he did. But first, I need to face my problems, Lily. That's my priority right now."

"Well, I'm glad you said that because I've arranged for you to go to the best treatment centre in the country. I've had a word with your doctors here and they're happy to release you under the condition you start treatment tomorrow at the latest."

I nod my head in agreement. Thank fuck I can finally leave this place I was getting agitated being stuck in this little room. I've had to stay hidden so word of my overdose wouldn't get leaked to the press.

"They wanted you to go straight there, but with a few of my stellar negotiation skills, I got you one night," she looks towards Rosie. "I thought you might appreciate a night together before you disappear for ninety days."

"Thank you, Lily."

"Don't worry about it. You're my brother, and contrary to what you might think, my black heart loves you. I also love that girl in your arms. You're well aware, I've been rooting for you both since day one. Ever since I made you both get married as kids with my teddy bears as witnesses," she laughs at that memory.

Typical Lily, a hopeless romantic hidden under her hardened exterior.

"So, when can I leave here?"

"The doctors want to check a few things first, and then you will have to sign some forms, but after that, you should be good to go. Maybe you should go shower. I'll sit here with Ro."

Crossing her legs, she pulls out a book from her handbag.

"Yeah, that would be great."

Gently, I pull my arm out from under Rosie, careful not to wake her. I climb from the bed and walk towards my sister. I extend my arms to give her a hug, but she holds her hand out forcing me to stop.

"Go shower, you smell worse than you look and right now that's like shit."

I sniff my pits and unfortunately, I've to agree with her. How Rosie didn't pass out is beyond me?

"Don't think you're getting out of this. Once I get out of that shower, I'm coming for that hug."

Lily scrunches her nose in disgust. "Whatever you say, Lurch."

Her eyes flick back to her paperback novel as she shoo's me away with her hand. I hope one day she realizes it is not too late to get her own happy after. She might seem tough, but deep down I know better. As I make my way to the small private bathroom in the corner of my room, the only thing on my mind now is how to convince Rosie to spend the night with me.

Chapter Thirty-One
I Won't Let You Go by James Morrison

Rosie

Lily heads up the long drive leading to Cillian's house, the only sound is the gravel of the driveway, crunching under the tyres of her orange mini cooper. Staring out the side window, I watch as the house where our demise began comes into view.

This is a house I was meant to love. My dream home. A place where Cillian and I could have lived happily ever after.

But instead, it only reminds me of the worst moments of my life. The day I lost Cillian, and then the day I found him lying on the floor. Pushing down the dread churning in the pit of my stomach, I remind myself why I am here. I'm here because he asked me to be, and for him, I would do anything. Who knows, maybe I can learn to love it.

The car comes to a stop right outside the front door, but I don't move. I just sit there, staring.

"Snow, are you okay?" Cillian's voice echoes through my thoughts.

Looking up at the man peering back at me through the gap between the front seats, and all the doubt dissipates. A small smile forms on my face, just the sight of him makes everything better. As long as he is by my side, it doesn't matter where we are.

"I'm perfect."

Leaning forward, I kiss him softly on the lips.

"Gag, can you please wait until I leave before you two start fucking each other with your tongues?" Lily complains from the driver's seat.

Cillian's rough laugh rings through the small space. "Don't pretend you are not happy to see us together again, Lily. You have been rooting for this for years,"

"So! That doesn't mean I want to witness you two consummating your relationship. Now get out before I have to wash my eyes with acid."

"Love you too, sis," Cillian responds by pulling Lily into a hug.

She squeals in protest before finally wrapping her arms around him. "I'm glad you're okay, even if you annoy the shit out of me."

Pulling back, she pokes Cillian in the chest. "I'll be here at ten a.m. Don't worry about packing, I've already done it."

"You're my favourite sister."

"I'm your only sister, now get out before I kick you out."

* * *

Cillian closes the door behind us, silence fills the large hall as we both just stand there. Cillian's eyes roam over my body with such intensity, my body reacts instantly. My centre tightens with anticipation for what's coming.

The need for his touch against my skin is almost unbearable. He takes slow steps towards me until his face is hovering over mine. My heart is beating loudly in my chest, the quickening beat vibrating in my eardrum.

Cillian's gaze lands on my mouth and my tongue darts out, running over my bottom lip. The fire in his woodsy eyes touches my soul before his hands even reach my body.

I want him to kiss me.

I need him to kiss me.

More than I've ever needed anything in my life.

"Snow."

That one word falls from his lips like it's the answer to every question he ever asked.

He raises his hand to my face, his fingers brushing my hair from my cheek. The sensation his touch ignites inside me is indescribable. Nobody has ever made me feel the way Cillian does. The way he is looking at me now makes me feel like the most beautiful woman in the world.

With his free hand, he grips my hip, pulling me in against his chest. "I need to make you mine again," he whispers against my lips, his eyes never leaving mine.

"I was never, not yours, even when we were apart—I belonged to you."

Linking my arms around his neck, I force our bodies closer, if that's even possible.

"As much as I want to kiss you right now, I can't. If I start, I won't stop; and you deserve more than me fucking you in a hallway." He rests his forehead against mine.

"Well then, you better take me to bed," I wink. "Then you can love me the way you think I deserve to be loved."

A deep groan escapes his mouth. He places his hands on my ass lifting me with ease. Wrapping my legs around his waist, he carries me across the room and up the stairs.

His lips trail along the skin of my neck, filling my stomach with the flutter of a thousand butterflies. I moan in pleasure as he teases me with each flick of his tongue.

Finally, we make it to his room—which thankfully, Lily had professionally cleaned. You would never know he trashed the place. I push the images of that night back down. Right now, I want to concentrate on us.

Cillian moves to the bed, dropping my body against the mattress. He climbs up over me and takes hold of my wrists, lifting them above my head. My body arches towards his, silently begging him to touch me.

"I need you," I plead.

"You got me."

His lips crash against mine and the only thought I can form is... finally. It's just a kiss, but somehow it makes my heart lose balance. And although I never stopped loving Cillian, I fall a little further, a little deeper.

Our kissing becomes frantic, while we tear each other's clothes off in desperation. It doesn't take long before we have nothing between us.

We are skin to skin.

Lips to lips.

Soul to soul.

"You are mine, Snow."

He kisses his way down my naked body, each brush of his lips against my skin sets my body on fire. He slips the hardened bud of my nipple into his mouth, gently teasing it between his teeth. Every nerve in my body is electrified by his touch.

I moan in pleasure as his hand travels along the inside of my thigh, right to the place I need him most. His fingers run through the wetness pooled between my legs.

"Fuck me, Snow. You're soaked."

He lifts his hand to his mouth and sucks my juices off his fingers. "I missed the taste of you on my tongue."

"Cillian."

I'm so turned on; my body is squirming under his.

"Patience, baby," he chuckles. "We have all night."

His deep laugh adds fuel to the flames only he can distinguish. He runs his tongue along my bare stomach, finally settling between my legs. He blows air against my clit, making my hips buck.

"Stop torturing me."

"As you wish, Snow."

Burying his face between my thighs, he laps up the need he created. My hands grip his head as his tongue works my clit in a way, only he ever could.

"Oh... my... God."

A cry of pleasure rips out as my body begins to shake from the orgasm building under the surface.

"Cillian. Oh, Cillian."

Sucking on my clit, he adds just the right amount of pressure and my body erupts like fireworks on the fourth of July. He continues to lick and suck until I can't even remember my own name. My legs are spasming from the intensity of my release.

"Cillian, I need you inside me."

He kisses his way back up my body until his lips meet mine. I can taste myself on his tongue and somehow it turns me on even more. His length is pressed against my entrance, begging for entry.

"I'm on the pill," I tell him.

I want to feel him with nothing between us.

"I'm clean, I haven't been with anyone since your engagement party," he adds.

"Me neither."

I feel like he needs to know that. It's him, it always has been.

"Make love to me, Charming."

He replies by taking my lips with his, kissing me with a passion so fierce, it leaves me breathless. Pushing his hips forward, he enters me in one thrust. My walls tighten around his length as he embeds himself deep inside me.

"Yes," I cry out as he picks up the place, lifting my hips higher so he can go deeper.

"Fuck, baby. I missed this. I missed you."

He pumps in and out with greedy thrusts. My hands grip the sheets as my orgasm begs to be freed. With his thumb, he circles my clit in time with each thrust. It doesn't take long before we both fall over the edge, moaning out our releases.

Cillian's body collapses onto mine and we both fight for breath. Rolling onto his back, he pulls me back against his chest, kissing me right where my neck meets my shoulder.

"I love you, Rosie Mulligan."

"I love you, too."

And I do. Endlessly.

* * *

Waking to a cold bed, I reach out, seeking Cillian but he isn't there.

That's when I hear it, the piano softly playing down the hall. I crawl from the bed and pull Cillian's discarded t-shirt over my naked body.

Following the melody, I reach Cillian's music room. There he is, sitting on the piano stool, his eyes closed as his fingers run over the keys.

It's very rare you see him sitting at a piano. The guitar is his main instrument, but he is just as good on the keys.

Standing in the doorway, I listen to the beautifully haunting melody. He has a long road to sobriety ahead of him. I just hope he knows he doesn't have to walk it alone.

When he opens his mouth and sings, tears fill my eyes. The words are filled with emotion.

I don't wanna feel this way no more, I don't wanna feel it. I don't want it in my veins no more, tell me how to free it. I know that I can't keep running, but my demons keep on coming, strong.

I'm sorry for the pain I keep on causing, I know I didn't mean it. I'm sorry for the hurt that I brought on you, I wish I could delete it. I know that I said forever, and I promise you I'll get better, now.

I'm gonna set them free. Release the demons inside. Clear their thoughts from my mind. No more hiding. No more fighting. I will set them free. So, they have no control, no more hold on my soul. I'm done hiding. I'm done fighting. Time to set them free.

I can see your light it keeps on shining, hope that I can reach it. I can feel the love you keep giving, Lord knows I'm gonna need it. I know that this road's a long one, but with you, I will keep on walking strong.

I don't wanna feel this way no more, I don't wanna feel it. I don't want it in my veins no more, I no longer

*need it. I know that I can get through this. With your
love, I know I can do this, now.*

*I'm gonna set them free. Release the demons inside.
Clear their thoughts from my mind. No more hiding. No
more fighting. I will set them free. So, they have no
control, no more hold on my soul. I'm done hiding. I'm
done fighting. Time to set them free. Set them free.*

Wiping the tears from my eyes, I move towards
him and take a seat beside him.

"That was beautiful, Cillian."

I lean my head to rest against his shoulder and he
places a kiss against my forehead.

"Thanks, baby. Sorry if I woke you, I couldn't
sleep."

"Are you worried about tomorrow?"

He nods his head yes. "I know it's something I
need to do, and I want to. But ninety days is a long
time, Ro. I just got you back, I don't want to lose
you."

His hand over my cheek as his forehead creases
with worry.

I sit up, taking his face between my palms. "Look
at me, baby."

His eyes find mine in the room's darkness.

"I am not going anywhere. I will be right here
waiting for you. You are my forever, Cillian. My
Prince Charming. I will be here every step of the
way, right beside you. I love you. You are not alone.
I've got you."

Kissing each of his eyelids, I pull back and take in his handsome face.

His eyes stay locked on mine as he opens his mouth, the words that come out shock me speechless. "Marry me?"

He takes my hands in his. "I know I have a long bumpy road ahead of me, but I love you, Rosie. All my life, I've wanted only you. This," he points to his chest, "it only beats for you. When I look at you, I see forever in your eyes. Everything in my life that matters is in your arms. You hold my future. It belongs to you and nobody else," he takes a breath.

"Snow, you've always been the light leading me through the dark. I want to spend the rest of my life loving you the way I should have been all along. If I have learnt anything over the past few days, it's that life is short. We aren't always guaranteed a tomorrow."

Tears fall from my eyes at his words, words I've wanted to hear all my adult life.

"When I'm out of rehab and I'm doing better I want to marry you. I want to make you mine the way I should have all those years ago. So, what do you say, Snow? Will you marry me?"

I nod my head because I can't speak through the tears.

"Is that a yes, baby?"

"Yes."

Leaning forward, I grab his face and plant my lips against his.

"I love you, Snow. Forever."

"And always

Chapter Thirty-Two

Recovery by James Arthur

Cillian

91 Days Later

Running my fingertips along the edge of the small circular bronze medallion resting in the palm of my left hand, I read over the words written across the top of the coin.

One day at a time.

I've been repeating those five words like a mantra for the last ninety days.

My fingers move to the lettering embossed across the bottom.

To thine own self be true.

That one was a little harder to achieve, and probably what I struggled most with during my three-month stay here at Recover Right Rehab.

The ninety days I've spent here will help set the tone for every day after I leave. I'm not going to lie and say my journey will be an easy one because it will be anything but. The road to sobriety is the most difficult path I have ever walked. I am still walking it — and will continue to do so, every day for the rest of my life.

Am I still an addict?

Yes. I will always be an addict.

That title will never go away. I still have days where I want to reach for the nearest bottle, but the important thing is... I don't.

It took me a long time to admit to myself, my recovery must come first so that the most important people in my life don't come last.

I hit rock bottom, and thankfully, with the support of my family, my friends and most importantly my Snow, I used my lowest point as the foundation for a better future.

Now, as I stand in front of the other inpatients here at RRR, expressing my truth, I find a sense of freedom, a burst of strength, a glimmer of hope.

Taking in a deep breath, I step up to the podium and look around the room at all the faces. Some have helped me on my recovery, some have only just begun their journey through the twelve steps, but each face staring back at me is here for a common goal — to kick their habit and become a better version of themselves.

Pulling some courage from the ninety-days-sober chip I received this morning; I adjust the microphone with a shaky hand. This is always the hardest part — sharing my story — but I know there is no judgement here.

"Hi, everyone. My name is Cillian," I swallow back the lump forming in my throat, "and I'm an alcoholic."

I still remember the first time I admitted my addiction out loud. The second, those three words left the tip of my tongue, I felt the weight of the disease lift off my shoulders.

That's what alcoholism is — a disease.

"Hello, Cillian," the group calls in unison.

"I was fourteen when I took my first drink," I pause. "I still remember to this day when my little sister — who was twelve at that time — had been ill. She had spent the night before, and all day, curled up in a ball in her bed."

I rub the crease between my brows with my hand. "My Ma had been tending to my sister the entire day and completely forgot to make my Da's dinner. When he came home, full as a coot and his dinner wasn't on the table... he lost it. He gave my mother a left hook to the jaw. The fear in my Ma's eyes that day is something I'll never forget." Closing my eyes, I blink back the emotion threatening to escape. I draw a breath in through my nose before continuing, "I remember thinking in my naive mind, whenever my Da drank, it made him stronger. He only hit us when he was drunk, so maybe if I drank too... I would be strong enough to hit him back."

I release a pathetic chuckle. "My fourteen-year-old self thought alcohol would somehow turn me into Superman. That night, I raided his liquor collection and drank half a bottle of whiskey. I ended up passing out with my head hanging over the toilet. That night, I didn't find the strength to take down my monster of a father, instead, I found an escape. With every sip, the pain inside me dulled. With each shot, I was able to forget. After that, I kept drinking; it left me yearning for the emptiness, and numbness it brought."

My grip tightens on the small coin in my left hand, I draw from it, the strength I need to continue. "For a while, it worked. Alcohol became an escape. I drank to forget; I partied every night. I slept with countless girls, sometimes not even remembering it. I was a mess. One night my sister tried to call, when I didn't answer she eventually called one of our friends she knew I was out with. My Da had completely lost it. He trashed our house and had beaten my Ma unconscious. I rushed home with my two best friends to find my Da standing over my sister's frightened frame. He was tearing her clothes from her fragile body."

Tears begin to fall from my eyes. I wipe them away with the heel of my right hand. "I still harbour guilt surrounding my sister's struggle and everything she went through at the hands of our father. I was always wasted, and selfishly, I overlooked all the times she locked herself in her room, pretending to be sick, and refusing to come out for days. I drank myself to oblivion while my sister was being abused. The guilt was too much for me to live with."

My eyes scan the room as I continue telling my personal story. I share the worst, most painful moments and explain how my addiction nearly cost me my life. My gaze lands on my sister and she mouths the words, *'I'm proud of you,'* making me falter for a second. I give her a softened smile. Lily, Rosie, Ma and the 4Clover lads here to witness this significant moment.

Step five in the recovery process is: *Admit to God, to ourselves, and to other human beings the exact nature of our wrongs.*

I want them to know I take full responsibility for my actions, and I am sorry for all the years of pain I put them through. My eyes connect to the crystal blue ones I love so much. Rosie.

"I love you," she whispers across the crowded room.

I need to get off this stage, it's been three months since I held my fiancée. Ninety days since I kissed her lips and I can't wait another minute. Finishing up my prepared speech with a smile, I hold the precious chip up to show the audience, showing them that I made it.

"My name is Cillian O'Shea, and I am a recovering alcoholic. Thank you."

The room breaks into applause. I make my way off the stage with a fierce determination.

"You did it," Rosie squeals, jumping into my open arms. I wrap her legs around my waist and try not to laugh when she covers my face with kisses. "I missed you, I missed you so, so much."

Spinning us around, I squeeze her slim frame closer to my body. "I missed you, too, Snow."

God, I can't wait to get her home. Capturing her lips with mine, I give her a quick, yet passionate kiss.

"Stop hogging him, Rosie," Lily argues from behind me. I set Rosie back on her feet and turn to face my sister.

Her normal badass facade is not in place. Her mascara is streaked down her stained cheeks and for the first time, she engulfs me in a hug without protest. "I love you, Lurch. I'm so freaking proud of you," She holds my waist a little tighter, burying her head against my chest. "It wasn't your fault. My cross... it was never yours to carry. You need to stop blaming yourself, Cillian. You need to forgive yourself."

Pulling out of my grip, her hand disappears into her handbag. She pulls out a white envelope. "Here, this is for you. Do yourself a favour and read it."

I take it from her grasp. My eyes study the government official stamp in the top right corner — Mountjoy Prison. Looking back at my sister, I search her face for answers.

"It's from Da. I went to visit him last week. He asked me to pass it on."

Staring down at my name scribbled across the front of the envelope, I suppress the urge to rip it to shreds.

Lily's hand covers mine. "Read it, it might help you put the past to bed."

I nod my head and stuff the letter into the back pocket of my jeans and greet the rest of my family and friends with a hug and some manly back slaps.

Finally, it's time for me to go back to my own house. I have ninety days of pent up frustration that needs taking care of, and luckily for me, I know just the raven-haired beauty who can help me with that.

* * *

God, it feels good to be back in my bed again with my arms wrapped around the most precious thing in my world.

My Snow.

There was a time, I thought I would never get to hold her again. I thought I had lost her. I thank God every night for giving me a second chance at happiness.

The letter Lily gave me earlier rests on top of my bedside locker, taunting me. I'm still debating if I should read it or leave it alone.

Then I remember Step nine: *Make direct amends to such people wherever possible, except when to do so would injure them or others.*

Slowly, I remove my arm from Rosie's waist, being extra careful not to wake her from her slumber. Sitting on the edge of the bed, I plant my feet against the floor, seeking some sense of grounding from the hardwood beneath my soles.

I reach for the white envelope and take a deep breath before flipping it over. I tear open the seal, my eyes scan the words and something inside me cracks.

Cillian,

I hope this letter reaches you well. I do not deserve for you to read my next words, but I am hoping you will. If not for me, then for yourself.

First of all, I want to apologize to you, for all the hurt I caused both you and your sister. I'm not asking for your forgiveness – because that is something, I am unworthy of. I should have been a better man, a better father, the man both you and Lilyanna deserved.

I do not have a good excuse for my actions. My addiction shut down my senses a long time ago and for years, I hid behind my illness foregoing any, and all consequences. I realize now, after two years of sobriety – I was solely to blame.

I hate what my addiction has done to me, to us, and what our relationship should have been. I know I forged a wedge between us that can never be filled. I hurt you and Lily in ways I am not proud of, and I will never be able to forgive myself for the despicable sins I committed.

I've had a lot of years sitting in this cell – and many more to go – to contemplate my behaviour, and what I did to the people I was meant to love, was unacceptable and frankly sickening.

I wish I could erase those years and start again, but unfortunately, that is not how life works. I cannot take back all the abuse I inflicted, but know that I bear the cross of your pain every damn day of my sorry life.

I'm writing to you because I do not want you to fall victim to the same fierce disease, I let destroy my life. You are better than that, better than me. I know you will never forgive me for the nasty, hateful childhood I betrothed to you and that is no fault but my own.

Please know, from the bottom of my heart, how truly sorry I am and if you only take one thing from this letter, let it be this: Inside you, there are two people. The alcoholic and the recovering one. They will both continue to fight for dominance. It is up to you to decide which one you feed.

Feed love, Cillian.

Feed happiness.

Feed life.

It's not too late to turn your life around.

Don't become your addiction.

Don't become me.

Love, Dad.

Tears fill my eyes, I never realized how much I needed those words.

His words.

Finally, I feel free.

Free of my demons.

Free of my past.

Free of the chains.

Free... to love.

Epilogue

Is That Alright by Lady Gaga

Cillian

One Year Later

I tug at the too-large suit jacket Lily stole from Mr.
Mulligan's closet. I don't like it; it makes my skin itch.

"Lil, why do I have to wear this? It's ridiculous."

My sister really gets on my nerves sometimes. The
only reason I agreed to this silly game is, for the first time
in forever, Lily is smiling.

"You can't marry a princess in rags, Cillian," she
protests. "You have to wear a suit."

Taking my hand, she drags me across the freshly cut
wheat field — towards the treehouse. I don't want to get
married. I'm only twelve, but my sister can be very
persistent when she sets her mind on something.

In the distance underneath the large oak tree, I see four
makeshift rows of seats. Lily has pulled over a few of

farmer John's straw bales and is using them as seating for the teddy bear guests in my pretend wedding to Rosie.

"This is stupid, Lil."

"You're stupid, Cillian. Why my best friend wants to marry you, I'll never know?"

She continues to pull me forward until finally, we're standing under the tree that holds our treehouse.

"Wait here," she demands, running off behind the nearby hedging.

Ciaran's head peeks out from the treehouse, and I watch as he carefully climbs down the wooden planks we use as a ladder. His shoulder-length blonde hair, blowing wild in the Irish summer breeze.

In his hands is a little pink and white radio, I recognize from Rosie's house.

He stands by my side and shouts in the direction Lily ran towards. "Okay, we're ready. You can come out now."

He presses a button and the cassette begins to play. Music flows from the tiny speakers, but for the first time in well, ever, I don't hear the melody.

The reason I can't tell you what song it is: my eyes are solely focused on the pretty girl carefully marching towards me. Her little white sundress is blowing in the cool summer breeze. Her hands carefully placed in front of her stomach, holding on tightly to a bunch of wild daffodils.

I forget all about going to play at Cian's.

Rosie is the most beautiful ten-year-old I've ever seen.

I know, there and then, I would marry her every day for the next one hundred years if it kept that beaming smile on her face.

My princess.
My Snow.

The soft rustle of leaves on the oak tree behind me brings me back to the present. It's a beautiful mid-July evening and the sun is setting past the horizon, reflecting a kaleidoscope of pinks and purples across the sky.

Large white lanterns and blush-coloured rose petals make up the outdoor aisle. Standing under the floral archway — beneath the treehouse — I wait on my bride.

Fairy lights are strung all-around, lighting up the dusky summer's sky while the guests wait patiently for the ceremony to start.

In the front row, I spot my Ma and Maggie sitting together, large smiles lighting their faces. The two of them have been planning this day since Rosie and I were kids.

Conor is seated over to the right, playing a soft melody on the keyboard while Cassie — 4Clover's photographer — snaps picture after picture of everyone in attendance.

The more time passes, the faster my heart pounds in my chest. I've been anticipating this day for over half my life. I want everything to be perfect.

Rosie deserves perfection.

Pulling at my too-tight collar, I struggle to get air to fill my lungs.

Where is she? What's taking her so long?

Ciaran places his hand on my shoulder, giving it a tight squeeze. "There's still time to run." The laughter lacing his tone confirms he's joking.

There isn't a person at this wedding who doubts my love for my soon-to-be wife.

"Have you got the rings?" I ask for the twelfth time in four minutes.

Patting his chest pocket, he eases my concern. "Right here. Can you take a breath or something? You look seconds away from passing out."

It is moments like this I question why I chose him to be my best man, then I remember I was out of options. Cian is accompanying Rosie down the aisle, and Conor is looking after the music.

Speaking of music, Conor begins to play the opening melody of the song Rosie and I chose together. The lyrics of this song describe us perfectly.

The guests all stand as my sister, Lily, begins her walk up the aisle. She looks beautiful; her emerald green bridesmaid dress makes her red hair stand out against her pale skin. When she reaches me, she gives me a one-armed hug.

"You're sweating, Lurch. Take a chill pill, she's coming." She gives me a wide smile, nodding her head in the direction she just came from before stepping back into position.

Following her head motion, my breath hitches in my throat. There she is. The love of my life.

I must be dreaming because she looks like a vision walking towards me. I swallow back my emotion, but a tear still escapes.

She is radiant.

Her long black hair is swept off her face, flowing down her back in elegant waves. Her flawless skin holds very little make-up, just the right amount to make her skin glow. Her white strapless mermaid gown hugs her body like a second skin.

You would never know that she is twelve weeks pregnant with our first child.

She is beautiful, all I see is her.

The lyrics of the Lady Gaga song Conor sings echoes in my ears as Rosie comes to meet me. The words reflect how I feel at this very moment.

It doesn't matter what life throws our away, as long as I have Rosie by my side, everything will be alright.

"Cillian and Rosie have decided to write their own vows." Fr. Jack looks at me. "Cillian. You will go first."

I pull the worn-out piece of paper from the inside of my tux jacket. I don't need them, I've memorized these next words over the last few weeks, but still, I need to hold something in my shaky hands.

"My fairest Snow."

I swallow, closing my eyes to heed the emotions brewing behind them. Once I get them under control, I lock my eyes to her crystal blue ones.

"Today, I give you my life and my love. There was never a time where my heart did not belong in the palm of your hands. Your love is so fierce; it knows no doubt, no hesitation, and no bounds."

Passing the page back to Ciaran, I take Rosie's hands in mine.

"You have stood by me through my darkest days, guiding me towards the light that is your heart and soul. Throughout my recovery, you were my strength, my hope, and my motivation. Your undying support is what gave me the courage to become the man who deserves to stand before you today."

Tears slide down her cheeks at my words, and it takes everything in me not to reach up and wipe them away.

"I vow to you, in front of all these witnesses, to love and cherish you every day for the rest of my life, and every life after. I vow to be the man you see me as. To hold you at your weakest and cheer you on when you are strong. I vow to be your partner, your friend, your confidant, and most importantly, your soulmate. Together we can conquer whatever life throws our way because we choose to love. I love you, Rosie. Forever and always."

Sliding the diamond-covered platinum band on to her finger, I release the breath I didn't know I was holding and wait for her to begin.

"Cillian, today I give you my heart and my soul." Rosie pauses, dragging in a deep breath before continuing.

"All my life, my heart has only beaten for you. Even when we were apart, it was you who I belonged to. All my firsts belong to you, and all my lasts are yours too, if you will have me." Rosie blinks back her tears. "I choose you, to be no one, other than yourself. I love you for who you are and what you have overcome. I vow to you today to stand beside you through your darkest days and to always be the light that guides you home. I vow to love you endlessly, without bounds from now until the end of time and beyond. Our hearts sing a song of true love, and when we are together, they beat in perfect harmony. I love you, Cillian. Forever and always." Rosie lifts my left hand and slides the matching band onto my ring finger.

The guests clap and cheer when the officiant pronounces us, Husband and Wife.

Now, if you will excuse me... I need to kiss my bride.

The End

Acknowledgements

To Joshua & Benjamin, although I hope you never read this, this one is for you. As your mother, I try to encourage you to follow your dreams. But, how can I expect that of you when I was too afraid to follow my own. So, this is me, shooting for the sky, feeling the fear and doing it anyway. One day, when you are both older, I hope you will do the same.

Andrew, I love you. Thank you for that one sentence. Without it, this book would be incomplete. LOL!

To my wild at heart mother, thank you for showing me that without struggle, we can never truly be strong. For teaching me to never let anyone dim my sparkle; and that the "f word" is not a curse but a sentence enhancer. Love your favourite child.

To my siblings, Paul, Tony, Emma, David, and Aisling, I love you all. Thanks for supporting me on this crazy ride. Sorry if I became a hermit, ignoring all your calls. I promise to answer now. (Kidding, the next book won't write itself)

To my Hoes, Emily, Cheryl, and Louise, Thank you

for being my ride or dies. Your friendships are invaluable to me.

To Ruth and Sarah, I cannot thank you enough for all the time and effort you put into making this book readable. Thank you, for your patience, your time, your medical knowledge and most of all your support throughout this 4Clover journey.

To Daria and Dani, my soul sisters, and my ALPHA beta readers. I'm so glad I found you both on the little, strange, orange website that is Wattpad. All the love for you two and all your crazy. Thank you for being my biggest supporters. You've done so much to promote my work and I love you so much for it. You truly are the greatest friends. Thank you for holding my hand, and for being my rock when I was on the verge of giving up. You both are truly are amazing. I cannot wait for the day I get to meet you, for real, and not over the internet.

To Traci, thank you for all your support over the past year. You're amazing, inside and out. Traci's book, Just Love Me is available for preorder now, and will be released May 1st.

To Elle Maxwell, without you, my social media game would be weak. Thank you for teaching me all things tech. You designed everything, from images to this amazing cover, and for that, I will forever be grateful. Check out her book Us, again. It's available on Amazon NOW! You will not be disappointed.

To all the other Wattpad ladies, I love you all. Thanks for pushing me (in a good way) to publish.

To my Wattpad family (The best of Wattpad Ladies), without you, this book would've never reached its full potential. Thank you for giving me the push I needed, and for pulling me out of meltdown mode on more than one occasion; Most importantly, sending me all those hot Insta pages when I was lacking inspiration. I love you all.

A big thank you to all the bloggers and readers who took the time to read this book. I appreciate it so much. Please leave a review on any (or if you're feeling generous) all, of my social media platforms.

Much Love

Shauna x Xx

4Clover Series

Luck, 4Clover Book One (Cian) Available Now

Love, 4Clover Book Two (Cillian) Available Now

Hope, 4Clover (Conor) Coming Soon

Faith, 4Clover (Ciaran) Coming Soon

Connect with
Shauna Mc Donnell

Enjoyed LOVE? Make sure you stay in the loop with UPCOMING BOOKS!

Join my reading group: Shauna's Steam Queenz.

Follow me on Instagram.

Like my author page.

Find me on Goodreads.

Printed in Poland
by Amazon Fulfillment
Poland Sp. z o.o., Wrocław